Appalachian Slam

Doyle Johnson

Published by Doyle Johnson, 2019.

This is a work of fiction. Similarities to real people, places, or events are entirely coincidental.

APPALACHIAN SLAM

First edition. March 4, 2019.

ISBN: 978-1386361534

Written by Doyle Johnson.

Dedicated to Chelsea,

the type of catch every fisher dreams of.

"No man ever steps in the same river twice, for it's not the same river and he's not the same man."

- Heraclitus

CHAPTER 1

It was dark outside, but it wasn't quiet. It never was this time of year. In other parts of the world, the comforting blanket of night brings with it a peaceful stillness interrupted only occasionally by the soothing call of some nocturnal creature. But not here. It was late June in the North Georgia hills and although the air surrounding the little white house was still and the darkness was deep, the noises of the night were powerful.

A chorus of voices swelled from the darkness of the pine trees looming at the edge of the carefully manicured lawn. Katydids took the lead with their long rasping melody, while the crickets joined in on rhythm accompanied sporadically by the short, high trill of tree frogs. Underlying it all was the constant, almost electric screech of cicadas providing background vocals while an ancient air conditioning unit well past its expected lifespan thumped a low, steady beat.

The cacophony of discordant sounds would have been unnerving to anyone unaccustomed to it but to Jim Cavanaugh it provided a deafening tranquility which he welcomed. His dark eyes, surrounded by the creases of time, pierced through the screen of his back porch and into the darkness beyond the moonlit grass.

Jim creaked back and forth on a wooden rocking chair as he sipped black coffee from a chipped mug. A ceiling fan whirled slowly, doing nothing to mitigate the heat and oppressive humidity that not even the early hours could scare from the screened porch. Periodically the cicadas took a break from the nighttime orchestra and thudded loudly into the screen, attracted by the light from the ceiling fan's lamp. The setting in which Jim Cavanaugh rocked back and forth was almost too stereotypically southern. One would not be surprised to find a lazy hound dog curled up on the floor of the porch. Instead Walt, a meticulously groomed black and white shih tzu-poodle mix sat perked up on an empty rocking chair next to Jim's. The small dog stared at him intently as he sipped his coffee.

The heat, the humidity, the noise. Jim didn't mind it. In fact, he appreciated it. This was the time of the day he loved the most. There was so much promise as he sat with his warm mug contemplating what the sun might bring. There was no frustration or disappointment.

Today is the day. His mood rose with the wisps of steam from the mug. Nevermind the fact that the same thought entered his mind almost every morning before he ventured off with his fishing pole into the surrounding streams and rivers. Today was different, he could feel it. Something about it felt distinct and hopeful.

Jim wore thick, waterproof waders over his clothes. They stretched from his feet, where they were tucked into heavy rubber boots, up to his chest. He used to carry his waders with him to the riverbank and don them next to the water's edge before stepping in. But as age had gotten the better of him, it had become more difficult to carry them through the woods with the rest of his equipment. Now he put them on in the comfort of his own home which meant paying extra attention while making his way to the water's edge so as not to snag them on branches or briars. No matter how hard he tried, a stray thorn always found a way of making some small puncture and it had been years since he had ended a day of fishing fully dry.

Leaning against the frame of the screen door was a long, narrow fly fishing rod. Normally, when not in use it was broken down into three pieces and stored in a round, aluminum case made especially for it. But Jim had already pieced the old rod together in preparation for the day. The neon green fly line, wound tightly around the seasoned reel, was so bright it seemed to produce an unearthly glow in the dark corner of the dimly lit porch where it rested. Next to it, a well-worn, wooden handled net was set aside, along with the rest of his gear. In the gravel driveway outside Jim's pickup truck waited patiently for its driver.

Today is the day. Jim thought again as he planned out which stream he would drive to first and from then, where he would travel if the morning proved unfruitful. At the urging of another stray thought, Jim gently placed his half-drunk coffee on the wicker table next to his chair and unzipped his breast pocket from which he pulled a plastic Ziploc bag which contained a small, black notebook and pen.

Jim's calloused hands shook slightly as he struggled to separate the bag's seal. Eventually, after some effort, he set the bag aside and turned to the next available blank page in his journal and began writing. The peaceful noises continued outside but the world was silent to Jim as he focused intently on the words flowing from his pen.

This was another reason Jim loved this time of the day. It was at this time, alone in the darkness, that his thoughts gathered most clearly. Throughout the day, when dealing with his responsibilities, or the self-inflicted frustrations which come with fly fishing, his thoughts scattered and rarely coalesced into valuable insights. But as the sun prepared to break over the tree line, flashes of ideas pierced through the solitude. Jim wrote quickly, attempting to capture these thoughts before the sun scared them away with the dew on the grass.

His pen moved across the page, pausing only for brief coffee breaks. After a few minutes, the tremors in Jim's hands became too violent for him to continue and he laid the pen on the pages of the book and placed them in his lap, sighing in frustration.

His hands continued to shake as he placed them on the armrests of his chair. In an effort to take his thoughts off the more-increasingly intrusive signs of age, he turned his gaze again on the world beyond the screen porch. The scene outside was just slightly lighter and more visible as the sun started to warm the dark sky. With the coming morning, the orchestra of nocturnal voices began to dissipate. Jim knew it was almost time to go.

He sipped the last of his coffee and turned back to the open journal in his lap. His hands were still trembling, but only with the usual agitation that they always showed. Over the last few years, as what little hair was left on his head had frosted completely white, Jim had learned to live with the expressions of age. Shaking hands, aching back, slower movement, they were all par for the course now.

Two years before, Jim had suffered a bad fall on the stairs leading down to the basement which had put his knee in a brace for two months during the best part of the fishing season. The doctors had told him he was lucky nothing worse had happened. But all Jim saw were fellow anglers pulling in monster trout during a record-setting run while he sat on the banks and watched. It was hard for him to feel lucky. Helen, his wife, had forbidden her husband from returning to the dark basement, swearing he would end up dead at the bottom of the staircase. But as soon as the brace came off, Jim was back downstairs, tying flies and arguing loudly with the hosts of local political stations crackling from an old radio nestled on a nearby shelf.

While his body was clearly feeling the effects of time, Jim considered himself blessed that his mind was as sharp as ever. He had watched as close friends had begun to forget important aspects of their lives and became increasingly more confused by the world around them. Jim was glad that he had, as of yet, not suffered the same fate.

He looked down at the pen trembling slightly in his hand. He had picked it up and positioned it over the paper, ready to resume his writing. Over and over again he read the last sentence he had scribbled on the lined paper. *Where was I going with this?* After a moment of staring, he capped the pen in frustration. Maybe he wasn't as mentally sharp as he thought. Hopefully the thought he had been chasing would return.

Slowly, Jim pulled the ribbon tight between the pages of the old journal, marking his place, and closed the cover. He dropped the small book with its pen back into the plastic bag, sealing it and folding the excess plastic around the contents of the bag before stuffing it back into the pocket of his vest.

Jim's eyes closed as he breathed in the smells of the morning. His head hurt. It had been aching slightly since he woke up, but he was sure that the fresh air of the mountain rivers would chase any headaches away. This morning was more difficult than most. His temples were aching and his face and fingers had an odd numbness that he hadn't felt before. But it was fine. Jim knew that as soon as he descended into the river and felt the cool water whirl around his body, kept at bay by the waders, all of that would disappear. Like a baptism, the water never failed to chase from his body, and his mind whatever troubles beset him. While wading through the water, flipping his line back and forth over his head, he was made new again, however briefly it might last.

A new pounding entered his head and Jim opened his eyes. He was ready for the cathartic power of the river. Grunting against his aches, he pulled himself from the rocking chair, grabbed his now empty mug and moved across the creaky, wooden floor of the porch to the back door of the house.

Walt jumped from his own rocking chair and followed his owner into the kitchen, dancing and whining anxiously as soon as the door closed behind them. Jim set the mug on the counter and proceeded to fetch Walt his daily cup of dry dog food from its bag in the pantry. Walt happily crunched through his bowl of food while Jim took his mug to the sink in the still dark kitchen. He was content to stand in front of the sink without flipping the switch to turn on the overhead light. From the window in front of his slightly numb face, a small amount of light from the rising sun gave him all the illumination he needed. For Jim, natural light, no matter how dim, is infinitely more beautiful than the stale glow of man's artificial counterfeit. He considered the hum of a light bulb almost sad when compared to the silent hues provided by dawn.

As Jim rinsed the mug out in the sink, a mechanical moan escaped from the bowels of the house. With it, the rush of warm water sputtered slightly as it escaped the tap. Jim cringed. He hoped the sound of the water heater had not awakened Helen. She was still asleep upstairs and would remain so for at least another hour if he could keep his noise to a minimum while he prepared to leave.

He had been promising Helen for years that he would replace or repair their old water heater. He was determined to do it next week. He always was. All it did was moan and sputter, it rarely stopped heating the water. When it did, it was easy enough to hit it a few times to get it going again. For now, he wasn't too concerned with it as long as it didn't wake up his wife.

Quietly, he dried his mug, gently placed it in the cabinet, and tiptoed across the linoleum and back to the porch. The vision of the new day standing in front of him almost brought full feeling back into his limp cheeks, still numb from whatever was ailing him this morning. His head still ached, even more sharply now. But he took a deep breath and imagined the feel of his line in the water.

Today is the day. He thought again.

Jim picked up his rod, which was still leaning against the door frame, waiting like a loyal companion to accompany him on his next adventure. He leaned over to retrieve the rest of his fishing equipment piled on the floorboards next to the door. At that moment a sharp pain splintered through Jim's head. He jerked up straight, dropping his rod in the process and grasped both sides of his head with his hands. Almost instantly the agony was gone. For a moment, the pain subsided and Jim wondered what had happened. Never before had he had such a sharp, painful headache. He pulled his hands away from his forehead and looked at them shaking in front of his face.

In an instant the pain returned with a newfound intensity and Jim's knees gave out beneath him. He fell forward to the ground in a heap, hitting his forehead sharply on the floor. However, he couldn't feel the force of the floor hit against his head. The pain inside his brain was too intense for him to notice anything else. Sprawled out across the porch, Jim's hands and feet shook violently as he once again attempted to grasp his forehead in his hands.

"Helen!" he tried to yell out. But the slurred voice that escaped his mouth was nothing more than a whisper.

"Helen..."

His trembling hands started to shake less violently and he closed his eyes to the bronze light of the morning sun streaming in through the screen porch. Jim's panicked movements seizing across his body slowed and his breathing softened as he began to pass out.

"Jesse..." he breathed in desperation. "Jesse..."

Mercifully Jim's breathing became subdued as he drifted into unconsciousness.

Outside, the chorus of nocturnal voices grew quiet as the day began, giving way to a flurry of bird's songs accompanied as always by the steady beat of the old air conditioning unit thumping along in the background.

CHAPTER 2

The sun was setting over the New York skyline. Bold streaks of gold, pink, and red radiated across the city, piercing through the noise erupting from the streets below. The light from the setting sun passed through the windows of a corner office on the forty-first floor of a tall, stoic building overlooking 6th Avenue. The waning sunlight set ablaze the minimally decorated office, reflecting its beautiful colors off the shiny, flat surfaces.

Jesse Cavanaugh sat straight in his leather chair behind a large desk with his back to the fiery, crepuscular vision of the city beyond the window. The gentle click of his mouse occasionally penetrated the silence of the office. His fingers tapped across the keyboard in a flurry of noise as he made minor updates to the multiple documents staring back at him. Most of the staff had gone home for the evening and the office building was quiet, which allowed him time to work in peace.

The office surrounding Jesse was clean and professional. There was an almost sterile feel to it, like an operating room before the ordered chaos of surgery. His desk was large and tidy, with only the essentials. Besides the twin monitors, the only other items on its surface were an office telephone, an iPad, a pen with a small pad of paper, and a modern-looking silver lamp. No photographs or knick-knacks made the desk feel like home.

In fact, unlike his colleagues, who decorated their offices with family pictures, sports memorabilia, and other personal items, Jesse's surroundings revealed nothing about him. Nobody could enter the room, examine it, and tell you anything about his personal life, where he was from, or what was important to him. On the vast expanse of the far wall, hanging by itself, was a framed diploma from Harvard Law School. Nowhere on that, or any of the other walls hung a similar document evidencing what undergraduate institution the attorney had attended. On the far right of the office was a long bookshelf that held several unused code books and transactional guides. Sprinkled throughout the dust-free shelves were a number of professional accolades in the forms of plaques and trophies. The only item in the room that had any personality at all was a live fern centered on a round metal table nestled next to the large window. Janice, the attorney's loyal secretary had forced him to allow her to place the plant in his office but he had insisted that she be the one to keep it watered and cared for.

Jesse continued working at his desk as the sun continued its descent. He switched on the lamp to illuminate the room with something other than the glow of his computer screen. Nelson, Johnson, & Christensen employed hundreds of people in its Manhattan office and there were always lawyers like Jesse who worked late into the night, taking advantage of the silence. Among the attorneys on the forty-first floor who specialized in mergers and acquisitions, it was not uncommon for a handful to remain in their offices well past sundown to accommodate the many overseas companies involved in their complex transactions. Walking down the hall late at night, Jesse could often hear associates speaking into their phones or webcams in a myriad of different languages.

When Jesse worked on international deals, like the one currently occupying his attention, he specialized in corporations operating out of Brazil. Rio de Janeiro was actually an hour ahead of New York so there was no one to communicate with now that most offices had closed for the day. However, Jesse still took advantage of the peace and quiet, often staying late before returning home to his one bedroom apartment on the Upper East Side. His quiet apartment had the same, minimalistic, modern feel as his office so it didn't matter to him where he spent his evening hours. He figured, if it was all the same, he might as well get work done.

Jesse Cavanaugh was a tall man with an athletic build. At 40 years old he was in remarkably good shape, which he maintained by early morning trips to the gym located near his apartment. A heavy diet of salads and regular exercise offset the time required to stay seated in front of his desk, constantly working on the documents required for his clients' businesses. His hair was a dark blonde or a light brown depending on the lighting, trimmed short and presentable with a defined part down the left side of his head. It was not uncommon for him to run his fingers through his hair on difficult nights like tonight but he somehow always seemed to maintain a professional composure.

A soft knock came from his office door, causing Jesse to snap out of his intense focus. Looking up, the door opened and two men stepped in the room, one an older attorney, and with him a younger attorney at his side.

"I thought you'd still be here," said the older man. "Mind if we have a seat?"

"Sure thing," replied Jesse, leaning back in his chair as the two men closed the door behind them and sat down in the two chairs facing the desk.

Ted Willows crossed his legs and rested his elbows on the armrests of the uncomfortable chair. Ted was the managing attorney of the mergers and acquisitions practice at Nelson, Johnson, & Christensen and carried an aura of authority and command about him. His short hair sat tight to his head and his trimmed flat line mustache accented his upper lip. Jesse was sure Ted had been at the office since before the sun had risen that day, but you couldn't tell by looking at him. The knot of his gray silk tie was tight against his collar and his expensive suit still seemed freshly pressed.

Ted and Jesse shared a professional, yet friendly relationship, but it was still rare for the senior attorney to show up at his office door after hours. Jesse wondered to himself what was going on.

"How are you doing?" Ted asked, genuine concern clearly underlying his query.

Jesse gave a slight shrug and a smile as he responded, "I'm fine, how are you doing Ted?"

"Really Jesse, how are you doing?" chimed in Gabe Harbour, from the seat next to Ted.

"You mean since an hour ago when we were talking baseball in the breakroom?" replied Jesse, leaning back further in his chair. "Not much has changed since then. I'm doing great. Just trying to finish things up for the night."

If Jesse had any real friends, he considered Gabe one. The two of them had been at the firm together since they were interns in law school. Gabe was a good attorney and had risen with Jesse through the practice. Five years ago, Jesse had been Gabe's best man at his wedding. Jesse usually trusted Gabe implicitly but he couldn't help but feel he was being ambushed in his own office.

"How's your father doing?" asked Ted.

"Oh," said Jesse, realizing what was happening. He should have known this was coming. "How did you find out?"

"Janice told us," replied Ted.

"Of course she did."

"She was just looking out for you." Ted said defensively, "She's worried about you. Your dad had a massive stroke just this morning and you go about your day like it's a normal Tuesday. Janice came to let me know the situation and asked me to check up on you."

Janice was a fantastic employee whose only real fault in Jesse's mind was that she cared too much about his personal matters. She had been with the firm for longer than he had and always seemed to concern herself with his well-being, even when it was not needed or wanted. Earlier in the day, with her eyes watering, she had insisted that he take a call from his sister whom he had been ignoring all morning. Apparently, his sister had updated Janice on his father's condition before breaking the news to him when she couldn't reach him directly. He had been hoping to avoid these types of conversations all day.

"Well, Janice needs to mind her own business."

"You are her business, Jesse." Responded Ted. "Now how is everything?"

"He's stable," Jesse answered, "I appreciate you asking. It seems that it was a little touch and go there, and he'll probably be out for a while but it looks like they've got it under control."

"Janice said he's not expected to come out of the coma," said Gabe.

"Well, like I said, Janice needs to mind her own business. I spoke to my sister more than she did. They don't know what will happen. It was a big one, but they've got him under control and they're going to keep us updated. Hopefully, we know more soon, but for right now we know very little."

"And how are you doing?" Ted asked again.

Jesse sighed. "I'm doing okay Ted. I mean, it's not every day you find out your dad will probably die but I'm taking it in stride. I'm eager to hear more, but I'll be fine."

"Why didn't you say anything, Jesse?" Gabe said, clearly frustrated as he leaned forward on his elbows. "Come on man, we were just sitting around talking about the game and the whole time you're dealing with this?"

"Dealing with what?" Jesse shrugged. "Yeah, my dad's in bad shape, but like I said, it's under control. I'm on top of it. I don't need to cry it out or anything. I'm fine."

Gabe sat back in his chair looking at his friend. Jesse was naturally a private person who rarely spoke about his life outside the firm with his co-workers. Except for Gabe. Over the years, little by little, Jesse had let Gabe peek inside his outer shell. Gabe was well aware of Jesse's relationship with his father. The two Cavanaughs were not estranged exactly. They were just different. Jesse had revealed to Gabe how their differences had put a strain on their relationship during the more difficult times in Jesse's life and how the two almost never spoke anymore.

Suddenly Jesse regretted ever talking with Gabe about his father, or anything else.

For a brief moment the three men sat in silence, staring at each other. Outside, the sun continued to dip down. The last of the colored rays of the sunset stretched across the city as though they were fleeing desperately from the sinking sun threatening to pull them below the horizon with it.

"I'm sorry about your dad Jesse," Ted said, breaking the silence. "I really hope he's able to pull through."

"Thanks Ted," replied Jesse sincerely.

"Jesse, I think it'd be a good idea for you to take some time off," Ted said lacing his fingers together on top of his knee.

Jesse thought quickly. This was a delicate situation and one he needed to address carefully. "I think you're right Ted. Thanks for bringing it up," Jesse said to his boss. "Once we close on this Carvalho deal I'll take a couple of days to go down and visit my family."

"I was thinking a little sooner than that," Ted answered.

"Ted, come on. This deal could close any day now. Really we're just waiting on the buyer to finalize their financing and then it's good to go."

"Jesse, you know as well as I do it could take them a couple days to complete that financing or it could take a couple months. If you wait for that deal to close to go take care of your personal business you could be waiting a very long time."

"Or it could be within the week," Jesse responded sharply. "Ted, this deal is setting up to be the third largest merger of steel companies in history. This business is unprecedented for our firm. It's by far the largest merger we've done in the past decade."

"I understand Jesse, but..."

"And I've overseen it from the beginning. Every negotiation, every draft, I've been a part of it. I can't just take off right when it's on the verge of closing." Jesse was calmly punctuating every syllable of his speech, making a concerted effort not to speak with his hands more than necessary to get his point across.

"Jesse, I appreciate your professionalism," Ted interjected as soon as there was a free opportunity to speak. "But the fact is, I spent all afternoon looking over the agreement and all the necessary documents and this deal is as good as done. You've done a fantastic job. All that's left is to dot some I's and cross some T's. And you've already done most of that as well."

"Ted, there's plenty left that needs to be done."

"I know, but most of what's left are little things. As you said, we're just waiting at this point. You can wait as easily in Georgia as you can here."

"Well, if I'm not here to finish it off who's going to oversee it?" asked Jesse shrugging his shoulders and holding his hands up in a questioning gesture. Ted glanced over to Gabe shifting uncomfortably in the chair next to him.

"Really, Gabe?" Jesse said incredulously. "You know how hard I've worked on this."

"Come on Jesse, the two of you are the best M&A guys we've got," Ted reasoned. "You just need to take a few hours to get him up to speed and then it's good to go. You know it'll be in good hands with him."

"What about your big telecommunications deal?" Jesse asked, turning towards Gabe. "I know for a fact that's taking most of your time right now. How are you going to handle both?"

"The Carvalho deal is all but finished," Gabe responded. "As soon as that financing gets ironed out I'll throw some associates at the minutiae, get it all polished up nice and be able to wrap it in a bow without cutting too much into my own stuff. You've done all the hard work buddy, I get to just be the pretty face."

"That's such a relief," Jesse responded sarcastically.

"In all seriousness, Gabe will do just fine with both projects," Ted interjected. "He'll take good care of your baby. And you will get all the credit you deserve. I'll make sure of it. Jesse, you've worked yourself to the bone on this project. And now this thing with your dad. Listen, you guys are our best assets. We built this firm on good attorneys like you. Your health, whether that's physical health, mental health, or emotional health is a top priority. If that goes downhill we're screwed. So don't think this is some kind of altruistic decision. You taking some time to take care of yourself ultimately benefits all of us."

"Trust me Ted, my emotional health is just fine."

"I know," Ted continued. "But I think it would be wise if you took some time off to go visit your family and get a handle on this thing. You haven't taken a vacation in a couple years now, you work late, you're here on holidays. HR has been begging you to use some of those vacation days Jesse, now is the perfect time. Go take care of your mom at least. How is she doing?"

"I haven't spoken to her yet but my sister is back home, everyone is well taken care of." Jesse replied.

"That's not the point Jesse." Ted's demeanor was less relaxed now, his natural authority was starting to permeate the room and Jesse was beginning to feel that he didn't have much of a choice in the situation anymore. "This isn't the old days where we expect our attorneys to work all hours of the night, on holidays, and weekends with no regard to personal well-being. And even if it was, that's what associates are for. You've been a partner for a while now, it's time to enjoy the benefits that come with that."

Ted stood up from his chair, buttoning the top button of his suit jacket. The conversation was over. That much was clear. Ted walked behind the chair he had just been sitting in on the way to the door, placing his hands on its backrest he turned to face Jesse.

"Listen, when my dad had his heart attack I didn't have time to say goodbye. It happened like that." Ted snapped his fingers. "I don't know what I would have done differently but I probably wouldn't have been sitting in my office which is what I was doing when I got the call. You don't have to go say goodbye or anything, but I want you to take time and just make sure you and your family are doing okay. Here's what I want you to do; go home and get some rest, come in tomorrow, spend a couple hours with Gabe getting him ready to go on the Carvalho deal, and then get out of here. Two weeks minimum, take more if you need to. That's not an offer, that's an order."

Ted turned and headed towards the door. "And call your mother for heaven's sake!" He bellowed while stepping out of the office.

"Thanks Ted!" Jesse called after him.

As soon as the two were alone Jesse turned to Gabe. "Really? You're really going to nudge me out of the biggest deal of my career?"

"Don't get mad at me man," Gabe retorted. "He came to me, I had to hear about this whole thing from our boss. You don't think you could've taken a minute to mention that your dad had a stroke."

"I'll mention what I need to mention," replied Jesse.

"See. That right there. That rock hard Cavanaugh shell is why no one likes you."

"People like me," Jesse responded.

"Who?"

"People."

"Well, I for one agree with the old man." Gabe continued, "I think it'd be good for you to head down to Mayberry for a while, pick on your banjo, skin some opossums and whatnot. Meanwhile, I'll finish off your hotshot deal, giving you all the credit, and you can come back to a hero's welcome."

"You're so kind," Jesse said, rubbing his eyes with the palms of his hands. He could tell he wasn't going to get any more work done this evening. It was dark out now and since he needed to book a flight, he figured he might as well head home for the evening.

Gabe had already stood and loosened his tie. "We'll get started in the morning. It'll be fine, and if I have any questions, I'll call you. Assuming you have cell service down there.

"Thanks man," Jesse said while saving and closing the documents on his monitor.

"For real though," Gabe said before leaving the room. "I'm real sorry about your dad. Let me know if I can do anything."

"Will do Gabe. I'll see you in the morning."

Gabe left the office and Jesse gathered his things, straightening the notepad to line it square with the corner of his desk. The sky outside was almost black now. Draping his jacket over his arm Jesse picked up his iPad and turned off the light, plunging the office into darkness.

CHAPTER 3

"Welcome to Hartsfield-Jackson International Airport," a bubbly voice chirped from the intercom. The Boeing 737 rumbled across the runway towards one of the many terminal gates lined across the massive airport. "It is now permitted to use cell phones and other mobile devices, however we do ask that all passengers remain seated with their seat belts securely fastened until the plane has come to a complete stop and the pilot has turned off the seatbelt light."

Immediately the cabin erupted in an explosion of disobedient clicks as passengers unfastened their restraints and prepared to make a speedy escape as though they were being held captive on the large plane. Sitting in first class, Jesse did not join his fellow travelers in their rebellion against the seat belt policy. He elected instead to sit quietly and read from one of the magazines in his seat back pocket with his seat belt pulled tight across his waist. This was not due to any loyalty he felt to the flight attendant, who continued to speak over the intercom, but simply because he was in no rush to disembark the aircraft. Doing so only meant he was that much closer to the place he had spent so much time avoiding. He would have been perfectly content if the two and a half hour flight from New York to Atlanta had taken all day.

One by one the passengers retrieved their overstuffed bags from below seats and overhead bins and shuffled past him. Jesse was skimming an article on recommended restaurants in Kansas City. He had never visited Missouri but the article was making him interested in someday using his large cache of frequent flyer miles to visit, if only for the cuisine that the magazine so highly touted.

Eventually, the stream of exiting passengers slowed to a trickle. Finally the last flyers, a family desperately herding young children down the narrow walkway, blew through the cabin in a fit of noise. After the father, who carried the majority of the family's cargo, walked past the first class cabin and exited the airplane, Jesse was left alone. In resignation he closed the magazine and dropped it back into the pocket in front of his seat. He had read somewhere that the seat back pocket was the dirtiest, and most germ-infested location on an aircraft. He made a mental note to find hand sanitizer soon.

"Thank you for flying Delta Airlines, enjoy your stay in Atlanta!" The same bubbly stewardess who spoke over the intercom earlier said to Jesse as he passed by the crew on his way out.

Jesse felt a small blast of muggy heat as he cleared the minuscule gap between the plane and the narrow walkway leading to the terminal. Unlike his fellow travelers, he carried nothing with him. No carry on, no backpack, no computer bag. Jesse preferred to check his bags and avoided the unnecessary burden of extra luggage when possible. It was a hassle that he didn't appreciate and he could afford the extra charge, so why worry about it? Dressed in a business casual outfit of gray slacks and a neatly pressed blue button-down he strolled up the walkway and into the terminal. Like a laser, Jesse shot immediately for the nearest dispenser of antibacterial foam before powering up his phone which was still resting quietly inside his pocket.

Six new text messages and one new voicemail. Jesse smiled to himself. While he was not thrilled with the prospect of returning to his hometown there were at least a few people he was looking forward to seeing again. One of them was his sister Aubry, the author of all six text messages glaring up at him, all a different variation of the same question: "Have you landed yet?" Jesse pressed the phone to his ear to check the voicemail. It too was Aubry, again inquiring as to whether he had arrived.

Aubry had always been impatient and Jesse imagined it was frustrating her to no end that he hadn't responded to any of her messages, all sent within minutes of each other. He imagined that her frustration would no doubt manifest itself when he saw her in just a few moments. In an effort to postpone that inevitable confrontation he avoided calling his sister, instead texting her back simply that he had indeed arrived and upon retrieving his luggage would meet her at the curb.

The airport was buzzing with activity, it always was. Jesse traveled frequently through Atlanta and the only thing that seemed to change about the world's busiest airport was that it had somehow gotten busier. He made his way calmly toward the underground train which connected the terminals while travelers from all over the world hurried around him in all directions. Once, many years ago, while traveling out of this airport he had decided to walk between the terminals instead of utilizing the train. Halfway between the first two subterranean platforms he had come to regret his decision. He had misjudged the distance between the stops and even for someone like himself who enjoyed exercise, the walk was too much. He had boarded the train at the next platform, allowing it to whisk him to his terminal in a fraction of the time. Learning from his past mistake, Jesse entered through the sliding door of the train and headed towards baggage claim.

Before long, Jesse had retrieved his luggage from the rotating carousel and walked toward one of the brightly lit doors. Far above him, positioned in a meandering line, lifelike sculptures of fire-ants the size of small dogs hung from the ceiling and walls, making it appear as though a monstrous infestation was wreaking havoc on the airport. Jesse had forgotten about this strange art exhibit which had greeted world travelers at the airport for over a decade. As he walked towards the sliding doors he wondered to himself what the appeal of horrifyingly large ants could possibly be. Who would commission and pay for such an exhibit in the middle of a busy airport, and why?

The thought disappeared from his mind as he left the comfort of the air-conditioned building and stepped into the bright light and crushing heat of the Georgia summer. It was mid-morning, and Jesse estimated that the temperature was already well into the nineties. Although it was hard to tell. The humidity, which, during the summer, was intensely high, made it feel hotter than it actually was. As Jesse unfolded his black Wayfarers and put them over his eyes to shield them from the cloudless day he thought about the saturated air and immediately regretted wearing a blue shirt. After feeling the blast of Southern heat from the space between the airplane and the runway he had attempted to prepare himself for the stifling heat to no avail. Setting down his two black bags he reached into his pocket to find his phone and let his sister know he was at the curb.

He didn't need to though. She had found him already. Jesse looked up at the sound of a horn blaring from the steady stream of cars drifting past the airport entrance. A huge, bright red, Ford F-150 was weaving in and out of the traffic creeping past the airport entrance. Jesse was amazed that the massive vehicle was able to fit through some of the gaps in between cars but it somehow effortlessly glided through. It was clear that motorists sharing the road were perturbed by the driver's reckless disregard for proper roadway etiquette. In one smooth motion the truck pulled into a spot behind a departing van directly in front of Jesse. A taxi driver who had been patiently waiting to pull into the available space threw his hands up in disbelief and honked his horn before driving past while flipping off the driver of the truck. *So much for southern hospitality.*

Jesse hadn't ventured outside New York City for anything other than business in some time. His life was completely contained within the confines of Manhattan and he hadn't seen a pickup truck driven by anybody but a city worker in years. The behemoth rumbling in front of him would have been as puzzling to see on the bustling streets of New York as a unicorn. He wondered how much gas the beast consumed and what the emissions were, silently judging his sister for her irresponsible choice in vehicles.

The driver's side door opened and a hand waved over the roof of the truck. "Jesse, it's me!" His sister yelled, as though he or anyone else in the general vicinity hadn't noticed her already.

"Yeah, I see you." Jesse called, wheeling his luggage across the sidewalk towards the idling truck.

Jesse's younger sister came bounding around the truck like a puppy being reunited with its master after a long day at work. In contrast to the enormous truck which she drove, Aubry Quezada was a diminutive creature whose head full of long brown hair barely reached the side mirrors of the Ford. Like her older brother, Aubry had big blue eyes. But, where his often expressed either cynicism or possibly minor enjoyment, hers reflected excitement and happiness. With a smile larger than her face seemed capable of containing Aubry rounded the corner of the vehicle with outstretched arms.

"Hey there Mr. New York!" She practically screamed.

"Hey Aubry, thanks again for..." The wind was nearly knocked out of Jesse's lungs as his sister wrapped her short arms around him without bothering to decelerate from her rapid sprint.

"Holy crap, it is so good to see you!" She said, her arms still locked around his torso. Jesse let go of the handle to one of his two pieces of luggage and wrapped his arm around his sister, holding on to his other bag with his free hand.

Finally, after a few more seconds Aubry pulled out of the hug, still smiling at her older brother. Glancing over to a security guard glaring at her from a few yards away she grabbed Jesse's bag and rolled it towards the truck.

"C'mon, let's get out of here," she said heaving the bag, which was almost as big as she was, over her shoulder and haphazardly into the bed of the truck. "That rent-a-cop there was getting on me earlier 'cause I was sitting here waiting for a while. He made me pull out and I had to drive around this place a few times."

"You could have just parked in the deck." Jesse said, lifting his other bag over the side of the truck and placing it gently in the bed next to the one thrown there by his sister.

"And pay for an hour of parking! No sir, that's how they get you."

Jesse wondered who "they" were and why his sister believed they were out to get her. He glanced at the security guard still staring intently at them and tried to imagine what exactly his sister had done to get on this man's bad side before his arrival. Trying to avoid the man's stare he opened the door and pulled himself up into the passenger seat of the truck.

Aubry practically had to scale the side of the seat to climb up behind the wheel. Even with her seat raised well above his own, Jesse worried about her ability to see over the hood of the vehicle. "Jayden, you remember your Uncle Jesse, don't you?" Aubry inquired as she pulled her seatbelt across her chest.

In confusion, Jesse turned to look in the back seat of the four-door truck and to his surprise found his nephew Jayden seated quietly in a booster seat behind him, swinging his legs back and forth. It made sense that he would have accompanied his mother to the airport to retrieve him but for some reason it had never entered Jesse's mind. He was unfamiliar and awkward with children and so had not considered the fact that the five-year-old boy would be accompanying them. There was a time when Jesse had found the idea of children fun but since he spent little time around them now he disliked being in their presence at all. Jesse found his sister's question to her son odd since it was almost certain that Jayden did not remember him. The last time he had seen the boy he was a small baby, less than a year old.

"Well hey there buddy, it's good to see you." Jesse lied.

"Hi Uncle Jesse!" the boy said, flashing a wide grin and waving at his uncle while kicking his feet even harder.

Despite being wary about having a kicking child seated directly behind him for almost two hours Jesse smiled to himself. He liked the name "Uncle

Jesse". It reminded him of *Full House* which he had watched when he was younger and he didn't mind being compared to John Stamos.

Aubry pulled into traffic and directed her bright red tank away from the airport and towards the heart of the city. Like before, Aubry weaved the truck in and out of the busy traffic, merging into whatever lane seemed to be moving the fastest at the time. Jesse spent a large amount of time at the mercy of New York City taxi drivers who were notorious for their reckless driving in urban environments but he was still unprepared for how nervous he felt as his sister barreled down the interstate.

"You know, you really didn't need to come pick me up," Jesse said, as he attempted to nonchalantly buckle his seatbelt which his sister's driving had reminded him he had forgotten. "I was planning on just renting a car. You didn't need to come down here."

"Are you kidding me?" Aubry retorted. "No. My brother is coming into town for the first time in God knows when. I'm not going to let him rent a car and make the drive home by himself."

"Well thanks, but it really would have been fine."

"I know. I was just excited to see you." Aubry said, reaching across the wide expanse of the center console to pat her brother's knee. She continued, "Besides, Jayden and I needed to get our minds off of dad, huh Jay?"

"Uh huh," Jayden said, obviously not too concerned with his Grandfather's situation.

Jesse had truly missed his sister. Growing up, even though there was a five year age gap between the two, they had always been close. It had been over four years since he had briefly visited the family but she looked exactly the same. She wore khaki shorts and a red Georgia Bulldogs t-shirt with rough looking work boots showing that as a contractor's wife she was a woman of the people. On top of her head she wore big round sunglasses that she almost always forgot to put over her eyes despite how bright it was.

Aubry talked on and on as they drove through Atlanta interrupted only intermittently when Jayden pointed at various skyscrapers and asked questions about the buildings. Aubry spoke a hundred miles a minute with a southern twang which let everyone know exactly where she was from. Jesse had expended a considerable amount of mental effort and dedication ridding his own tongue of the southern drawl that was spoken around his childhood dinner table but appreciated that Aubry had maintained the accent.

While Jesse was usually reserved around people and reluctant to say anything, let alone reveal any inward thoughts or emotions, with Aubry he tended to open up more than usual. Long ago, before he had left for college he couldn't wait to leave their small town and over the years his relationship with his father had grown more and more distant. As events unfolded in his life that further drove a wedge between the young lawyer and his father it was rare that he reached out to his family, preferring his solitary life in New York. While he rarely regretted his decision to leave his past behind him he did feel bad about the distance that had grown between himself and Aubry. The two should be close and he knew that the only reason they were not was because of him. It must cause Aubry an immense amount of emotional pain that the two had drifted so far apart.

As they drove, Aubry spoke about Jayden, his school, his sports. She told Jesse all about her husband Marco's thriving business as a contractor in North Georgia. She updated him on various characters from their childhood and high school days and brought him up to date with all the town gossip. Jesse didn't provide much input but was happy to sit back in his seat and listen. As they made it past the last of the skyscrapers in the metropolitan area, the highway emptied and Aubry had little need to merge suddenly between lanes. Finally Jesse was able to relax as they headed north, past the city.

It was almost a two hour drive home. At Kennesaw they turned off the major interstate and moved along a winding highway through residential areas and towns that grew smaller and farther spaced as they drove northward. All the while, Aubry talked. Periodically she would inquire into aspects of Jesse's life which she considered glamorous and enviable. He could tell she was impressed when he spoke about the city and his job.

On the other side of the passenger window fields and forests rushed by, interrupted momentarily by buildings and cities. Jesse had forgotten how green it was here. The northeast had its own magnificent foliage as well but here, even in the sweltering heat of the summer, everything seemed to be overtaken by verdant growth. At the edge of a field a small barn had been completely enveloped by a wave of kudzu vines which had grown off the nearby pine trees and wrapped themselves around the decaying building.

There was no hope of reclaiming the forgotten barn from nature's grasp. But what was left, a combination of manmade and natural structure made the field more beautiful than if only one of the entities had been allowed to remain at the expense of the other.

The road began to softly incline and the North Georgia mountains were gently popping up on the horizon. The mountains of the southern Appalachians were not massive, rocky fortresses like those found elsewhere in the country. In fact, people living in the western part of the United States would likely laugh at those who called them mountains at all. But they were beautiful nonetheless and the rolling green peaks were welcoming to all those who visited them. After some time they eventually entered the Chattahoochee National Forest near Elijay, although you couldn't tell. It was just as green and forested as before. Even on a wide highway like this, the evergreens loomed tall on either side of the sweltering blacktop.

Jesse was so used to looking up at the gray monolithic buildings of the city that it seemed strange to have his vision bombarded by the vivid greens of the forest and blue of the clear sky. He loved the vibrant life of New York although he generally only experienced it from his office window. Over the years he had rarely spoken of his southern mountain roots with his peers at the firm, convincing himself that what he had left behind was beneath what he had become. He was still sure of that fact but found himself hypnotized by the canvas of colors speeding past his eyes.

"Jesse...?" Aubry said, emphasizing his name in an indication that it was not the first time she had tried to get his attention. Jesse whipped his head around, snapping out of the trance induced by the mountainous scenery. Aubry was staring at him waiting for him to respond.

"Sorry, I was... it was a long flight. What was that?" He replied.

"Have you even called Mom yet?" She asked again.

"Oh, um, no. We were texting earlier."

"Well, whatever, you'll see her in a few minutes. She's really looking forward to seeing you. You wouldn't even guess that Dad is in a coma based on how excited she seems for you to come. It's a shame it took this to get us together."

Jesse could sense in her voice an undertone of judgment which he had been hoping to avoid. "Yeah," he said, letting it go. "Has there been any change with Dad?"

"Nothing," Aubry answered. "Personally, I'm glad you weren't here when it happened. It was so scary. Mom called me, freaking out. When I got there the ambulance was just leaving. It was so sad. He was just on the porch getting ready to go fishing, you know, like he always does."

Fishing. Aubry had told him everything already. A few times. It wasn't surprising that something like this would happen while his father was doing something involving fishing. The man fished like it was going out of style which, as far as Jesse could tell, it was. Jesse thought to himself that it was probably best that it happened while the old man was at home and not in the middle of some river in the woods.

At that moment a sign appeared on the side of the highway. *Fannin County*, it read, in large green type above a picture of a rainbow trout leaping for a fly, *Trout Capital of Georgia*. Jesse smiled at the timing as they crossed the county line. *Almost home*, he thought, knowing that they were only five minutes or so from his parents' house. The drive had taken longer than he thought and Jesse was ready to stretch his legs. As they got closer to town, businesses and homes started to appear by the side of the road. They passed tractor dealerships, barbecue restaurants, and churches as they ascended a gentle slope. Aubry led the truck off the larger road and onto Old Highway 76. The two-lane road weaved around the bend, past a weeping willow blowing softly in the welcomed summer breeze.

Blue Ridge City Limit, a green metal sign read as the truck crossed into the Cavanaughs' hometown. Jesse smiled to himself as they passed Fannin County High School. There was a new sign out front but from what Jesse could see, past that it looked the same as when he had graduated over twenty years earlier. Up ahead at the next intersection he knew they would turn right on Industrial Boulevard to wind through back roads to his family's reclusive home.

They reached the intersection and Aubry continued on without turning. Looking behind them as they drove past Jesse asked, "Where are we going? Mom and Dad's place is back there."

"We're not going to the house Jesse." His sister said in a matter-of-fact way, as though he was crazy to suggest such a thought. "We're going to the hospital. Mom's waiting there. She hasn't left in two days."

It shouldn't have surprised him. It made sense that they would meet his parents where his father was being treated but for some reason Jesse had assumed he had more time. More time to prepare. More time before being forced to see his father again. If he had more time he would calm the conflicting emotions that battled under the calm surface of his stoic demeanor. But there wasn't enough time, there never was.

CHAPTER 4

If a line of demarcation were drawn which separated reality from the mythic idealism of Southern nostalgia, it would run through Blue Ridge, Georgia.

Located less than ten miles from the point where Tennessee, North Carolina, and Georgia meet, the small town is nestled in a fertile valley along the banks of the Toccoa River. Overlooking the city are the tree-covered hills of the southernmost peaks of the Blue Ridge Mountains which stretch from the Deep South to Pennsylvania. It is estimated that at one time the Appalachians were taller than the Rocky Mountains which loom over the American West. But the gradual changes wrought by a few million centuries had transformed these mountains into beautiful, smooth domes rolling gently across the landscape.

The city of Blue Ridge was founded in the late 1880s but its heritage extends much farther into the past. Through much of the tumultuous history of the United States, the small pocket of society lay tucked away under the watchful care of the surrounding hills, unperturbed by time's constant march. Even when the country was ripped apart in the waning days of the Civil War, and a path of destruction was torn across the state, the natural beauty of the area was spared the destructive fate met by many valleys in the South.

For generations, the Cherokee inhabited the mountains, calling them *Sah-ka-na'-ga*, "The Great Blue Hills of God." It was the Cherokee who first heard the call of the rivers and streams that flowed over the land. Much like Jim Cavanaugh and other modern anglers, the Cherokee answered the call and descended into the river. Just north of town, in the middle of the Toccoa River, there still stands a rock wall built by the ancient people. Constructed in a V shape, pointing downstream, the natives would stand at the center of the point and catch the fish forced there by the current. From the rushing waters these fishermen pulled similar trout that modern anglers would catch in the very same river. Where this wall once traversed the body of water from bank to bank, it now remains, crumbling under the daily wear of the river, as a silent reminder of the people who once called the forested hills home.

For hundreds of years the Cherokee built a sprawling empire across the natural beauty of the southeast. In 1540 the first known contact with Europeans occurred when, under the banner of Spain, Hernando De Soto traveled across the South. The Cherokee, and other eastern tribes were decimated by disease brought by the new settlers and their numbers dwindled rapidly as the land was slowly overtaken by Europeans in search of a new life in a new world. The earliest mention of the area now within the borders of Fannin County comes from the pages of a journal kept by a preacher who traveled through the area in the 1790's referring to the settlers there as "...an intemperate bunch." A description of the frontier lifestyle that remained accurate for many years.

In 1830 President Andrew Jackson signed the Indian Removal Act and eastern tribes made preparations to relocate to "Indian Territory" west of the Mississippi. By 1838, Gold had been discovered in and around the city of Dahlonega in North Georgia and to make room for the coming economic surge, the Cherokee nation was forcibly removed from the state. Approximately 2,000 to 6,000 people would perish in the arduous trek leading from their mountain homeland to Oklahoma.

Fannin County was founded in 1854, formed from portions of neighboring Gilmer and Union counties. Unlike the plantation owners to the south, counties in the northern part of the state were divided on the issue of secession as war loomed dark on the horizon. Roughly two-thirds of Fannin's citizens remained loyal to the Union while only one-third supported the Confederate cause. Men and boys left the community in droves to enlist in the respective armies of their choosing.

While the battles themselves never reached Fannin County, the war did. In the absence of honorable men who left to fight for a greater cause, general lawlessness overtook the area. Like many counties, Fannin was overseen by Confederate Home Guard units tasked with protecting the home front during the war. However, due to the government's focus on the conflict, no oversight was established to control the Home Guards and corruption was rampant. By the end of the war, many in the secluded settlement were left destitute and a large number of the county's citizens moved west to pursue the promise of a better life.

In the 1880's Blue Ridge finally burst into existence as the Marietta and North Georgia Railroad was controversially routed to bypass the county seat in Morganton. The town was incorporated in 1887 as a terminus for the rail line and eventually became the county seat itself. The Railroad no longer transports passengers or goods to the Blue Ridge Depot but to this day the Blue Ridge Scenic Railway provides tourists a twenty-six mile round trip from Blue Ridge to McCaysville, on the Tennessee border. The train attracts visitors from across the country who relax in the open air cars rumbling over the winding rails as the engine snakes through the mountains. Eager faces of children, watched over by their parents, gaze up at the green canopy overhead and down at the river below as the scenes flash before their eyes. When riding the train on a hot summer day it is easy to feel as though the old metal wheels creaking along the steel tracks are carrying you back in time to a simpler era.

With the arrival of the rail line, the newly formed town experienced unprecedented growth. Visions of a great mountain city booming from the raw forests, mineral springs, and plentiful mines brought investors to the depot at every arrival. Blue Ridge took center stage in North Georgia as high society flourished with the influx of capital. Luxurious new homes were built for white collared families leading the charge for a new, developed, and economically profitable South. Water and spa retreats were constructed in and around the valley. It was not uncommon for the who's who of Atlanta to travel to Fannin County for weeks at a time to take advantage of the mineral springs found across the mountains. Touted as one of the healthiest cities in the country because of its rich environment, salesmen made a fortune in Blue Ridge selling access to the minerals so highly spoken of in urban circles.

By the early 1900s the intensive progress experienced by the area began to subside. The railway was extended to Tennessee and with it the machine shops, with their jobs, moved up the line, and out of town. The mines in North Georgia and Tennessee remained plentiful, however the costs of extracting the minerals increased to a point where investors began to move their capital to businesses with higher margins. By the 1920s it is estimated that somewhere between 60%-80% of the forest had been lost to logging or defoliation due to copper mining. In an effort to create one final burst of growth an ambitious dam project was undertaken. East of Blue Ridge, workers and material were brought in and the structure was stretched across the river. In July 1931 Lake Toccoa was created and the dam began producing power for the surrounding valleys. To this day Lake Blue Ridge still provides power to local residents as well as a tourist destination for watersports, camping, and fishing.

In the 1920s, as legitimate businesses began to fold or leave the North Georgia mountain area it became necessary for ingenious residents to find new sources of income. The Federal Government provided just the opportunity when the eighteenth amendment to the Constitution was passed prohibiting the manufacture and consumption of alcohol. Prohibition tightened the supply of alcohol but did nothing to decrease the demand and the moonshiners of North Georgia were all too eager to fill the gap.

Moonshine has been produced in Georgia since the late eighteenth century. Scots-Irish immigrants who settled in the Appalachian Mountains brought with them their knowledge of distilling whiskey and shared it with other settlers. The uneducated farmers of the region were able to master the difficult processes of fermentation and distillation, and stills were openly present on many farms across the countryside. Distillers were well-respected members of the community and their practical enterprises generated valuable revenue for themselves and the region. Corn, apples, and peaches were distilled and taken to market alongside the raw goods themselves.

During the Civil War, the Internal Revenue Service was created and high taxes were levied on liquor, tobacco, and other "luxuries" in an effort to balance the national budget. When Georgia returned to the Union, distillers in the Blue Ridge area found themselves subject to the tax and were forced to pay it or to disband their operations. Stills which were once openly run alongside farmer's harvests were hidden in the mountains and operated at night, giving their operators the nickname "moonshiners." The IRS sent "Revenuers" to collect and enforce the taxes at gunpoint and moonshiners resisted with equal force. The covert moonshine wars rippled across the mountains. As time dragged on and brutal tactics were adopted by the moonshiners, public sentiment turned against them.

The temperance movement led by evangelicals encouraged individuals to refrain from alcohol and accept federal taxes as a means to purify the country of its vice. Moonshining decreased in popularity but Prohibition brought it roaring back to life. Gangsters in Chicago and New York cornered the market and stills throughout the Georgia mountains were fired back up to meet the insatiable thirst of the black market. For years moonshiners found new and inventive ways of evading revenuers to transport hundreds of gallons of whiskey to the urban masses. Eventually prohibition was repealed and the practice fell off sharply to only a few moonshiners who continued to avoid federal taxes on liquor out of principle. To this day some moonshine stills continue to operate in the foothills surrounding Blue Ridge but the economic benefit which drove the practice in years before has long passed.

Today Blue Ridge, the small town, with a big history, is a popular destination for people who want to "get away from it all." Cabins surrounding the city are constantly filled by urban travelers taking advantage of the breathtaking views and clear air. At all times of the year the hiking trails are well used by vacationers seeking to take a glimpse into the mountain wilderness as it was meant to be, unspoiled, and pure. The lake and the rivers are common resting places for the Southeast's weary inhabitants hoping to find rejuvenation from the stresses of life. In downtown Blue Ridge a burgeoning arts scene has been well developed within the aged walls of historic buildings. Handmade crafts, art, and food are sold to tourists and locals who are drawn to the magnetic personality of the town's eclectic style blended seamlessly with archetypal Southern convention.

But still one of the city's primary attractions remains fishing. While the Toccoa River is the primary source for fly fishing in the area, Fannin county has, within its borders, dozens of streams and creeks which attract anglers from all over the world. On any given day, should one hike along the banks of any of the creeks, it is unavoidable that they would come across someone standing waist deep in the water, flipping a fly back and forth over their head as they move upstream. The cool mountain waters provide ample opportunity for men and fish alike to contemplate existence and its many meanings as they continue their back and forth game played between the species for millennia.

Today Blue Ridge is home to roughly 1,265 people. Staring down at his father, Jesse Cavanaugh couldn't help but think that it wouldn't be long before the population fell to 1,264.

James Cavanaugh lay peacefully on a hospital bed in a brightly lit room in Fannin Regional Hospital. Jesse, his sister, and his nephew had traveled directly through the heart of the city to the facility on the outskirts of town. It was noon when the trio checked in at the visitor's desk and made their way to the Intensive Care Unit. There, Jesse was reunited with his mother for the first time in years. When they entered his father's room Helen Cavanaugh had been asleep, curled into a ball on the meager couch under the room's window. She was sleeping soundly, and the only noise that disturbed the silence of the room was the whirring of machinery, the soft pumping of air, and a steady beep emanating from an electronic screen tracking heart rate and other vital statistics. At first glance it had been clear that what his sister had said was true, his mother had not slept in some time. This was probably the first time she had allowed herself to sleep since finding her husband convulsing on the floor of her back porch.

Jesse's first instincts were to let his mother sleep but the instincts of a five-year-old are much different, and Jayden immediately evaded Aubry's grasp and bounded across the room to his grandmother. Upon seeing her long-absent son, Helen sprung from her makeshift bed and greeted him as though she hadn't been fast asleep moments before. Wrapping her arms around Jesse you couldn't tell that her husband lay comatose only feet from where they stood. She was happy. After filling her in on his trip from New York the conversation quickly turned to Jesse's father and his current state.

"He'll make it through this Mom," Aubry reassured their mother. "He's a fighter."

For the life of him Jesse couldn't imagine what his sister was referring to. His father had been an insurance agent until he had retired fourteen years before. And a rather mediocre one at that. He wasn't known for being a pillar of the community, or a leader among his small group of friends. He wasn't known for anything, really. He certainly wasn't known for being a fighter.

"Yeah, I know." His mother responded, nodding her head as she wrapped her arm around her grandson sitting next to her on the couch. "Thanks baby."

"So mom, what have the doctors said recently?" Jesse inquired.

"Oh, you know, a bunch of doctor talk," Helen responded, looking over at her husband lying calmly on the bed. "I don't understand most of it. But they said he's stable. He's not responsive, but he's stable. I think he's going to start showing improvements pretty soon."

Jesse knew there was a difference between stable and improving. He suspected that his mother understood this as well but didn't want to show any doubts. Jesse was a lawyer, not a doctor, but he knew that with strokes the sooner a patient was able to receive treatment, the better. No one knew how much time had passed between the stroke and when his mother had found him but his physician suspected somewhere in the range of one to two hours. Too much time. The medicine needed to break up the clot impeding the flow of blood to his brain had been administered within an hour of arriving at the hospital, as recommended, but it would likely be ineffective given how much time had passed.

Jesse watched over his father who lay strapped to a number of different monitors, I.V.s, and tubes. Even if he was a fighter as Aubry suggested, and survived this ordeal, what kind of life would he have? Certainly there would be brain damage and limited motor functions he would cope with for the remainder of his days. Is that really the kind of life he would want anyway? Jesse told himself that he wasn't being callous, he was just trying to assess the situation analytically. And from an objective point of view it seemed almost impossible that his father would leave the hospital alive, let alone with the ability to function in society without extensive care. It could be today, or a week, or a month, but for all intents and purposes his father's life was over.

He understood why his family would not want to accept that conclusion but he had. And doing so made him feel ... he wasn't sure how it made him feel. He had expected it to make him feel at peace. Content with the cards dealt to his family and prepared to do the things needed to help his mother make preparations and move on. But instead he felt different. On some level he recognized that he felt sadness but he felt something else as well. Incompleteness. Staring at his father lying vulnerably on a stale white sheet, drugs being pumped through his veins and air through his lungs, it felt so anticlimactic. Not that his father's life suggested it would end in crescendo. This just seemed different than what Jesse had expected.

"Now what?" Jesse said, his eyes fixed on his father's closed eyelids.

"Now," said his mother. "We eat. I'm starving, and who knows what you've been eating up there in New York."

"It's fine Mom, you stay here, I'll get you something," Jesse said, rising from his chair.

"Nonsense, I need to get out of this hospital room anyhow and besides, your dad will be here when we get back."

CHAPTER 5

½ medium Vidalia onion, grated.

½ cup pimentos, diced, with the juice.

1 teaspoon ground cayenne pepper.

4 oz. cream cheese, softened.

3 cups grated sharp white cheddar cheese.

¾ cups Duke's mayonnaise.

It has to be Duke's. That's important. Helen Cavanaugh's famous pimento cheese sandwiches wouldn't be famous without it. And Helen Cavanaugh took her pimento cheese very seriously. Once, at a springtime gathering of the First Baptist Church of Blue Ridge, Winnie Roebuck, Helen's best friend of thirty years, challenged Helen's reign as the queen of pimento cheese. When her own sandwiches went untouched, Winnie loudly proclaimed that she did not care for Helen's recipe and declared it tasted as though she made it with Miracle Whip. The two women had not spoken since.

Helen Cavanaugh cradled a large metal bowl in her left arm which contained all the ingredients to her simple cheese spread. While pacing barefoot across the brown linoleum of her kitchen floor, she gently mixed the ingredients with a large wooden spoon. Mixed thoroughly, but still chunky, that was the secret to good pimento cheese. Helen hummed as she paced across the floor. She always hummed to herself when she was working on a masterpiece in the kitchen. And almost everything that went on her table was a masterpiece. The tune she hummed was indiscernible. They usually were. It drove her family crazy sometimes as she paced around the kitchen humming melodies that sounded almost like real songs. But it helped her think. Or sometimes it helped her refrain from thinking and dwelling on unpleasant realities. Such was the case today.

Helen and Jim Cavanaugh had been married for 49 years. They would celebrate their golden wedding anniversary next May. It was a big one, and they had already discussed traveling to some exotic location with one another to celebrate. It didn't seem like that would be happening anymore. Helen had been reading over the past day about stroke recovery. Even if her husband pulled through, it was unlikely they would be doing any traveling in the next year.

Helen was short, maybe a foot shorter than her son. Her hair, which was a mixture of her natural blonde and the graying of age, reached just past her shoulders. She often wore it clipped up in the back of her head as she did now. She was in remarkably good shape for her age and could be found everyday walking with two or three of the other women in the neighborhood, spreading town gossip as they exercised.

Unlike her husband and children, Helen had not attended college. She married young which most did at that time and kept the home while her husband went off to brave the exciting world of local insurance. But she was smart. While lacking technical training, Helen was as intelligent as any professional who came through Blue Ridge and had positioned herself as an important figure in the town's social circles. This was especially so at the church where she and her family had attended for many years. While Pastor Carmike was the spiritual leader of the congregation, everyone knew that nothing took place within the red brick chapel without the blessing of Helen Cavanaugh.

Helen's face and hands bore the creases of age with dignity. She had become more active as she had gotten older. Around her neck a strand of pearls given to her years before by her husband always hung regardless of whether she was attending Sunday services or on her hands and knees pulling weeds in the garden.

Helen and Jim had been at each other's sides for almost half a century now but it was Helen who acted as the voice of the couple. Jim was content to fish every moment available to him and was not one to intentionally interact with anyone outside of the two or three people he considered friends. Helen was just the opposite, looking for every available opportunity to expand her circle of influence. Where he was quiet and withdrawn, she was boisterous and unreserved. It was difficult to shake Helen Cavanaugh. But the last few days had shaken her. Finding her husband in the aftermath of a stroke frightened her more than anything else she had experienced. When she learned he had likely had the stroke a few hours before, while she lay asleep in her bed, she had been overcome with guilt. That guilt and fear had kept her by his side for two days straight. As she paced around her kitchen, mixing the pimento cheese, she let her humming carry away some of the fear and anxiety which she had been carrying.

Helen loved living so close to her daughter and grandson but Jesse's absence had always left a void in her life. It wasn't the physical distance which caused her to long for a time when her family was together but the emotional distance which she watched separate her son from his father and subsequently, herself. Having him under her roof made her forget about that distance and the stresses of the last few days.

Jesse was downstairs in his old bedroom tucked away in the basement. In high school he had elected to move from his room on the second floor of the house to the solitary recesses of the basement. Half of the space downstairs was unfurnished, used for storage and his father's workbench. The other half consisted of a carpeted bedroom and adjoining bathroom, lit by a sliver of daylight let in from the half-window on the room's far wall. When he was younger the space seemed so massive. A fortress into which he could retreat. Now, the room seemed smaller than ever. But he lived in New York City, he was used to small spaces, and Jesse was convinced that he would be fine for the short time he would be here.

His mother had left his room exactly as it had been when he had left for college years before. Of course he had been back since, but he found it funny how she had refused to change the room in any way or convert it into a more useful space. It seemed to him a museum of a forgotten time. On the wall were photographs of himself and high school friends. On top of the dresser stood various accolades much like his office back in the city. Instead of awards for his professional endeavors, the dusty plaques outlined his accomplishments in high school academics and baseball.

Jesse dropped his luggage at the foot of his old twin bed in the corner and took himself on a tour around the room, meticulously examining the pictures and artifacts. On one wall, next to his dresser, twin posters of the Atlanta Braves and the University of Georgia Baseball teams reminded him of when he had time to care about sports. He remembered lying on the uncomfortable mattress, listening to the Braves play through the static of an AM radio station.

I wonder how the Braves are doing?

It had been years since he followed the sport the way he used to. An old worn hat with the unmistakable "A" of the Atlanta team hung from a scratched up wooden bedpost. The hat, once a dark blue with a bright red bill had been transformed through years of use to an entire spectrum of red and blue shades. He picked the hat up and rolled it over in his hands before placing it on his head and pulling it down low over his forehead like he used to in high school. It still fit like a glove.

"Jesse, lunch will be ready in five minutes!" Helen yelled down the stairs.

"Alright mom, I'll be right up!" he yelled back.

He hung the hat on the bedpost and wandered out into the unfinished darkness of the other half of the basement. The light was turned on but only a few bare bulbs hanging from the cobweb-covered beams glowed in the darkness. It was not enough to illuminate any large portion of the cluttered space. When the garage door on the other end was opened there was plenty of light, but with it pulled down it remained gloomy and dark. As Jesse turned to start up the stairway something in the far corner caught his eye.

One of the lonely incandescent bulbs hummed over his father's work bench nestled into the far corner. On it lay a neat pile of clothing folded carefully on the center of the wooden surface. Jesse made his way through a narrow aisle surrounded by dusty boxes and lawn equipment to the desk-sized wooden counter. He tried to keep his clean outfit from rubbing on a dirt covered tool, or sawdust encrusted stack of lumber as he maneuvered through the maze to the illuminated workspace.

Jim's workbench was about the size of Jesse's office desk in New York but its surface stood chest high. Above the desk, a series of cubbies and small drawers covered the wall, each one marked with a label identifying its contents. Hooks, beads, feathers, fur, dubbing, cements, etc. While Jesse was unfamiliar with the practice himself, he recognized the materials used in tying flies. On the workbench itself, a wide array of tools and instruments were scattered across the surface. Scissors, tweezers, and forceps were interspersed with tools that Jesse couldn't recognize or name. A small vice of some sort was fashioned to one edge of the bench and a black and gray circular motorized machine with an array of clips outlining it was bolted into the other. Pushed to the back wall, a magnifying glass on a flexible accordion neck centered what little light passed through it from the bulb overhead into a bright point on the rough wooden plane.

Leaning against the bench and the wall, an array of fishing rods bent slightly as they rested in the corner. Some were fully assembled while others were broken down in a group of shorter poles leaning against one another or in the occasional wooden box. Jesse resisted his natural inclination to organize the mess. Instead he turned his attention to the pile of clothes stacked in the center of a cleared space on the counter. A pair of jeans, a short sleeve plaid shirt, and a fishing vest were folded methodically in a square pile seemingly waiting for the return of their wearer. The items which had almost certainly been stuffed into the pockets of the vest were laid neatly next to the clothes. A set of old, time-worn waders hung from a nail on the wall next to the bench.

Jesse remembered what Aubry had said. His father had been preparing to fish when he collapsed. These must have been the clothes he was wearing that morning, which explains the care with which his sister had left them on the workbench for their father. She obviously had placed them there so he would be able to use them when he returned from the hospital. Jesse felt terrible for his sister. He knew the devastation she would feel when she was forced to accept the fact that their father would not be needing the clothes.

On the center of the folded fishing vest, separated from the other items which had made up its contents, a small, black, notebook drew Jesse's focus. He reached down and picked up the book. It was a Moleskine 3 ½ inch by 5 ½ inch hard cover notebook held closed by an elastic band and marked by a gray ribbon bookmark. These notebooks had made a resurgence in recent years as the go-to notebook for journals and personal note-taking. Jesse himself had purchased one at one time but found the efficiency of electronic note-taking too enticing and after only a month he threw his own notebook in a recycling container outside his apartment.

Jesse removed the elastic band and thumbed through the water stained pages. Only about three-quarters of the lined pages were filled. It was apparent from the dates marking the beginning of each entry that his father did not write in the book daily. Sometimes there were gaps spanning several months between entries. Jesse didn't even try to make out his father's handwriting. The script would have been legible if he had truly attempted to decipher it but he wasn't interested enough for the headache that such a task would surely bring. Common words or phrases periodically were legible among the otherwise erratically written script. Most of it seemed to contain his father's thoughts about where to fish at what time of year, what flies to use, and records of fish caught. On the last few pages of the notebook his father had prepared a chart. Down the left side of the page were written dates, across the top were written three words, *Rainbow*, *Brown,* and *Brook* divided into three columns. In each column, in the rows created by the dates, tally marks were drawn. Some days had many tallies on one or two columns, but most had very few.

Jesse flipped through the book one more time, ready for the meal waiting for him upstairs. As he prepared to close the notebook and place it back where it had originally caught his eye, a phrase jumped out of the scribbled writing and hooked his attention. *Appalachian Slam*. Jesse had no clue what the phrase meant. He held the book closer to his face as he attempted to decipher the sentence in which the phrase appeared. It was written at the beginning of the book, only four pages into the record.

It's been almost five years since I started and I still haven't gotten the Appalachian Slam. It's coming though. I can feel it.

Jesse noted the date. The entry was over two years old. The rest of the entry outlined the lack of fish caught that day by the optimistic angler. Jesse flipped through the book again, keeping an eye out for the curious phrase. Every few pages it seemed to crop up in some form or another. *Appalachian Slam*, *The Slam*, *A.S.*, *A. Slam*. The closer Jesse examined the awkward writing the more references he was able to find. The notebook was filled with the phrase in some form or another. Jesse wondered what his father could have been obsessing over. It must be some legendary fish in the area he had never heard of or some accomplishment he had hoped to achieve. At each reference he attempted to quickly glean from the context what the phrase meant but was unable to do so. He continued rifling through the yellowed pages, looking for more references.

"Lunch is ready!" his mother's voice shouted down the stairs.

Jesse looked up from the notebook. He was sitting at the workbench with his elbows resting on the wooden surface. He didn't even remember pulling out the metal swivel stool and sitting down. He must have done it subconsciously as he searched through his father's handwriting. Jesse closed the book and laid it back where he had found it before making his way through the subterranean maze to the bottom of the staircase.

His, mother, sister, and nephew were waiting around the circular kitchen table, plates in front of them. Jesse pulled the empty chair out and sat down in front of a waiting plate of food.

"You get lost down there?" Aubry quipped.

"Something like that," Jesse responded, reaching for the sandwich on his plate.

"Ahem," Helen said, staring at her son.

Jesse looked at his mother. Her elbows were resting on the table and her hands were clasped in front of her face. Jesse immediately noticed that his sister and her son were likewise looking at him, their hands in the same position.

"Oh," said Jesse, awkwardly putting the sandwich back on the white, ceramic plate and interlacing his own fingers. "Sorry."

"Aubry, will you please." The matriarch requested.

The group closed their eyes and Aubry asked a short blessing on the food. Jesse had forgotten that his mother insisted on a prayer before each meal. It was a habit he had never adopted and was easy to forget. Upon the amen, Jesse was finally able to eat his sandwich free of judgment.

Jesse had one time attempted to make pimento cheese in New York, briefly indulging the inner Southerner he had spent so much time suppressing. It hadn't worked out. It just wasn't the same. Once, in a store in Brooklyn, Jesse had come across the familiar yellow and black labeled jar of Duke's. He hadn't seen the condiment for sale in the city before then. For some time he stood in the aisle of the store holding the mayonnaise and pondering whether he should attempt the meal again. Ultimately he decided against the idea and placed the jar back on the shelf.

Now, he wished he had bought the jar and tried his hand again at the delicacy. It was so simple, a cheese spread on white bread. But for a wanderer who has been away from home too long, a good pimento cheese sandwich is as good as home. The four enjoyed their sandwiches with a side of potato salad and ice cold sweet tea. They made plans for the coming days and it was determined that Helen would remain at home for the rest of the day getting

Jesse settled in. Aubry and her family would visit Jim that night to check on his status. As the meal drew to a close Jesse wondered if either of his other blood relatives could shed light on the enigmatic phrase scratched into his father's notebook.

"Have you guys ever heard of an 'Appalachian Slam'?" Jesse inquired leaning back from the table and his empty plate.

"Oh God, not you too," Helen muttered folding her napkin on the plate in front of her.

"What do you mean? Jesse asked.

"Did you see Dad's notebook downstairs?" Aubry asked, leaning over the table and brushing a long strand of dark hair out of her face.

"Yeah, I did."

"I flipped through that when I brought his stuff home from the hospital yesterday. I wondered what that was."

"You know what it is Mom?" Jesse asked.

"No, not really," she said, standing up and collecting the plates and forks from around the table. "He told me once, but I wasn't really paying attention. He's always talking about fishing and sometimes I just have to drown it out. But he was always saying something about it afterwards. God, it's been years. He's always talking about 'the Slam' and how he's going to get it any day."

"But you can't remember what it is?" Jesse asked.

"No," Helen replied. "You'll have to ask him later."

Jesse found that very unlikely.

"Or you can go ask his friends down at the bait shop. I've heard him talking with them about it before."

Jesse wondered again what it is that his father had been so fascinated by. What could have been so intriguing as to take up so much of the man's time and thoughts? Whatever the Appalachian Slam was, he was determined he would find out.

CHAPTER 6

"The secret to fly-fishing is..."

Buffering.

The red progress bar under the video on Jesse's iPad screen had stopped moving. Above it, a rotating wheel on the smooth, reflective screen indicated that the video was attempting to play faster than it could load. He had only been home for a day but he learned quickly that his parents had not upgraded their internet system in far too long. In frustration he paused the video, then pressed play, pause, and then play again, each time he tapped the screen harder than before. Nothing. The image of a half-blinking bearded fisherman in a wide-brimmed hat standing in the middle of a Rocky Mountain stream remained frozen on the device.

He had been attempting to watch YouTube videos on fly-fishing for the past hour but had only been able to watch a few short minutes before becoming frustrated and moving on to the next one. He sat at the dusty workbench in the recesses of the basement where he tinkered with some of the tools and equipment while he waited on videos to load.

Jesse had spent all morning with his mother at the hospital. Overnight there had been no change in his father's condition and today was more of the same. The hospital room was quickly filling up with flowers and balloons sent by well-wishers as word of Jim Cavanaugh's circumstances spread across town. Jesse wondered how many of them actually knew his dispassionate father on a personal level. It was more likely that the who's who of Fannin County simply didn't want to incur the disfavor of Mrs. Cavanaugh. After a few hours of meeting with visitors and staring at the same medical charts and computer screens, Jesse left the hospital and returned to his parents' empty house, promising to return later.

When he was younger, his father had taught him how to fish. Or at least had tried. Even then, before it had become such a major part of his father's life, Jesse could see that fishing was almost a spiritual experience to the elder Cavanaugh. It was not uncommon for him to wake his young son and with a gleam in his eye invite him to join him in the river while there was still mist rising over the water. As a child, Jesse enjoyed the hobby to an extent but by the time he began middle school his interest had all but disappeared. He never shared his father's love for the outdoors or the river, and he hadn't picked up a fishing rod in years. But he was hoping he still remembered some of the pointers that his father gave him years ago.

It seemed a shame that he should have so much free time, with all of his father's equipment at his disposal, in a place which bragged about its fishing and not at least give the activity a fair chance. There wasn't anything better to do. Besides, Ted, his boss, was a fisherman who spent vacations in some of the best fishing spots in the world. At least it would give him something to talk about when he returned to the office.

Jim Cavanaugh's attempts to teach his son the delicate art of fly fishing never took root. Now it was the internet's turn to try and impart the sacred knowledge. Jesse glanced again at the screen. Instead of a window teaching him how to cast a line across the water, an error message read that he had lost internet connection altogether.

"That's it!" Jesse said aloud to the musty basement as he switched off the iPad and swung around on the stool.

After a few minutes of gathering equipment, Jesse pulled open the metal garage door letting light from the cloudless day flood across the basement. Jesse was wearing his father's fishing vest and carried in one hand a long fly rod and the wooden handled net. He had left the waders hanging on the wall. Something about putting on another man's pants seemed too personal. Jesse had a few more hours before he needed to meet up with his family. Plenty of time to try his luck in the water. In no time at all he would have a great conversation starter for his boss. He may not have been able to have the YouTube lesson he was hoping for but Jesse was successful at most things he put his mind to and felt confident he would be just fine.

Jesse placed the gear in the back of his father's truck. Jim Cavanaugh bought a Dodge Ram new in 1987. He always bragged about what a deal he had gotten and how he had negotiated such a great price out of the salesman at the lot. Jesse was amazed that the old, faded brown pickup was still running. Over the years it had taken a lot of abuse carrying Jim across dirt roads and up mountainsides to find the best fishing spots North Georgia had to offer. Jesse would have expected it to tap out years ago. But it looked now as if the loyal four wheel drive companion would outlive its driver.

Jesse drove down the short, gravel driveway, leaving a cloud of gray dust in the humid air between himself and the little white house. Finding out quickly that the air conditioner in the vehicle had, in fact, met its demise, Jesse rolled down the window of the tuck with the hand crank. He welcomed the relief from the stifling heat brought by the wind rushing by as he rumbled down the road.

Appalachian Slam.

The phrase swept across Jesse's thoughts without any provocation. Last night he had gone to sleep with the odd phrase racing through his mind. He had laid in bed wondering what it was and why his father had been chasing after it. By the time morning arrived Jesse had forgotten all about it and had not given it any thought all day. Now it was back. Jesse remembered what his mother said the day before about the bait shop as he came to an intersection near the main strip of the town. Jesse tried to remember where the bait shop was located and turned left, making an educated guess based on spotty memory after a car pulled up behind him, forcing him to decide.

Jim Cavanaugh had been retired for roughly a decade. His career at the local branch of Lawrence Insurance Group was as low stakes and unexciting as any that could be imagined. For decades Jim arrived early at the office, dealt warmly with his clients, processed claims, and went home. On his last day at work his co-workers took a few minutes to enjoy some cake in the break room, present him with a set of kitchen knives engraved with the company's logo, and a Hallmark card, and then promptly went about their work as though the old man had never existed.

It appeared to Jesse that Jim had embraced retirement, throwing himself into the culture of fly fishing like never before. From what his mother told him almost every morning, before wading into the rushing waters of the surrounding rivers and streams, Jim stopped at "Daddy Ray's Bait & Tackle" on Appalachian Highway to replenish any supplies that he needed and lie about former conquests with the rest of the fishermen. According to Helen some days Jim never even made it to the river, he just sat on a wooden stool with the rest of the old men arguing about sports, and politics, and weaving ever more elaborate tales of trout that they had almost certainly not caught.

Blue Ridge was a destination for fly fishermen from around the country. Tourism, driven by the outdoors was one of, if not the primary industry in the county. Accordingly, there were numerous bait shops and sports and outdoor retail stores all over the area. "Daddy Ray's" was by far the least profitable. The old log cabin had been sitting by the side of the highway near the river since well before the days when it was a major travel artery through the valley. A yellow, hand-painted sign hung askew from the tin roof and the gravel parking lot surrounding the small building was never full. Most fishermen visited the larger outlets which offered every item an angler could want at discounted prices. "Daddy Ray's" attracted only the older generation who were more interested in the social atmosphere of the shop than the limited selection of merchandise. Jesse remembered being dragged there by his father a few times and waiting impatiently as the men told their stories.

Gravel crunched under his tires as Jesse parked the truck in front of the old wooden building. Moving swiftly, Jesse bounded up the steps onto the creaky front porch. *This isn't very ADA compliant,* he thought to himself, noticing there was no ramp leading up to the warped surface. Jesse swung the screen door open and entered the shop with a chime from a small brass bell positioned over the doorway.

Inside, the cramped walls were lined with rods, reels, nets, vests, and tackle boxes. Rows stretching across the store contained lines, backing, hooks, flies, and fly making equipment. Jesse walked slowly through the store looking at all of the unfamiliar equipment and pausing briefly to examine strange looking lures and flies. On the right wall, the cash register was positioned atop a wooden counter next to displays of rock candy, Necco wafers, and two clear refrigerators, one for live bait, the other for cold Cokes. Behind the counter, an old man, older than any person Jesse had ever seen, leaned back in a leather office chair fast asleep. His snores filled the bait shop.

In addition to the heavy snoring, Jesse could hear voices drifting through the aisles. Making his way towards the voices, Jesse found himself in the back corner of the shop which had been outfitted into a sitting area. On one wall, an ugly green sofa was positioned with a rustic coffee table directly in front of it. On the other wall, in front of a dirty window, a counter was stretched out with a few high seated wooden stools. Two men were seated on the sofa, one, an elderly black gentleman, had his feet propped up on the coffee table littered with newspapers and fishing magazines. The other man, a balding white man the same age, had his face buried in that morning's edition of The

News Observer, the local paper. The two men continue to talk softly until one noticed the new arrival.

"Jesse Cavanaugh!" The old man with his feet on the table said with a hint of disbelief in his voice. The other man looked up from his newspaper and gazed, slack-jawed, at the newcomer.

Jesse's mind raced. This man obviously knew who he was but he had no memory of him at all. *I hate it when this happens*, he thought, flashing through faces in his head of people he had met over the course of his life.

"I'm sure you don't remember me," the man said as he removed his feet from the coffee table and slowly rose, extending his hand. "I'm Abram Siler. You and I met a couple times when you were a boy. This here is Bennie Ledbetter. Bennie, it's Jesse, Jim's boy."

"Bennie Ledbetter, Pleased to meet you," Bennie said in a deep gravel filled voice, and reached out to shake Jesse's hand in a firm grasp. He was a stout, barrel-chested man with thinning pitch black hair brushed straight back. He wore a pencil-thin mustache and was dressed casually in a pair of khakis and a short sleeve button down. He carried with him a distinct military feel which Jesse immediately recognized.

Abram, on the other hand, had a much looser feel about him. He was amiable and smiled wide at Jesse as he shook his hand. Abram's curly black hair was peppered with gray and the goatee which surrounded his lips was almost completely white. The two men seemed perfectly at peace sitting in the back corner of the empty bait shop. Jesse could tell immediately that they were permanent fixtures in the store.

"I'm awful sorry to hear about your dad," Bennie said folding his hands in front of him.

"Have a seat," Abram said, motioning to one of the wooden stools. "Let me get you something." Abram walked over to the refrigerator and began to pull out a bottle of Coca-Cola.

"Oh, no thanks, I'm fine," Jesse said.

"Don't worry, Daddy Ray won't mind." Abram motioned to the old man sleeping peacefully behind the cash register. "Here, it tastes better out of a glass bottle."

"Unless you want something a little stronger," Bennie said, holding up a coffee mug containing what Jesse assumed wasn't coffee.

"Stop it Bennie. This man is a New York City lawyer. He doesn't want any of your hooch!" Abram exclaimed as he sunk into the cushions of the couch.

Jesse pulled up a stool and opened the Coke. Abram was right. It did taste better that way.

"It's good to see you in town Jesse," Abram said. "It's a terrible thing that happened to your dad and I'm sure he'll be happy to know you came down to see him. But what are you doing in this old dump?"

"I actually came to find you guys," Jesse replied.

"Well, I'm flattered," Bennie said, rolling up his newspaper and leaning back into the cushions.

"You guys knew my dad pretty well, right?"

"Sure did," Abram answered. "We all come here most days. He sits right there on that stool you're sitting on. One of these days one of us will kick the bucket and he'll get to graduate to the couch."

"Well, I'm not planning on going anywhere soon," Bennie said. "So you must be holding a spot for him."

"He talked a lot about you Jesse," Abram said.

Jesse found that very unlikely but appreciated Abram's attempt to flatter him. "Do either of you know anything about something called an Appalachian Slam?" Jesse asked.

Immediately the two old fishermen burst into laughter. Bennie's was a loud obnoxious laugh originating deep within his protruding gut. Abram was more restrained but chuckled at the mention of the phrase. Jesse turned the half empty bottle he was holding around in his hands as he waited for the old men to get control of themselves.

"Where'd you hear that?" Abram asked, still smiling at the thought.

"I read about it in my dad's journal. I've never heard of it before. My mom thought the two of you might know what it is."

"Your father went on and on about that stupid Appalachian Slam. He's been chasing it for years." Bennie said, fanning himself with his newspaper as he recovered from his laughing spell. He leaned forward and took a quick shot out of his coffee mug.

"So you guys know about it. Do you mind letting me know what it is?"

"It's really no big deal," Abram replied. "The Appalachian Slam is what you call it when you catch all three species of trout that live in these here waters in the same day."

"What type of trout are those?" Jesse asked.

"Here in this corner of the world we got three trout," Abram answered. "Rainbow, brown and brook trout. The Rainbows are everywhere, the browns are less common, and the brookies, those suckers are the tough ones to get."

"Hmm," Jesse said to himself. It wasn't quite what he was expecting. It had seemed so mysterious in his father's writings and he was disappointed in such an anticlimactic explanation.

"The thing you've got to remember though," Bennie piped in. "To be a true Appalachian slam they all need to be caught on a fly reel, using barbless hooks."

"So, it's a pretty hard thing to do?" Jesse asked.

"That's just it," Abram replied. "It's not. I mean it is rare if you only fish every now and then. And it's definitely something to get excited about when it happens. But when you hit the water as much as your old man and us do it's bound to happen. That's why he was so frustrated by it. With as much time as he spent flipping a line around he should have gotten a slam years ago. The statistics don't make any sense. No matter how hard he tried it always eluded him. And it drove him crazy. I feel bad for him whenever he starts going on about it. I myself got the Slam twice and I don't even fish nearly as much as he does."

"Three times for me," Bennie remarked.

"Like hell you did!" Abram exclaimed at his friend. "Jesse, don't listen to this old fool, he's only gotten it once."

"No, no, no," Bennie said, slamming a fist on to the armrest of the couch. "It's not my fault you didn't come fishing those other times."

"If you don't document it and no one's around to see it, it doesn't count!" Abram asserted.

"What? You can't just trust me?" asked Bennie.

"I wouldn't trust you as far as I could throw you."

Jesse let the two old fishermen argue. The explanation of his father's obsession was much different from what he expected. It didn't sound so hard now that it had been fleshed out. *I'm sure Ted has heard of this Appalachian Slam,* Jesse thought. He figured it would give him something to shoot for and even if he doesn't manage to get it before he leaves he will still have a good story to tell Ted when he gets back.

"I have a quick question," Jesse said, halting the two men's argument. He looked over at the sleeping proprietor. "Does he sell any waders here?"

CHAPTER 7

The Toccoa River rises deep within the Chattahoochee National Forest. Its headwaters are fed from small streams and creeks which spread through the wilderness like arteries carrying the precious lifeblood of the mountains. From its source, the river runs northwesterly, jutting sporadically here and there as it bends around mountains and cuts across gentle slopes.

The name Toccoa is derived from the Cherokee word for "Catawba place." The Catawba tribe, who came from the nearby Carolinas, were enemies of the Cherokees and the two nations often clashed over the course of their long history. The name of the river endured, showing that at some point in the distant past the Catawbas made major incursions deep into Cherokee territory, leaving a lasting impression on the land and culture. After meandering across the state for 56 miles, the river rushes past the twin border towns of McCaysville, Georgia and Copperhill, Tennessee. At the border, the name abruptly changes from the Toccoa to the Ocoee River as it continues across the Volunteer State.

Near the upper Toccoa, cool water from rainstorms and dew trickle drop by drop down the mountainsides. One drop merges with another, which in turn combines with more. Small rivulets of clear mountain water form larger streams as they come together from distant branches. As the streams of water, fed by rain, are fueled even further by frigid subterranean supplies, they gain speed and force as the courses combine with other streams to form the many creeks which serve as tributaries to the mighty river.

From stream to creek, to river, the water flows deliberately and constantly. At times, when the river is wide and deep, the water drifts slowly with nothing but a faint, almost imperceptible current. At other times, when sharp cliffs cut deep into the bank, narrowing the river, the water surges violently over smooth rocks and boulders. Eventually, the ancient path of the river continues to the point where it empties into the still waters of Lake Blue Ridge.

The lake encompasses over 3,000 acres of water which is surrounded by approximately 60 miles of pristine forested shoreline. Eventually, the water, which flows into the lake from the upper Toccoa, makes its way through man's concrete and steel structure and bursts from the dam's outlet into the Lower Toccoa river. From that point, the river continues its methodical journey past the town of Blue Ridge. It flows past log cabins and state parks. It creeps gently around waiting bends and rushes swiftly over rocks and downed trees, decaying in the moving waters. Sunlight flits in between swaying branches stretching across the surface before warming ever so slightly the moving water.

On this sunny afternoon, a cool rush of water, which had traveled so far on its pilgrimage from the mountain heights to the small town below, swirled around Jesse. He stood thigh deep in the middle of a wide stretch of the river lined by green overhanging trees on both sides. Jesse's body and clothes were completely dry, protected by the new pair of Hodgman waders pulled up to his chest. Behind him, an unnoticed price tag still attached to the neoprene garment spun in the current. Even though the water drifting past him was kept at bay by the waterproof material, its cool temperature penetrated the fabric and provided a welcome relief from the overbearing heat from the sun overhead. A bead of sweat trickled past the sunglasses shielding his blue eyes but nonetheless, Jesse was relatively comfortable in the chilled embrace of the moving stream.

After purchasing the only pair of waders Daddy Ray had left on the shelves of his small store, Jesse drove a short distance to a nearby city park with public access to the river. The park's easy access and proximity, along with the wide, slow-moving waters made it a favorite location for families and beginners. It also didn't hurt that the Georgia Wildlife Resources Division used the park as an input for stocking the river with young trout from their local hatcheries. After donning the new waders, his father's boots, and the khaki fishing vest, Jesse picked a random fly from a clamshell container in one of the pockets and stepped into the water to try and remember something from his brief experiences years ago and the few minutes of online instruction he had managed to view earlier.

He had been there for over an hour already. Almost immediately after entering the current Jesse turned against the flow and stumbled his way upstream. His thick boots were equipped with felt soles which allowed them to firmly grip algae and moss covered rocks. The popular footwear was banned in many states because of their ability to retain and transport harmful algae from one locale to another. But in Georgia, they were still legal, and the best way to traverse slick rocks hiding below the surface of the water. Even so, Jesse almost slipped and fell in the water three times while moving upstream but had managed to keep himself upright and dry each time.

Jesse decided to move upstream because the point where he entered the water was occupied by two anglers sitting on lawn chairs by the riverbank. One, a large man with a long, white beard wore a pair of overalls without any shirt underneath. His companion, a skinny, middle-aged man with greasy hair sat next to him with his rod in one hand and a can of beer in the other. The two were accompanied by the ugliest dog Jesse had ever seen. The small dog was missing almost all its fur and was well on its way towards losing the rest as it constantly scratched itself furiously. The two fishermen were not fishing with flies but with rooster tail lures which they threw out into the river and then lazily reeled back on their spinning reels. After the two men erupted into laughter when Jesse almost fell into the water due to a particularly slippery boulder, he thought it best to move upstream and away from an audience.

Now he was all alone. He preferred to be alone. In New York he worked best when he was holed up in his office with no one to distract him. Here, in the river, he enjoyed the solitude as the water rushed by. Or at least he did at first. After an hour of shuffling over rocks and sweating under the beating sun he was beginning to rethink his decision to take up his father's hobby.

Jesse remembered something about casting the fly upstream and letting it drift down before casting it upstream again. He pulled the line off the reel as he remembered doing years before and started to gently whip it back and forth over his head. Eventually, picking a spot upriver to place the fly he cast the line forward. The line noisily slapped against the surface of the water as the small hooked fly landed far from its intended target.

That doesn't seem right. Jesse thought.

Over the course of the next long hour Jesse continued to whip the line over his head, back and forth. In short time he was able to avoid that initial slap of the line on the water, which he was sure scared any fish in the area away. After some trial and error he figured out that if he released the line earlier in the air it would gently drift down onto the moving water. He still was no better at aiming his cast. Although, Jesse was pleased he was able to place the fly in the general vicinity of where he aimed but even he recognized that was giving the term "general vicinity" a very liberal definition.

Over and over again, he cast the line somewhere upstream and watched it drift gently towards him in the moving water. Periodically Jesse reeled in a few feet of line floating across the swirling surface to keep it from doubling up on itself as it drifted. Eventually the line would reach Jesse and pass him by, moving lazily downstream until it straightened out and he began the process of another cast.

His patience was wearing thin. Jesse recognized this was a bad sign because he had always heard that fishing required a great amount of patience. He had arrived at the river determined to catch, over the next couple of weeks, what had eluded his father for so many years. Now, after standing in the hot sun with not even a single strike from a trout since his first cast, it didn't seem as important.

What am I doing out here? He questioned. *I need to be following up on Carvalho's deal, not splashing around in a river trying to catch some stupid fish.*

Jesse cast the line back upstream. Once again, it landed a good distance from the point where he had aimed the throw and began to drift downstream. He decided that after one or two more tries he would pack up and head back to the house. He had had enough and was already beginning to kick himself for coming out in the first place.

"You're not going to catch anything on that fly." He heard from behind him. The voice was clear and unmistakable.

Jesse turned slowly to find Jim Cavanaugh staring at him. His father stood in the water not far from him wearing the old rubber waders which Jesse had left hanging on the basement wall. He had just been with his father earlier but the man standing in front of him was not the frail, comatose person he left lying in the hospital bed. This man seemed lively and alert, maybe even a few years younger. His voice, deep and smooth, with a slight southern drawl, was the same voice Jesse knew from years of hearing his father lie about the fish he caught.

Jesse would have been surprised or frightened if he believed on any level that what he was seeing was real. But he understood almost immediately that the voice he heard and the image he saw were merely figments of his imagination. He did not know why his mind would project the image of his father onto his subconscious but there it was, channeling his own thoughts and impressions and attributing them to the figure standing before him.

"You're not real," Jesse said, turning back towards the line which was drifting towards him. Jesse hoped he hadn't said that out loud. There was no one around to hear him talk to himself but he would still rather avoid it. He determined that anything else he felt to say would take place within the secure confines of his mind.

"Of course I'm not real." His father said, crossing his arms. "But you're still not going to catch anything on that fly."

Jesse ignored the voice as the line slipped past him with the flow of the water.

"Suit yourself. It seems to me like you could use some advice but it's okay if you don't want it." Jim said turning with his son to watch the line move onward.

"You can't give me any useful advice because you're not real," Jesse said calmly. "You can't say anything that I don't already know."

"Well, now that's thinking like a lawyer," the old man said with a chuckle. "I guess you got me there. You always were smarter than me."

"Please stop talking," the younger Cavanaugh begged as he began to reel in excess line.

"I'm your subconscious you know," Jim asserted. "I just might have some valuable insights. Think about it. You've been reading my journals, you came out here when you were just a boy. You could have gleaned something of worth that just might help. I'd be happy to share it with you."

"Don't you have somewhere to be?" Jesse asked the imaginary specter of his ill father. "Like dying in a hospital." Immediately Jesse felt regret for the response even though the figure he was arguing with didn't actually exist.

"That's a little harsh, don't you think? Besides, I'd rather be out here with you."

There was an awkward silence as Jesse whipped the line back and forth over his head before casting it off again.

"Diving caddis" Jim muttered.

"What was that?" Jesse asked the apparition.

"You should try using a diving caddis." His father said slowly. "You're fishing a Parachute Adams. Those should really be used more in the fall and winter. Not in June."

"You don't say?" Jesse responded sarcastically.

"C'mon, what's it going to hurt to give it a try?" Jim inquired. "Besides, the diving caddis is a wet fly. Those make for an easier cast. They're much better for a beginner."

"Fine," he said reeling in his line and pulling in the seemingly useless fly at the end. Jesse was ready to go but he figured he would give it a few more tries with another fly if not to just get it out of his mind.

He remembered reading briefly about the difference between dry and wet flies. Dry flies float on the surface of the water, imitating mature nymphs and caddis. Wet flies on the other hand sink below the surface. They are pulled underneath by the current and are meant to resemble the early, underwater stage of the insect.

Jesse let the fishing rod and reel float on the surface of the water as he pulled in the almost invisible leader and the fly tied securely to the end. Using a small combo tool he snipped the line and secured the hook of the used fly in the foam of a small case he had pulled from a separate pocket. The handheld, floatable case contained a few dozen flies, each one painstakingly crafted by Jim's elderly hands. Every one of them was beautiful in its own right, adorned with colorful thread, felt, hair, and feathers. Jesse stared at the layout before him trying to remember from some brief passage or lesson from his father which one was the diving caddis.

"It's that brown and white one right there." His father said, pointing over Jesse's shoulder.

Jesse, still annoyed at the illusion's presence plucked the small fly from the case and tied it to the end of the waiting leader.

"With that one you want to cast it quartering downstream."

Jesse wasn't quite sure what that meant but he had read it somewhere and so he turned himself around so that he was now facing in the same direction the river was flowing. He brought the line up over his head and worked it back and forth as he pulled the line out from the reel with his left hand, lengthening the line in the air with each swing. He cast forward and the line flew downstream before landing and being pulled underneath the water.

"You've got to work on that cast," his father chided.

"I think I'll be okay," Jesse responded. "I'm not really planning on coming out here again."

"I thought you were going to try for the Slam?" His father asked, obviously disappointed.

"Yeah, well I thought I was going to as well. But believe it or not Dad, some people have more to do than waste their time standing out in the water all day."

"That's too bad," Jim said, looking down at the moving water. "It's beautiful out here. I think you'd like it if you gave it more than a couple of hours. You know, I don't think I'm going to be coming out here anymore. What I wouldn't give to waste my time standing in the water all day one more time."

Jesse felt the current pulling his line as the underwater fly was carried along with the water and he let more line out to allow the fly to move freely.

"There you go," his father said. "Let it sit there for a minute and then reel it in a bit."

"I know what I'm doing,' Jesse said quietly as he cranked on the reel a few times, moving the fly upstream. The heat from the blazing sun beat on his scalp through his thick head of hair.

"Next time you should bring a hat." Jim piped in, watching as his son smoothly pulled in more line.

"I told you Dad, there's not going to be a next time."

All of a sudden Jesse felt the line move. The current of the river had been moving the line since he first cast in but this was different, more erratic. Something had definitely struck the fly. He grasped the rod with both hands.

"Whoa, calm down." His father said, wading up next to him. "Wait until it really takes it, then set your hook. Don't get too jumpy."

"I know, I know," Jesse replied in frustration.

Jesse stared intently at the line. Below him, the noise of the water swirling around his legs disappeared along with the sounds of the birds above. Everything was still in his mind as he focused on the line and the unseen trout dancing around the fly at the end. An eternity passed, and then another. Still nothing. Eventually, his heartrate slowed and Jesse came to the conclusion that the curious fish had moved on.

Suddenly the tip of his rod bent forward as the line was pulled tight. Instinctively Jesse gripped the rod and pulled back sharply, setting the hook into the fleshy mouth of the unsuspecting fish. He pulled the rod back with one hand and cranked on the reel with the other. On the other end of the line the fish darted back and forth, attempting to escape the snare, the line followed it across the water. The fish fought hard, moving every which way as Jesse continued to reel it closer towards him.

"Give him some room to run." Jim's voice chimed in, "You've got him, don't worry, just bring him in nice and steady."

Jesse eased up ever so slightly. Just enough to give it some space but not enough to let the hook loose from the fish's mouth. He could feel his heart pounding and a rush of adrenaline seethed through his blood. Jesse imagined a prize-winning fish waiting under the turbulent surface of the water. He was sure it wouldn't be any record breaker but it felt like a monster battling at the end of the line. Finally he pulled it close enough to see flashes of color from its bright side scales as it darted beneath the water. He reached behind him and retrieved the net he had attached to his waist.

"Be careful there," Jim said, "keep that line tight."

Jesse held the long fishing rod upright keeping the line tight as he pulled the fish close enough to scoop the net underwater and retrieve his prize. He pulled the net to his face and gazed upon the most beautiful rainbow trout he had ever seen. He easily pulled the barbless hook from the fish's mouth and extricated the trout from the net, holding it in front of him with both hands. The back of the fish was dark green with brown spots all over it. Along both sides, a swath of bright pink scales stretched from its gills to its tail. Jesse didn't feel like measuring the fish but estimated it to be about eight inches long.

"That is a beauty right there," Jim's southern voice remarked. "We'll call it 9 inches."

Smiling, Jesse crouched down and plunged the fish underwater, holding it for a few seconds while the water rushed over its body before letting it go. The trout flipped its tail and with deep lateral movements of its slender body it propelled into the river. Jesse remained crouched, enjoying the feel of the cool water as it swirled around him. After a moment he became acutely aware again of the heat bearing down on him from the sun above. *Dad's right. Next time, I should bring a hat.*

CHAPTER 8

"Hurry up, it's time to go!" Helen yelled down the open basement door to her son.

She paced across the kitchen in her high heels while screwing the backs on to her earrings. She wore a bright yellow dress with her usual pearls and carried a fashionable white clutch in her manicured hands. It was Sunday morning and at the rate at which Jesse was moving, Helen feared they would be late to church. And Helen Cavanaugh was never late. Every Sunday for decades Helen had been seated next to her husband in their usual spot in the chapel well before Sunday services began. She was not about to let her son ruin her streak now.

"Jesse! Did you hear me?"

"Yeah mom, I heard you," his voice called up from the descending staircase. "Do I really need to wear this?"

"No, you didn't if you had packed a suit like an adult. I mean for God's sake, Jesse, you're a lawyer, you don't have a jacket you could have brought?"

"I have plenty of suits Mom," Jesse added. "But it's so hot down here and I wasn't really anticipating a need for one."

"Well, that's not my fault." His mother snapped. "That's the only suit in the house that fits you. Now get up here right now!"

Dutifully Jesse climbed the stairs heavy footed and stepped into the kitchen. He wore a slim-cut blue and white striped seersucker suit over his white shirt and navy blue tie. The look on his face and his slumped shoulders indicated even further that he was not happy about the outfit.

"What are those?" Helen asked pointing at her son's feet.

"What?" He inquired, looking down at his polished black dress shoes. "My shoes?"

"You can't wear black shoes with a seersucker suit." She said calmly, trying to temper her frustration. "What are we, animals?"

"You've got to be kidding me?" Jesse said, looking at his mother in disbelief. "I don't want to wear this thing in the first place, now I need different shoes?"

"And a belt too." She said. "Jesse, these types of rules are what separate us from the beasts. I will not have my son showing up to church dressed like he just wandered in off the streets. There's a pair of brown loafers in your closet, go put them on along with a matching belt."

"You know Mom," Jesse responded, "I brought some nice slacks and shirts. I would look perfectly presentable in what I have."

"These are church services Jesse, not some night at the bar. Winnie Roebuck's boy doesn't wear a suit to church and look at what's become of him."

Jesse had no idea who his mother was talking about but didn't inquire further. He'd rather not find out what tragedy had supposedly befallen this person as a consequence of his refusal to wear a proper Sunday outfit.

"You will wear a jacket." His mother demanded, pointing at him. "More specifically, you will wear *that* jacket unless you have a different one hiding in your pocket. Now go change your shoes, we need to go now."

Jesse contemplated telling his mother that he would rather not go to church at all. But he knew that would just raise issues that didn't need to occupy their time right now. And it would be pointless anyways. He knew the rule. If you stayed under Helen Cavanaugh's roof, you went to church. No exceptions. He obediently went each week as a child, and even a few times in college. But ever since moving to Manhattan he hadn't stepped foot across the threshold of a chapel.

"Fine," he replied with a sigh and turned back to the basement. After finding the appropriate footwear and belt he returned to his waiting mother.

"Now don't you look handsome," Helen said, straightening the lapels on her son's chest. "If you're going to be a southern lawyer you might as well dress like one."

"Well, I'm not a southern lawyer so..." Jesse trailed off.

"The way I see it you're a lawyer and you're from the South, that makes you a Southern lawyer. You could practice law on the moon for all I care. Every southern lawyer should have a seersucker suit."

Seersucker, the all-cotton fabric with alternating puckered and flat sections was a common summer suit among barristers who resided below the Mason-Dixon line. Fictional Southern attorneys such as Atticus Finch and Matlock had kept the tradition alive, and in 21st-century courthouses across the region it was still common to see lawyers clad in the vintage striped outfits. The fabric was light and airy, making it a comfortable alternative to traditional suits in the sweltering heat of the summer. They were typically worn for the first time on Easter Sunday, but were traditionally not worn past labor day. Such fashion decrees had been all but abandoned in most parts of the country but in Blue Ridge, Georgia they were not only alive, but were strictly adhered to.

The First Baptist Church of Blue Ridge was packed. Services hadn't begun yet but almost all of the pews of the large white chapel were filled with chatting congregants or items marking that the seats were saved for someone who had stepped away. To his great displeasure, Jesse noted a number of attendees without suits or jackets who looked perfectly fine, and not a bit out of place. Jesse tried to keep a low profile as they moved through the aisle but his mother was stopped every few feet by an acquaintance expressing their condolences for her husband.

"Jesse! Jesse! Over here!" a voice called out in a sort of loud whisper.

Jesse turned to see his sister at the front of the chapel waving to him. He glanced back at his mother, who was speaking to a concerned group of women, and figured she would catch up. Aubry was waving to him from the second row in the crowded room, her purse and a book were marking spots on the hard wooden pew next to her, obviously reserved for himself and their mother.

"Nice suit fancyman." His sister said to him as he approached.

"Do we really have to sit way up here?" Jesse asked. "I saw a few spots left back there."

"You know how Mom is," Aubry replied. "These are her seats. Everyone knows it and she won't sit anywhere else."

Just then Jayden came running through the legs of the standing churchgoers and wrapped his small arms around his uncle's knees. Behind him, Marco strode through the crowd.

"Oh hey there buddy," Jesse said, clearly shocked at the child attached to his legs. He patted him awkwardly on the head like a dog.

"Jesse," Marco said, shaking his hand and embracing his brother-in-law with his other arm, "long time, no see. Nice suit. You look very dapper."

"Thanks Marco."

Marco Quezada, the son of Cuban immigrants, was raised in Miami. After meeting Aubry Cavanaugh while working for a construction company out of Atlanta he moved to Blue Ridge and began his own contracting business. Over the years he grew the business into a rather lucrative presence in the community, even weathering the difficulties of the financial crisis which had bankrupted many of his competitors. His athletic frame and Cuban accent made him a local heartthrob among the ladies of Fannin County but he only had eyes for Aubry.

While Marco was a welcomed addition to the family, the Quezadas harbored a secret. Marco was a graduate of the University of Florida. The small community of Blue Ridge was predominately made up of fans of the nearby University of Georgia and the two schools were bitter rivals. In the South, college football is serious business and long-standing rivalries are not trivial matters. The family therefore never spoke of Marco's alma mater. Jim Cavanaugh even went so far once as to lie about it altogether, telling a business associate that his son-in-law had attended the University of Miami. Jesse had always liked Marco, and while he had not spent enough time to get to know him intimately, he was pleased to see that his sister was married to a good man that made her happy.

The services were as boring as Jesse had feared. He had hoped to bury himself in his phone for the majority of the sermon but, anticipating his plans, his mother had insisted he leave his phone in the car. Luckily, he had come prepared with a backup. As the sermon began, Jesse pulled his father's small notebook out of the inside pocket of his jacket and opened to a marked page near the beginning.

Jesse was hooked on fly fishing. He was hooked worse than the rainbow trout he had pulled out of the Toccoa a few days ago. That first fish had struck at precisely the right time. It almost seemed that it had been waiting until Jesse was prepared to leave the river, determined to never return, before striking. Ever since reeling in that first rainbow Jesse could think of little else. Even though he didn't receive a single strike for the rest of that afternoon he had returned home with the rush of that initial catch still present deep within his chest.

Jesse soon concluded that's just how fishing goes. You never catch enough to truly call the outing a success, just enough to keep you coming back. And Jesse had gone back. On both of the following days, after visiting his father in the hospital with his mother and helping with minor chores around the house, Jesse retreated to the same park, waded upstream to a secluded area and cast his line downstream.

Now, shaded by both his sunglasses and his old Braves ball cap, Jesse was comfortable moving through the cool water to try and find new spots in the stretch of river near the park. On both occasions Jesse was rewarded for his perseverance. His second afternoon on the river he caught another rainbow and on the subsequent day he reeled in two more. All were roughly the same size but none were as breathtaking as that first. Having caught only rainbow trout, Jesse was nowhere closer to achieving the Appalachian Slam than he was on his first outing but he understood that he had only tried one spot as he began to learn the subtle art of fly fishing. He knew that to have any hope of progress in catching all three species he would have to venture to other, more challenging, locales. For now he was happy to spend a few hours at this one, easy location until he got his feet under him.

Each time Jesse was accompanied by the illusion of his father standing in the river next to him. It was concerning to him that his mind created the fantasy so vividly. He supposed that he simply associated the act of fishing with his dying father and so his own thoughts on the subject were manifested as advice from the old man. He was sure that a psychiatrist would love to spend some time with him on the topic but Jesse wouldn't give anyone the satisfaction. For the most part he attempted to drown out the voice constantly attempting to correct his casting technique but periodically, when a suggestion sounded particularly promising, he gave in and followed the instruction.

In between the hospital visits, the chores, and the fishing, Jesse had spent some time over the past two days reading through his father's journal. Half of the writing was illegible. His father was never known for his penmanship. Most of it was notes on locations to fish, flies to use, and recordings of what he had caught. Peppered among all of the notes were recordings of personal thoughts and insights into a number of different topics ranging from sports, to religion, to politics. On some pages, small words were scribbled into the margins of the lined pages, making adjustments to prior notes.

The book was almost completely full. Only a handful of untouched pages remained inside the back cover. Jesse was interested in extracting from the old notebook any useful facts regarding locations, fly choices, and techniques. Although he sometimes wondered how useful the information really was since his father had never caught the Appalachian Slam in spite of his best efforts. Holding the small journal low against his lap Jesse looked over the poorly written words and began to read.

Rock Creek, August 24: It's about two o'clock. Plenty of time left. I've been catching rainbows all day. I can't keep them off my flies. Wouldn't want to anyways. Caught me a brookie just now. It wasn't anything to get excited about. Maybe six inches. Didn't even put up a fight. But those are the tough ones to get! I haven't gotten a brookie in months. Now all I need is a brown and I got me a Slam. I felt it this morning. Today is the day. I can still feel it.

I caught it with a hare's ear nymph. 1:45pm. I caught some of the rainbows on the same fly, some on a wooly bugger. Not even sure where I am on the creek. I went up one of the side streams quite a ways. The farther up I go, the better luck I have, so I'm gonna keep heading upstream until I can't no more. I don't think I'm going to make it anywhere else today. I saw Richie a couple of hours ago and he caught him a nice brown up the main creek. If I don't get nothing here I'll head back to the main creek and move up that.

Home, August 24: No Slam today. I thought for sure it was gonna happen. I caught a nice brookie and everything. All I needed was a brown. Those suckers aren't even that rare. After catching that one I got me a little rainbow. I headed back down to the main part of Rock Creek a little bit later where Richie said he was. I got a few bites but nothing grabbed on. I don't think Richie caught anything. I think he was lying. Oh well. I'm going to head back there in a couple of days and give it another shot.

I've been reading more about the Bighorn River out in Montana. I've never fished one of those Western rivers but I'd sure like to. When I do, I think the Bighorn will be my first stop. That or the Madison River. From what I read, those rivers are lousy with monster fish. And there aren't any trees hanging over the water to tangle my line on. One of these days me and Helen are gonna take a trip out there. She'll love the view. I wonder if I could get the kids to come? As soon as I get the Appalachian Slam that's where we'll go. Montana.

That was the way most of Jim's entries went. He gets his hopes up, talks about what is working that day or what is not, gets disappointed, and then gets introspective. He ends a number of them talking about Montana. Apparently Jesse's father, who had rarely traveled outside of the Deep South and never been west of the Mississippi, had a fairly intense desire to take his fly fishing skills to the storied waterways of the American West. Jesse had never heard anything of the sort from his father in all the years he knew him. Jesse wondered if he had ever even expressed the desire to his wife. But it was peppered throughout the intimate notebook. Jesse disregarded the travel wishes and disillusionment of the journal entry and made a mental note to find out where Rock Creek was and to try out a hare's ear nymph and wooly bugger on it sometime soon.

The rest of the sermon dragged on as Jesse attempted to decipher some of the more unreadable handwriting in the book. Jesse didn't listen to a word of the discourse and as soon as the services were over he found the shortest route out of the chapel and made his escape. Helen stayed behind, greeting fellow church members who wanted to express their concern for her husband. Jesse followed his sister's family to their truck, catching up with Marco until his mother emerged from the crowd.

Jesse had wanted to go fishing after church. However, when he expressed his plans to his mother earlier that morning she had informed him of her strict no fishing on Sunday policy. Apparently she did not permit his father to venture out on the water on the Sabbath and she would not permit him to do so either.

That evening, the smell of fried chicken filled the small house, and his sister's family helped mash potatoes and shuck corn in the kitchen. Meanwhile, Jesse excused himself and ventured into the soft grass of the backyard with his father's fishing rod. His casting technique over the last few days left much to be desired and his father had made a note in his journal about practicing on dry land. Jesse removed the fly from the end of the leader so as not to snag anything while throwing the line across the lawn. At first he was afraid that the weight of the line wouldn't be authentic without anything tied to the end but after feeling the line slide through the air overhead as he moved his arm back and forth, he came to the conclusion that the fly didn't add any measurable weight. It was the weight of the thick line itself that provided balance in the cast.

Jesse chose a target in the yard and cast towards it. He was making progress but the perfectionist in him was unhappy with his inconsistency.

The neon green line cut through the air, disappearing in the golden sky before drifting to the ground. Again and again he let the line fly. Again and again it dropped around the targeted location, but never on it.

"Keep your wrist straight."

Jesse turned. Aubry was standing behind him, one hand on her hip, and the other gripping a fly rod.

"I am keeping it straight," Jesse replied, reeling in some of the excess length laying on the ground at his feet.

"No you're not," she said. "You're moving it all over the place. And your elbow too."

"What are you doing out here anyways?" Jesse asked.

"You looked like you could use some help. Here, watch, I'll try to hit that rock." Aubry pulled a long portion of line out of the reel and cast it up and behind her before bringing it forward smoothly. The line jumped off the ground, through the circular guides on the rod and sailed through the air. Aubry expertly landed the end of the line on a gray rock at the edge of their mother's garden.

"You've got to be kidding me," Jesse exclaimed.

"Just keep your wrist and elbow locked. Use your shoulder to move the rod." She pulled the line back to her, preparing for another cast. "And when you change direction do it smoothly, don't snap the line. It's not a whip."

"I'll keep that in mind."

"Mom told me you've been out fishing the last few days," Aubry said.

"Yep," Jesse responded. He was wary of his sister's tone. He appreciated the casting tips but wasn't interested in the psychoanalysis that usually accompanied his her conversations. Up until now, no one had attempted to talk to him about his feelings or his thoughts. He could tell his sister intended on doing just that and he wouldn't let her do so.

"It's kind of weird, don't you think?" she asked.

"Nope." He responded. He turned his back slightly to his sister as he adjusted the line, attempting to signal to her to back off.

"I mean, you couldn't care less about fishing your whole life. I've heard you call it stupid so many times. Then, all of a sudden, Dad's in the hospital, and you're out there every day."

"I'm just trying to pass the time."

"What are you looking for out there Jesse?" Aubry asked, staring at her brother with a look of genuine concern on her face. There was a long pause before Jesse turned back to her.

"Fish," he simply responded. Another long pause filled the space between them.

"Well," Aubry finally spoke. "You're not going to catch very many with that cast. Here watch me again."

CHAPTER 9

The sun rose, and the sun set. And Jesse fished. He had been home for over a week and with the sole exception of Sunday, Jesse had spent a portion of each day standing at the river. With his sister's help, Jesse had vastly improved his casting technique. While he was not nearly as proficient as some of the local anglers who he occasionally met on his daily excursions, Jesse was proud of the progress he had made.

The day after his first lesson with Aubry, Jesse ascended the creaking stairs at Daddy Ray's to speak with Abram and Bennie. The two old men gave him increasingly incoherent directions to what they considered the best access point to Rock Creek. For some unknown reason, both Abram and Bennie preferred to use landmarks to give directions instead of road names. At first, Jesse tried to follow along with their ramblings but when Bennie advised him to take a left "where Jack Rabun used to sell boiled peanuts before he died," he decided it was best to leave it to Google.

While the two weren't helpful at giving directions, they had a wealth of knowledge regarding proper flies to use and techniques that would be useful at that particular creek. As the two men loudly debated which flies were better at that time of year Jesse took mental notes. When the conversation began to devolve into a heated argument Jesse politely thanked them for their insights, slipped past Daddy Ray, asleep behind his counter, and made his escape.

Unlike his father, Jesse only caught rainbow trout on his first visit to Rock Creek. Once again, just enough to make him want to come back. Jesse found the narrow confines of the creek more difficult to manage than the wide open waters of the Toccoa. On more than one occasion Jesse hooked one of the many overhanging tree branches which made up the intersecting latticework of greenery above the water. Sometimes, depending on the way in which the small hook entangled with the branches, Jesse was able to free his trapped fly with the right flick of the line. But most of the snags resulted in a broken line and a lost fly. Jesse wondered how many trees across the southeast were decorated with the lures and hooks of frustrated fishermen.

The change in environment required that Jesse adjust the cast he had so diligently worked to improve. Instead of long, slow arcs, Jesse moved the tip of his rod quickly resulting in shorter bows passing quickly overhead. He concentrated intently to avoid the snapping whip motion his sister had warned him against. He even experimented with the side casts he had observed from more experienced outdoorsmen downstream but quickly decided he needed more practice with that technique before real-world application.

In the end, the lost flies, the setbacks, and the frustrations bore fruit and Jesse left Rock Creek with more experience in the artistic science of fly fishing. He took that experience and moved on to other creeks in the surrounding area. Each stretch of water brought new knowledge and Jesse began feeling comfortable immersing himself in the beauty of the flowing waters and their surrounding blanket of green woodlands. It was rare now that Jesse even thought about the work waiting for him in New York. When he did, he felt anxious and guilty, wondering what catastrophe had befallen his precious deal due to his neglect. But the feelings never lasted long. Anxiety and remorse are easily cured by a bent fishing rod.

Normally Jesse's cleanly shaved face accentuated his sharp masculine jawline and his parted hair portrayed the deliberate image of consummate professionalism. However, over the last week, Jesse let his facial hair grow a few days before shaving, deciding that since he was not meeting with clients in the woods it wasn't necessary. His light beard was nothing more than a few days growth but it was longer than it had ever been. Jesse was surprised when he looked in the mirror and saw how much gray was sprinkled into the short hairs on his chin. He had worked hard to keep himself in shape and was proud that he had maintained the body and stamina of a much younger man. But the face with the graying beard staring back at him, while distinguished, looked significantly older than he had expected. Time had marched on without him even realizing it. The evidence had been there all along, he had just been shaving it off every day.

Every day or so Jesse made sure to perform his family duties and visited his father's hospital bed. His mother preferred to have someone there as much as possible in case something happened. Helen was there most. She often read aloud from the many outdoor and fishing magazines to which her husband subscribed. Jesse appreciated her kindness as well because it left reading material for him when he took his shift in watching over the old man.

The Jim Cavanaugh lying in the hospital bed was not the Jim Cavanaugh with whom Jesse regularly communed on the river. This man was weak and frail. The man conjured by Jesse's vivid imagination was strong and vibrant. This man was strapped to numerous machines and tubes, just barely clinging to life. The man who accompanied Jesse each day to the water was always ready to impart a minor criticism or timely advice. This man was completely silent.

It was mid-morning. Jesse had traveled to the hospital early, hoping to do his time and then slip out around lunchtime. He had heard from Bennie and Abram that the day before a number of anglers had good luck at a creek south of town, and Jesse was anxious to give it a try. The room was quiet. Except for the steady beat of his father's heart rate monitor and the Darth Vader-like breathing machine, Jesse sat in silence, flipping through a copy of "Field & Stream" he had read before. Jesse, who usually relished silence, whether at his office or while fishing, was unnerved by the stillness of the hospital room.

There was no conversing with his father here. No figment of his imagination bothered him as it did while he was on the water. This was reality. The whir of the machines and the drip of sustaining fluid from the I.V. bag were real. His father was dying. Jesse understood that. He would never say it in front of his mother and sister, but it was true. They continued to insist that the family patriarch would beat the odds and make it. He was surprised their optimism had lasted this long.

Jesse laid the magazine aside and watched his father for a moment as he lay silently on the hospital bed. Jesse wanted to be angry with his father. He wanted to feel resentment for him for his distancing himself from his only son at a time when Jesse needed him. The same resentment he had felt for years. He wanted to feel offended at having been largely forgotten and ignored by the man who maintained an outward appearance of family unity and love. But he didn't. Or at least he felt like he couldn't feel those emotions at this time. No, right now all Jesse felt for the man was pity. Even with how distant they had grown, Jesse never wanted to see his father in this position, facing such hopeless odds. He wished he could feel the anger and resentment he had kept buried within his soul for so many years but he simply couldn't.

He shook the thoughts from his head. It was late into the morning already but he needed coffee. In reality, he needed a break from the deafening silence of his father's room, but coffee was as good an excuse as any. Jesse closed the door behind him and strolled through the wide sterile hallways to the hospital's small diner. The sitting area was sparsely populated. Only a handful of hospital employees nursing large lattes and frappuccinos, no doubt using the caffeine to endure a long shift. The smell of roasted coffee and the undecipherable conversations taking place in the open space were welcome reliefs from the hospital room where Jesse had spent the last few hours. The warm cup felt good in his hands even though the temperature outside had passed ninety degrees a few hours ago. It was always so cold in hospitals and Jesse was grateful for the comfort provided by the steaming hot black coffee. Just as he was turning to find a seat he heard someone call out to him.

"Jesse Cavanaugh!" a woman's voice said just loud enough to reach him without drawing any unnecessary attention.

Jesse turned and saw an attractive brunette in floral pink hospital scrubs standing up from her seat at a small table. He racked his brain trying to place a name with the slender face. He had worked hard since coming to town to avoid situations where he would run into people he knew, hoping to avoid this very situation. Jesse had been gone for a long time and had no communication with anyone from his adolescence except for his family. When he had received an invitation in the mail for his high school reunion he hadn't thought twice before dropping it in the nearest trash can. Now he was faced with someone obviously his same age who recognized him. His mind fired rapidly as it sifted through the many names of his high school classmates.

All of a sudden it hit him. How could he have forgotten?

"Karen?" He said calmly as a bolt of electricity surged through his chest.

The woman standing in front of him with her dark brown hair pulled back into a loose ponytail was Karen Hunter. The two had been good friends in high school, even dating briefly during their senior year. In an instant, a flood of memories swept over Jesse. He had visions of sneaking home late at night, the senior prom, and high school football games.

In Blue Ridge, unless somebody moved into town, which almost never happened, you knew people your age from the time you were small children for as long as both of you lived in the community. Jesse and Karen had been in classes together from elementary school through their last day at Fannin County High School. In the second grade she had forced him to marry her on the school bus and she gave him a hard time about it for years. For roughly twelve years they attended everything from birthday parties, to Fourth of July cookouts, to Christmas gatherings together. Aside from the second-grade wedding, Karen had been Jesse's first awkward kiss and only real high school girlfriend, although the relationship only lasted until graduation when he left to attend separate universities.

Of course, Jesse had thought about her over the years. They even kept in touch briefly as they started their college studies, but not for long. Soon they developed separate lives and like most of the people he knew from his days in Blue Ridge, Jesse hadn't seen her for quite some time. He had hoped not to run into anyone while he was visiting his family but all of a sudden, seeing Karen in front of him, he didn't mind at all.

"Jesse," she said, putting her arms around him in a kind hug. "I cannot believe it's you. My God, I couldn't believe my eyes when I looked up and saw you."

Her voice sounded exactly the same as it had when they were in high school, with just the right amount of Southern inflection to denote where she was from but without overpowering her melodic voice. Jesse, still somewhat surprised to see her, forced himself to stumble through a response.

"I wasn't expecting to see you here. How are you doing?"

"I'm fine," she said, brushing a stray strand of hair out of her face. "Do you need to run off somewhere? Have a seat." She motioned to the extra chair across from hers at the small table.

The two sat across from each other and Karen pushed aside the magazine she had been browsing through. It was obvious that she had been at the hospital for some time already. Her dark hair, while pulled out of her face, fell here and there, framing her delicate features. Slightly smudged eyeliner surrounded the same deep emerald eyes that he remembered staring into as a teenager. Even now, clearly caught off guard running into Jesse during a long shift, Karen was a stunning sight in the dull context of the hospital diner.

"Jesse, I am so sorry," she said, reaching across the table and placing her soft hand on his. "I heard your dad had a heart attack."

"Stroke actually," he responded. "Thanks, I appreciate it. Yeah, I came to town to see the family and help out."

"How's he doing?" She inquired.

"Well," Jesse said, pausing, "I don't think he's doing so well. My family is optimistic but you probably know how it is. I think it's just a matter of time."

"I'm so sorry. It's such a shame. He's a good man. I remember he used to always give me extra pancakes at the Memorial Day breakfast at the church every year."

"Yeah, we'll be okay," Jesse responded, not wanting to talk more about his father. "What about you? I didn't know you worked here?"

"Yep, a few years now," she said, nodding and sipping her coffee. "I work up in oncology."

"I'm surprised you're here. I thought after getting your nursing degree you worked at a hospital in Atlanta?"

"Well, you know what they say," she answered, "There's no place like home."

Jesse all of a sudden remembered something else he had heard about Karen through his mother a few years before. "That's right," he said, leaning back in this chair, "You're not Karen Hunter anymore, you're Karen Corrigan."

He recalled how Jesse's mother had excitedly told him that Karen had married another one of Jesse's classmates, Roddy Corrigan. Roddy had socialized in the same circles as Jesse and Karen. Jesse had known him for most of his life as well and the two had been friends, having played for years on the same baseball teams. Jesse couldn't remember what Roddy's profession was, but he thought he had heard that he was still in town. He remembered when his mother had told him about their wedding which she had attended because she had lamented the fact that Jesse and Karen had not ended up together.

"Actually," Karen said awkwardly, "it's Hunter again."

"Oh," Jesse said, feeling embarrassed. He inadvertently glanced at her ring-less left hand, still close to his on the table. "I'm sorry. I didn't know."

"No, it's fine." Karen countered. "Believe me, it's okay. I wouldn't expect you to have known. Word gets around pretty quickly down here but it takes a while to reach a fancy lawyer up in New York."

Jesse smiled, laughing slightly at her jab.

"So how about you?" She inquired. "How have you been? What have you been up to?"

"Well," He said, holding the cooling cup of coffee with both hands. "I've spent the last few years..."

"Oh my God!" Karen said gasping as she glanced at her phone's screen. "I have to get back upstairs. I am so sorry."

Unexpectedly, Jesse felt disappointed. He hadn't anticipated running into Karen but now that she was beginning to stand up and gather her things, he was sorry to see her leaving so soon. He stood as well, as she was preparing to turn away.

"I'm sorry Jesse, I lost track of the time. I'd love to catch up. I really want to hear everything about what you've been up to. How long are you in town?"

"Probably another week or two," Jesse replied. "You know, depending on what happens with Dad."

"Okay, um," Karen muttered, looking around the area close to their table. She spotted a discarded pen with the logo of an insurance company and grabbed it. "Let me give you my number, shoot me a text so I can put your number in my phone. Call me maybe tomorrow, or you know, sometime, and let's get together." Karen ripped a corner off a page in her magazine and hastily scrawled a telephone number across it. She handed the small piece of paper to Jesse and gave him another hug.

"All right," Jesse said, holding up the torn page, "to be continued."

"I'm serious Cavanaugh," She said, pointing a manicured finger at his face. "If you don't call me I'm going to kill you, or worse, tell your mother."

"All right," he laughed. "Go save somebody's life or something."

Karen turned, and half jogged from the sitting area toward the elevators around the corner. Jesse tucked the ripped page into the back pocket of his jeans and smiled. He took a sip of his coffee. It had grown colder than he preferred but he hardly noticed as he sat back and watched as Karen rounded the corner and disappeared.

CHAPTER 10

Dust swirled across fluorescent beams of light cutting through the stale basement air. Jesse didn't notice the roiling waves of tiny particles flitting in and out of the light surrounding the workbench. He intently focused on the task at hand. But periodically, when he stretched in the uncomfortable seat, feeling the vertebrae in his spine pop, we would notice the floating dust as it danced across the light. It was beautiful. It moved waywardly through the air, swirling, resting, and then moving again, carried on the slightest breath. Finally, the dust disappeared into the darkness of the basement, having strayed from the boundaries defined by the buzzing overhead lamp.

Jesse stared attentively through the convex surface of an enlarged magnifying lens positioned between himself and a number of tools laid neatly across the workbench. On the other side of the lens, a small, barbless hook was grasped at its curve by the minuscule jaws of a fly tying vise. The small hook appeared double its actual size as Jesse peered through the oversized lens. In one hand, Jesse held tight a length of black thread which he had already tied to and wound around the shaft of the metal hook. In the fingers of his other hand, he pinched a dozen or so long fibers from a reddish-orange feather. He had found the feather, along with many others, in one of the many cubbies on the back wall of the workbench. Each cubby held a different material. Feathers, fur, foam, thread. They were crudely labeled and terribly disorganized. It annoyed Jesse just thinking about the materials let alone having to search through each one to find what he needed. He vowed to organize it properly before returning to New York.

Around, and around and around. The black thread wound around the shaft again and again, this time fastening the fibers to the hook along with it. Still holding the thread tight, Jesse folded the long fibers over the side of the shaft and wound them back around the hook towards the eye. Moving carefully and deliberately, Jesse tied the fibers in place. It was warm in the basement and a bead of sweat dripped onto the magnifying lens. Finally, breathing slowly, Jesse folded the excess length of fiber backwards over the length of the shaft and tied the fibers down using a small, metal tying tool called a whip finisher. Holding his breath, Jesse clipped the extra, unneeded thread and applied a small drop of thin head cement to the finished product.

Jesse admired his creation. It was a simple nymph, nothing special. Its fibers fanned out downward, away from the eye of the hook. Jesse released it from the grasp of the vise, holding the small fly in between his thumb and forefinger. It wasn't perfect by any means but he was proud of the result. He opened his father's fly case and placed it next to the other two flies he had tied previously, plunging the hook securely into the foam lining to hold the fly in place. All three were the same design and Jesse was happy to notice a vast improvement from the first one to the third.

Jim Cavanaugh's large collection of hand-tied flies had been greatly diminished since his son had begun using them. Jesse had decorated branches, vines, and trunks along the banks of the rivers and streams he had visited over the course of the last week with the delicate creations. He felt bad for losing so many of the objects his father had spent so much time making. While he had accepted the fact that his father wouldn't be using them anymore, he still felt a need to replace them. First, he had attempted to purchase replacement flies from Daddy Ray's but Abram and Bennie, who never seemed to leave the bait shop, talked him into tying his own since all of his father's flies had been handcrafted by the old man. After a few frustratingly slow loading internet videos and a brief once-over of a fly tying book he found on top of the old wooden workbench Jesse took a shot at the procedure.

Initially Jesse consulted the yellowed pages of the book at each step of the process. But as he continued, the intricate process became easier and more natural. The first one was ugly, there was no way around it. It was just ugly. Jesse wondered if any self-respecting trout would give the lure a second glance. But he kept it anyways. There were plenty of materials scattered through the cubbies and he wasn't worried about depleting them. Now, as he secured the third nymph in his father's fly case, he was happy with the time spent on it. *Any fish would be proud to be caught on this fly.*

Attached to a small metal clip on the front of one of the cubbies was the ripped magazine corner upon which was scrawled Karen's phone number. It had been two days and Jesse still hadn't called her. He had spent those two days fishing and debating whether to get in touch with her as promised. It was a surprisingly difficult decision to make. Jesse had simply wanted to get done what he needed to, make sure his family was handling things reasonably well, and then go home. Calling an ex-girlfriend to catch up would accomplish exactly the opposite of those plans.

However, Jesse was surprised at how much he enjoyed seeing her. He hadn't thought about Karen for ages but sitting at a table across from her brought back memories he forgot he even had. Back in New York he was married to his work. He casually found himself on a date here or there but had kept himself distanced from developing a serious relationship with anyone for quite some time. He had no interest in getting involved romantically with Karen or anyone else, but he still debated the pros and cons of spending time with her while he was there.

It was Sunday once again. The weather was perfect, and Jesse had been hoping to try his new creations at Stanley Creek sometime soon. However, his mother had reiterated to him the rule against fishing on Sunday, as though he had forgotten. It was obvious she recognized his desire to get to the water and she cut him off as soon as she could. Helen was now at a luncheon, which Jesse had deftly avoided, and the house was quiet while he worked away on his flies. The warm sunlight beaming through the open garage door mocked him as the cool breeze that drifted in taunted Jesse in his basement prison. Jesse had come to enjoy the outdoors much more than he ever had when he actually lived here and the thought of squandering the optimal weather conditions on a day of rest pained him.

She's not even here. He wondered how his dad, the most devoted angler he had ever met, lived with the archaic rule that Helen enforced along with all of her other household regulations. He leaned back on the stool and gazed out the open door into the bright world outside. He could hear birds singing as though they were calling his name. Somewhere from within the basement, the faint sound of an old clock ticked the seconds away. He glanced around at his surroundings before finally making a decision.

Jesse bolted out of the chair as though he were struck by lightning. His mother's rule was outdated and idiotic at best. What made fishing any less reverent than sitting in an uncomfortable pew? He'd probably be back before she returned home anyways and even if not, he wasn't worried, she should just be happy that he is here at all. He grabbed his waders, hanging from a nail next to his father's, and slung them over his shoulder as he gathered the vest, his hat, a fly rod, and the rest of his equipment. As he reached for the fly case containing what was left of his father's collection along with his new additions, his hand accidentally knocked the small plastic box and it slid across the table before falling into the dark space between the workbench and the rough concrete wall. Jesse sighed. He placed his gear gently on the workbench and crouched down, peering into the gap between the piece of furniture and the wall.

It was dark, He couldn't see anything but he knew that somewhere in that four-inch space lay the flies he needed. Jesse reached into the pocket of his jeans and retrieved his cell phone, activating its powerful flashlight. The gap was surprisingly full of debris, trash, and discarded fly making material. He was disgusted at the disorganization.

"Come on Dad," he said aloud as he stretched his arm through the space, past the debris, and grabbed the corner of the box sticking up above the trash.

He pulled the case free and brushed dust off his arm. At the last moment, as Jesse was preparing to power down the phone's light, something caught his eye at the back of the gap. He pointed the phone into the space again and peered past the discarded trash to a tall box standing up against the back wall at the end of the narrow space. It was pink and somewhat shiny, which is how it had caught the phone's light so well in the dark, dusty space.

"What the..." Jesse mumbled to himself as he stretched his arm back through the space to retrieve the mystery item. His fingers just barely reached the smooth packaging of the box and he pulled it out into the light.

It was about three feet long and completely wrapped in pink and white striped wrapping paper. It was obviously a gift, but for whom? The end of the package was covered in layers of dust. It had obviously been wedged between the wall and workbench for years. Jesse turned it over in his hands, examining it as he stood. Finally his eyes landed on a small flap of extra paper which had been taped to the box and folded over as a makeshift label. Jesse flipped the scrap of paper open. The underside of the wrapping paper was beginning to yellow with age. Written across it in his father's unmistakable scrawl was a single name.

Elle.

Jesse threw the box on the workbench. It landed with a loud thud that echoed across the expanse of the basement. Jesse stared at the box in dismay.

He clenched his jaw and his nostrils flared as he glared at the motionless gift. The basement was silent but if there were anyone else in the room with Jesse they would have felt the rigid anxiety hanging in the air. After a few, tense moments, Jesse relaxed. He exhaled sharply and loosened his hands from the tight fists he had been holding at his side.

It's okay Jesse. He told himself. *Just forget about it and move on.*

Jesse decided what he needed was to get out to the water. He picked the fly case up and tucked it into the pocket of his vest. After gathering the rest of the equipment he put aside moments before, Jesse glanced one more time at the gift laying across the workbench and walked out of the basement, pulling the garage door down behind him.

The drive to Stanley Creek took longer than expected. Along the way Jesse's mind kept returning to the dusty gift he had uncovered. Each time it entered his mind Jesse anxiously sought to force it out. Sports radio, talk radio, music. They all worked for a few moments but not long after fleeing his mind, the thoughts returned. He knew it shouldn't affect him the way it did but finding the surprising gift made him angry. Thinking about it made him angry. It was obvious that the gift had been arranged by his father with the best of intentions. That's what gifts were. But still. it made him angry, no matter how irrational it was.

Finally, after what seemed like hours, Jesse arrived at the entrance to the creek. Jesse parked the truck along the side of a dusty gravel road, donned the waders and boots, and took his gear down to the running water. He didn't welcome the coolness of the water contrasting the blistering heat of the sun as he normally did. He didn't hear the different melodies of the birds flitting in and out of the greenery overhead. The sweet fragrance of honeysuckles hanging from a group of bushes near the creek passed by Jesse completely undetected. He couldn't focus on the experiences which had drawn him to the water in the first place. Instead he just cast his line as he moved upstream. And he cast, and he cast, and he cast. An hour passed, and nothing changed. Jesse continued to cast his line across the water. Nothing. Not a bite, or a strike from anything.

"You want to talk about it?" Jim's voice inquired.

In his mind, the man was standing in the stream next to him, his arms folded over a plaid button-down shirt covered up to his chest in his own thick waders. Jesse peered at his father's image from under his baseball cap and sunglasses. He had wondered when he would show up, surprised by the fact that he hadn't until now. Jesse then turned back to the line in front of him, reeling in a few feet as it drifted downstream.

"Really?" his father said. "You don't want to talk about it? Come on Jesse, I'm only here because you're thinking about me. Obviously you want to talk about something"

Jesse continued to stare forward, focusing intently on the line even though it didn't require it.

"All right. We can just fish if you want."

"What's in the gift?" Jesse asked without breaking his unflinching gaze from downstream.

"How should I know?" Jim asked, shrugging his shoulders and raising his hands. "As you so often remind me, I'm just a figment of your imagination. If you want to find out, open it."

"I'm not going to open it," Jesse said resolutely.

"Why not?" Jim asked. "It was meant for Elle. She's obviously not going to be opening it."

"Shut up." Jesse quickly responded.

"I'm just saying. You might as well open it up and see. It's just going to keep gathering dust unless you do."

"Drop it." Jesse calmly said. "Never mind. I never should have brought it up."

"Well, you obviously want to know," Jim said, wading next to his son.

"I said drop it." Jesse turned to face his Dad.

"I'd love to drop it. But I'm not real. The only reason I keep bringing it up is because you want me to." Jim's eyes stared straight into Jesse's. "I don't know what's in that box Jesse, but it's easy enough to find out. Just open it."

"What was it for? Why is it even there?" Jesse asked.

"You can figure that out as well as I can." His father said, speaking with his hands, the way he always did. "It's an old gift, it's obvious that I got it for Elle before she..."

"Stop it!" Jesse snapped, pointing his finger at the specter in front of him. He looked around, realizing he had just shouted out loud. Until now, the images of his comatose father and their interactions had all been kept securely within the confines of his own mind. He was alone at Stanley Creek. Had there been observers to witness his outburst they would have undoubtedly assumed he was insane.

"By the way, are you going to call that girl or what?" Jim asked in his long southern drawl.

"What?!" Jesse asked incredulously. "How can you...? Where did that come from?"

"I don't know Jesse, these are your thoughts. We can go back to talking about that gift if you'd like."

"No, I don't want to..."

Jesse's annoyed response was cut short by his cell phone buzzing from the pocket inside his waders. Normally while fishing Jesse was happy to let calls go to voicemail, but he welcomed the timely distraction. He unclasped one strap of the waders and awkwardly reached into his pocket to retrieve the phone. The display on the screen showed a picture of Gabe and Jesse hurriedly answered it.

"Jesse," Gabe answered back. "How's it going buddy?"

"Oh, you know," Jesse said calmly, still glancing at the image of his father standing in the water. "Just getting by down here."

"Good to hear. So you haven't been carried away by those giant mosquitoes down there?"

"Nope, I've fended most of them off so far." Jesse placed the phone between his ear and his shoulder as he used both hands to begin reeling in his line which had become taut as it drifted farther down the river.

"Ok Jesse, everything here is going fine."

"Why would you say that Gabe?" Jesse began to worry. Certainly Gabe hadn't called him to tell him that everything was fine. "Wait, are you at work? What are you doing there on a Sunday?"

"I'm just ironing some things out," Gabe responded.

"Wait, what are you ironing out?" Jesse was beginning to become very concerned.

"Ok Jesse, you can't tell Ted I called you. He explicitly told all of us to leave you alone. He's convinced you aren't handling this whole thing with your dad well. But I needed to ask you a quick question."

"What's going on Gabe?"

"So I've been working on the Carvalho deal and I wanted to ask you if you thought the other side would have a big issue if Carvalho had granted more licenses on their intellectual property than they originally thought?"

"Uh oh," Jim mumbled as he stared down the river.

"What?" Jesse began reeling his line in faster. "What do you mean? That due diligence has been done for months."

"Yeah, I know," Gabe continued, "It just looks like there were some old contracts that might not even be valid that they forgot about. It's probably nothing, and the other side didn't see it in their due diligence either, but then again we didn't even know about it until now. I just wanted to see if you thought it would be a big issue or not."

"Gabe, that is a very big issue. We have to disclose that and if it isn't handled correctly it could tank the whole deal. They might think that Carvalho was intentionally withholding information in order to make the deal happen. They are nervous enough as it is, this could reopen old fears that we already dealt with."

"That's no good," Jim said. Jesse turned away from his father to try to have some privacy but he could still feel his eyes behind him.

"I can talk to them and see what I can do to smooth things over." Jesse volunteered.

"No Jesse, you can't do that," Gabe said hurriedly. "Ted will kill me. He's serious about this whole 'not bothering Cavanaugh' thing."

"If you lose this deal Ted won't have to kill you because I will." Jesse wanted the threat to come off playful but he meant every word of it.

"Jesse, it'll be fine," Gabe said, trying to reassure him. "I just needed to gauge how important this issue was from someone who knows the deal better than I do. I'll be able to handle it."

"Send me copies of the contracts." Jesse pleaded. "I'll look over them and email the client."

"I can't do that, man. I shouldn't have even called you."

Jesse clenched his teeth in frustration. He had worked for over a year on making this deal a reality. If it didn't go through because he was stuck in his hometown, he would never forgive himself. He pulled his cap off of his head, running his fingers through his hair and pulled it back down even lower over his forehead. A vision of the pink wrapped gift flashed across his mind. He couldn't even concentrate on the crisis at hand.

"Well, can you at least keep me updated?" he asked Gabe.

"Of course," Gabe responded. "Listen, I've got to run. I'll get this figured out. Don't worry. Your baby is safe with me."

"It better be," Jesse said, and the two hung up.

It was quiet. The only sound was the bubbling of the water running across the stones under Jesse's feet. The specter of his father remained. No matter how much he willed it to leave, it remained in front of him with his arms crossed until it spoke once again.

"So," Jim breathed out awkwardly. "Do you still want to know what's in that present?"

Jesse let out a scream of frustration and heaved his cell phone at the unwanted vision of his father. As soon as he did he immediately regretted his rash decision as he heard the phone make a sickening *plunk* sound as it disappeared below the surface of the water.

"No no no no no!" Jesse said as he splashed the short distance toward where the phone had made contact with the water. He hurled the fishing rod he was still holding onto the nearest bank and knelt down in the water, searching with his hands for the phone on the river bottom. Chilling mountain water flooded his waders as his chest dipped below the surface. His fingers fumbled over stones, mud, and underwater plants until finally he felt the unmistakable shape of his iPhone. He pulled it out of the water and half stood as he made his way toward a large rock in the middle of the stream where he sat in exhaustion examining his phone.

"Well, are you happy now!?" he yelled.

But nobody answered. Jesse looked around him through water droplets sprinkled across the lenses of his sunglasses. He was alone.

CHAPTER 11

A handful of rice lay scattered across the uneven surface of a well-used butcher block. Most of the contents of the discarded bag had been emptied, uncooked, into one of Helen's favorite clear Tupperware containers. Buried somewhere beneath the grains, Jesse's drenched cell phone lay cradled in the arid embrace of the bleached kernels. Jesse sat in a wooden kitchen chair facing the butcher block with his arms folded and his eyes closed.

Upon returning home agitated at the afternoon in general, Jesse had, at the insistence of his mother, covered the phone in rice and sat back in the rickety chair to gather his thoughts. The idea behind the modern day folksy remedy is that the rice acts as a desiccant which absorbs the water from the saturated phone. Numerous scientific and pseudo-scientific studies suggest that the rice trick practiced by so many doesn't work any better than leaving the device in a dry spot to air out. However, thousands swear by it.

Jesse hadn't fallen asleep, but he had drifted off somewhere between thought and dreams. He was unsure how much time had passed but at some point he became aware that he had never changed out of his wet clothes and because of the humid weather they had hardy dried at all.

"That's why you don't go fishing on Sunday." His mother's voice jolted him back to reality.

"Really Mom," he said, leaning back on the two hind legs of the chair and opening his eyes, "that's why?"

"Yes, it is."

"So you're saying that the entire reason that you haven't let Dad go fishing on Sundays for decades, is because his phone might get wet?"

Helen rolled her eyes. "You know that's not what I'm saying."

Something delicious smelling was cooking in the oven which had been distracting Jesse from his brooding. It's difficult enough to dwell on bitter emotions in a comfortable home, add in the smell of a home-cooked meal and it becomes nearly impossible. Jesse returned his chair legs to all fours and pulled his damp frame out of the chair. Crossing the kitchen he pulled a cold bottle of beer from the inside door of the fridge. Before leaving the room he put his arm around his mother and kissed her on the top of her head.

"Sorry, Mom. I won't do it again."

"Damn right you won't."

Jesse smiled as he sipped his beer and proceeded downstairs to take a shower and change his clothes. He flipped on the light and moved across the basement towards his bedroom. In doing so, Jesse glanced towards the corner of the musty space and glimpsed what he expected to see but hoped to avoid. The wrapped gift was still lying where he had left it earlier that day. Its pink packaging was clearly visible through the dim light. He had expected that when he viewed it next the same feelings of rage and bitterness would overflow to the surface as they had before, but the only thing he felt now was curiosity.

Jesse took another swig of his beer as he made his way toward the workbench. He could still feel the water in his clothes as he sat down on the stool and turned on the overhead light. The bottom of the cold bottle, damp with condensation, instantly became covered with dust which clung to the minuscule droplets as he placed it on the workbench. Jesse picked up the package staring back at him and turned it over. This time there was no shock as he read the makeshift tag.

Elle.

Before that day Jesse had not heard that name for some time. For a while, it was not uncommon to hear family or friends whisper the name in hushed conversations when they believed he couldn't hear them. He knew they meant no harm and weren't talking behind his back. They only concealed their quieted discussions from him out of a concern for what they perceived to be his fragile emotions. Whenever he had heard the name whispered behind him Jesse felt a short sting of pain somewhere deep within his chest. It did not take long before the conversations ceased. Jesse had not heard anyone mention Elle for years. But he thought about her often.

Just a few hours before, Jesse had been agonizing about what could be wrapped in the gift which lay before him. He thought about his father's words from his own imagination at the river. *If you want to find out, open it.* His father was right. Elle wasn't going to open it. So why not him? If he didn't, no one would, and it would keep gathering dust as it had been for years. Maybe, thought Jesse, that was for the best.

Jesse placed the long, rectangular gift on the workbench next to his beer. With a sigh he slid it across the surface toward the gap between the work-bench and the concrete wall. He let the box tip slowly and fall over the edge into the dusty, trash-filled abyss from whence he had retrieved it. With a muffled thud it disappeared from sight.

He was still curious about the contents of the gift. The thought of his father preparing the present without ever speaking about it made him irrationally furious on some unexplainable level. But for the time being, he didn't want to open it. He recognized that might change within the next few days or even within the next few hours. In that event, he knew exactly where to find the gift. But in the meantime this ensured he didn't have to stare at the box, watching it taunt him.

The pipes creaked as Jesse turned the knobs in the shower of the bathroom attached to his bedroom. He stripped his wet clothes off and left them in a sopping pile on the floor next to the sink. The hot water streaming from the calcium encrusted shower head felt divine on his clammy skin. It was the middle of the summer but the rushing waters of the mountain stream were frigid. While the cool flow of the current had been a relief from the stifling heat of the afternoon, the rush of chilled water filling his waders had been a shock for which he had not been prepared.

After his short argument with the imagined presence of his father in the middle of the stream where he had thrown his cell phone, Jesse was left alone. No more snide comments from his father's voice or trite expressions about fishing. No, Jesse was left alone with his own thoughts, in his own voice. He was still angry, in fact, he was furious. Whether such anger was deserved was of no concern to him. Sitting on that rock in the middle of the flowing water the anger he felt didn't bother him. But something else did. Jesse Cavanaugh felt alone for the first time in years. Jesse hadn't been in a serious relationship for some time, he lived alone, rarely saw his family, and spent little time in social situations with friends and acquaintances. By all accounts, loneliness should have been an everyday feeling for him. But it never was. Jesse had always felt content with his life and the people that were part of it. But now, for the first time in a very long time, Jesse felt the pangs of loneliness and it unnerved him.

The shower helped. Jesse welcomed each second enveloped by the steam before it began to gradually cool. Jesse knew that if he did not get out soon he would be facing another round of frigid water for the second time that day. In an old house like this, with a heater almost as old as he was, hot water was a commodity that didn't last long.

Through the old floorboards over his head he heard a phone ring and the muffled voice of his mother as she answered the incoming call. The household telephone was the same one Jesse and his sister had fought over throughout high school. Jesse couldn't believe it when he heard its shrill ring for the first time after arriving home. Back in New York most people, like himself, didn't even have home telephones anymore. Jesse and everyone he knew relied solely on their smartphones for communication. Landlines were reserved almost exclusively for places of business.

But the Cavanaughs refused to let go of the device. Jim and Helen hadn't even upgraded to a modern home phone with its wireless handset and caller ID. No, the plastic, beige phone was still tethered to the wall by a comically long, curly cord which almost reached the floor when left unused. Jesse could remember fighting with his parents when he was a sophomore in high school, begging them to add a second line so that he could speak with his friends in the privacy of his basement retreat. But his mother had refused to give in. Instead, he spent countless hours sitting halfway down the basement steps with the cord stretched up the stairs and across the hallway.

"Jesse! Phone!" Helen's voice yelled down the stairs just as it had two decades before.

Jesse was just finishing buttoning his shirt when he heard his mother's announcement through his bedroom door. He was confused. Who would call him here? Who would even know to call him here?

"What!?"

"The phone. Someone's on the phone for you!"

"Yeah, Mom, I... I'll be right there!"

His mind raced. He thought about Gabe and his call earlier. His thoughts quickly jumped to the only logical conclusion. The deal was falling apart and Gabe needed help. His own phone was lying dead in a suspension of rice. He was unreachable. But how had Gabe gotten his parents' home phone number? His mind raced briefly. Janice, his secretary. She had spoken with Aubry on the day of his father's stroke. His sister must have given Janice the number. For all of Janice's unneeded meddling Jesse was suddenly thankful she had saved this information.

Jesse forgot about the last button and threw open the bedroom door. His long legs bounded up the staircase where he came spilling out into the hallway.

"Well, well well, someone's excited," his mother said, holding the heel of her palm over the mouthpiece of the phone.

"Give me the phone Mom."

"It's a girl..."

"What?"

"Oooo..." A chorus of voices rang out together from the open kitchen. Marco, Aubry, and Jayden stood around the table, setting plates and folding napkins in preparation for dinner. Jesse was thoroughly confused and as always, slightly annoyed at his family. He reached out and took the waiting phone from his mother.

"Go get 'em Jesse!" Marco yelled out from the kitchen, eliciting a playful smack from his wife.

"Hello?" Jesse said quizzically into the handset.

"So am I going to have to kill you or what?" A woman's voice asked from the other end of the line.

"I'm sorry?"

"You were supposed to call me Cavanaugh."

It finally hit him. Karen.

"Who is it?" Aubry's voice whispered. She had snuck down the hall and was standing uncomfortably close to him, trying to listen to the conversation. Jesse tried to wave her away as he turned his back to her.

"Karen, sorry I hadn't gotten around to calling you yet."

"Karen?" Aubry muttered to herself before excitedly turning to her mother and the rest of the family watching on from the kitchen. "It's Karen Hunter," she whispered loudly down the hall.

"Oh my," Helen said, holding her hand to her chest.

Jesse shot the two women an upset look and stretched the cord through the basement doorway. He gave himself enough slack and closed the creaky door on the cord. Jesse felt like he was in high school again, hiding on the stairs from his family while speaking to Karen on the old phone. However, now when he sat down on the steps he could feel his older joints pop.

"Yeah, you're in big trouble buddy. So, are we going to get together or what? I want to continue our conversation and really catch up. It was good seeing you the other day."

"Yeah, let's do it. I'm glad you called. I'm not sure how much longer I'll be in town."

"I know," she said matter-of-factly. "That's why I called you. I figured I need to catch you before you skipped town on me."

"Are you free tomorrow about lunchtime?"

"Mmmm... I was thinking more dinner. And yes I'm free tomorrow."

Jesse smiled at her forwardness. He had enjoyed spending just a few minutes with her over coffee and looked forward to reconnecting with his old friend. Just seconds before, his heart had been racing, assuming the most important deal of his life had come grinding to a halt in his absence. Karen's smooth southern drawl drifting through the earpiece of the phone chased the anxiety from his mind. His troubles at work were momentarily forgotten.

"Dinner sounds great."

"Oh, and you're paying. A big ol' fancy lawyer like you should be able to shell out for dinner and drinks."

"Well. I guess if I have to..." Jesse chuckled slightly.

"And who says chivalry is dead."

"How about I pick you up around seven if that works for you."

"Of course. Oh, and it has to be someplace nice. None of that crap you used to take me to back in the day."

"Have you seen this town?" Jesse asked. "We'll see how nice of a restaurant we can find, but we may end up at a Golden Corral."

"Come on, we've got great stuff here. And besides, the Golden Corral got shut down a while ago. Something about mice"

"We'll see what we can do."

"All right Cavanaugh, I've got a pretty important crossword puzzle I need to finish so I'll let you go but I'll see you tomorrow night."

"See you then Karen."

The phone line clicked and Jesse smiled in the dim light of the stairwell. For a moment he forgot about the unexpected loneliness he had felt earlier that day at the river. He actually had something to look forward to here. However he wished he could remain in the basement and avoid the barrage of questions he was about to receive from his mother and sister. But he knew it was inevitable. Jesse pulled himself off the steps, feeling his joints pop again as he rose. He opened the door to find the two women waiting for him on the other side, both smiling as they leaned against the wallpapered corridor. Jesse resigned himself to his fate and stepped into the hallway.

CHAPTER 12

Friction causes heat. During a thunderstorm, as precipitation and ice crystals move against one another, ions are charged by friction and build up static electricity. These charges grow and are eventually released as bolts of lightning. The average bolt of lightning results in a flash which is five times hotter than the surface of the sun. The increase in temperature in the column of air surrounding the bolt causes a shock wave from the rapid expansion of gases and results in the thunder which accompanies every lightning strike.

Sometimes the lightning is contained within the dark clouds looming over the landscape, sometimes it arcs between the clouds themselves, and sometimes it travels from the clouds to the ground's surface. On hot summer nights in the Deep South, it isn't uncommon for residents to spend their evenings sitting on front porches to enjoy the celestial displays of heat lightning.

In reality, heat lightning doesn't exist. The explanation given by many throughout the South is that the lightning bolts streaking across the sky are a result of the muggy air itself. Elderly family members give the explanation confidently and the myth passes from one generation to another. However, it is not grounded in scientific fact. Heat lightning is simply regular lightning generated by a distant thunderstorm. The lighting is far enough in the distance that the following thunder can't be heard and it is often too dark to see the clouds from which the lightning springs.

While the traditionally shared cause of heat lightning is at odds with its scientific explanation, there is something about it which has never been disputed. It is beautiful. On hazy summer evenings, lightning from dozens of miles away can illuminate the entire expanse of the cloudy twilight sky without a sound. Particles in the humid air, combined with the curvature of the Earth, and the different light provided by the setting sun can cause the lighting to take on an array of colors. Even after the sun has set, distinct and various hues of light flash suddenly against the sky as remote storms gather strength. White, blue, green, even pink veins of electricity spread instantly across the darkening sky and vanish as quickly as they appear.

Watching the flashes of light in the distance reminded Jesse of his summers as a child in Blue Ridge. The lightning streaking through the heavy Georgia air brought to his mind a specific night. He was probably twelve years old. Jesse and his father had been out of town at a baseball tournament all day. Jesse had been playing second base for his summer league. The two were driving home in the same pickup truck that Jesse had been driving while his father was in the hospital.

That night, the cab of the truck was deathly silent save for the rumble of the mountain road beneath the sturdy tires. Not even the radio was playing. Jesse suspected that his father had turned it off, believing his son, who was leaning against the inside of the passenger door, had fallen asleep. But Jesse was awake. His head was turned away from his father, towards the window, and his eyes were open as he stared into the darkness beyond. The inclined highway brought them to the ridge of the mountain and a break in the pines allowed Jesse to glimpse the dark expanse of the valley below. In the distance, lightning cracked across the sky like fireworks, reflecting bright flashes on the cool glass of the window. For brief, intermittent moments, Jesse and his father were independently awestruck by the vision of the mighty bolts arcing in the heavens.

Jesse thought to himself how odd that such a specific memory would be triggered by something as inconsequential as lightning in the distance.

He was seated at a small table on the front patio of the High Cotton Restaurant and Bar located just off Main Street in downtown Blue Ridge. Seated across from him, Karen twirled a lock of brown hair as she perused the menu. She mumbled to herself as her eyes darted across the surface of the page in front of her. The patio was sparsely populated with only a handful of dinner guests. While the restaurant was popular among locals and tourists, it was rarely full on a weeknight.

"I'm telling you Cavanaugh, this place is as good as any restaurant you'll find in Manhattan."

"How would you even know that?" Jesse asked as he placed his own menu on the table in front of him. "Have you ever been to New York?"

"It's on my to-do list." She responded, taking a sip from her glass of red wine. "I've been to Chicago. Does that count?"

"It most certainly does not."

"Well, I'll get around to it when I have a reason to go."

"When you do, I'll make sure to take you on a tour."

"But for real," she said, motioning to their surroundings. "Not too bad for small-town Georgia, huh?"

"Not at all. I was expecting to end up in a Waffle House or something."

"Well, the night is young. Waffle House is best after midnight anyways. And besides, don't knock it. I worked there for a year while I was in school."

"Oh, I'm sorry. I wasn't aware I was having dinner with a redneck."

"Well, then you don't remember much from High School."

The two laughed at Karen's self-deprecation. After much indecision on her part they finally ordered and enjoyed light conversation while they waited for their meals.

The patio of the High Cotton was situated directly in front of the restaurant itself which, like many restaurants in the region, was once a house in years gone by. Known as the historic Deacon house, the one-story white building covered by a tin roof was erected in the early 1900s by Colonel Harold Deacon, a prominent Blue Ridge attorney and member of the Georgia General Assembly. Notable authors and other local celebrities from the Atlanta social scene would make a point to attend the lavish parties held there when vacationing in Blue Ridge. To receive an invitation to one of the Deacon's celebrations was a point of pride among residents across North Georgia. In one of the dining rooms of the High Cotton, an original oil painting of the century-old power-couple watches over the patrons who frequent the establishment.

Jesse had been impressed by the effort and care put into restoring the old residence. Having been bored by a history lesson on the restaurant by his mother after Aubry convinced him to take Karen there, Jesse had not expected much from the restaurant. But the atmosphere was charming and the carefully crafted ambiance was inviting. He could tell that the marble steps leading to the large front door were original, as well as the distorted, rippled panes of glass in the windows. But it was obvious that the restaurant had been renovated in recent years with modern fixtures and styles mixed expertly with vestiges of an elegant past.

The patio where Jesse and Karen sat facing one another was surrounded by vintage edison-style light bulbs. The dim lights hung from lines strung between wooden posts on the perimeter of the patio. The light bulbs themselves, while providing some light were obviously more targeted at providing a final, romantic touch to the setting. However, they were easily overlooked when compared to the light show taking place in the distance over the darkening tree line. The heat lightning, which had jolted Jesse's mind into long forgotten memories, continued its noiseless display. The lights, both man-made and natural, reflected in Karen's dark eyes as the two spoke, drawing Jesse's gaze into hers.

Karen and Jesse continued catching up on one another's recent activities as they picked through their meal. The two reminisced about the years they spent together as children. In Jesse's attempt to erase his past and fully embrace his adopted life in New York, he had failed to remember the good memories he had developed with Karen and others. He had assumed they were few and far between but helping Karen recite the stories of their youth caused Jesse to wonder if they were so few after all. Perhaps, he thought, they were just forgotten until now. Driven from his memory until Karen pulled them back.

As Karen recounted her time in nursing school Jesse thought about how just a day ago he had effectively chosen not to contact her before returning home. He was glad that she was self-confident enough to call him instead, and give him the opportunity to spend the evening with her.

"So, I've got to ask Karen," Jesse said, leaning back in his chair, "and I know it's none of my business, so feel free to tell me to shove it if you want to. But, Roddy always seemed like a good guy. I mean, I know he and I weren't especially close in high school and I haven't seen him since, but he didn't seem too bad. What happened there?"

"Oh, Roddy's a great guy," Karen responded, sipping from her wine glass. "He really is. I mean, I'm not going to go set him up with any of my friends or anything because that would be really weird but he actually is very sweet."

"So what happened?"

"Well, after a few years we just both came to the conclusion that it wasn't working out. It wasn't a bad situation, I mean it wasn't particularly good, but I think we just saw that it wasn't the *right* situation."

"Ah, I see."

"We were both really young when we got married. I mean we were REALLY young. I don't think we fully understood the commitment we were making. Marriage is a big deal, and it's messy. You watch movies and TV and you see what you think are perfect marriages and they seem so flawless and you think that's what yours is going to be like, or what it should be like. But marriage is messy, even the ones that work are messy. Sometimes, they're the messiest of all because the couple is willing to stick it out and wade through all the mess together. I guess we just weren't willing to do that."

"That sounds to me like someone who's sworn off the institution."

"Are you kidding? Not at all. That's why we got divorced. Not because I didn't believe there was someone I should be married to. It was because I didn't believe it was Roddy, and I think he didn't believe I was his Mrs. Right either. We just needed to find the right people for us."

"I'm sure that's going well. The dating scene around here really seems to be on the move."

"You have no idea," Karen said as she pretended to hold a gun to her head and pull the trigger. "You know, sometimes I wish it ended worse than it did between Roddy and me."

"What? That's insane. Why would you say something like that?"

"I don't know." She replied, biting her lip, clearly regretting what she just said. "It just makes for such a bad story when people ask me that question. All I have is that we decided it wasn't working and amicably divorced. It makes me sound like such a quitter. Wouldn't it be great if I could tell people he cheated on me, or he was an ax murderer, or he had another family in Canada or something? Now those would be great stories."

"Come to think of it, it is really inconsiderate of him to leave you with such a boring divorce tale. Honestly, I fell asleep for a few seconds while you were telling it."

Karen smiled at the sarcastic joke and Jesse felt his heart jump in his chest ever so slightly as a short laugh escaped her lips. He quickly shook the feeling and reached for the bottle of wine between them, finding it empty.

"That's no good," Karen remarked.

"No it is not," he replied. "You want to cap this dinner off with some real drinks?"

"Now, you're talking my language Cavanaugh."

Jesse waved down their server for the check, paid it, and the two exited the patio in front of the High Cotton. It was dark now. In the summertime in Georgia the sun didn't fully set until almost 9:00 in the evening. Even then, the sky was normally laced with a subtle purple tint at the edges of the horizon.

"I haven't spent enough time in Blue Ridge since legally being able to drink. What's the best bar for us to grab something other than wine?"

"I don't recall the legal age ever stopping you."

"Well, we're old enough now so we don't have to hide it anymore."

"Alright, I've got a better place than any of the bars around here. *To the Swan*!" she yelled, pointing down the street.

"The Swan?"

In 1955, the Swan drive-in theater was built by two local businessmen off of Summit Street in Blue Ridge. Immediately upon its opening to the public, business boomed. People drove from miles around to park under the stars and watch the black and white films projected across the night. Families parked close to the front so that all of the little eyes in the car could soak up every inch of the screen. Young couples on dates would park toward the back where they could be left alone to engage in additional entertainment.

Drive-in theaters were common at the time of its construction but in recent decades they had all but disappeared. One by one they closed their doors and sold the valuable real estate to more profitable business ventures. But the Swan had survived. In fact, it had become a landmark and people still traveled to have the one of a kind experience that could only be provided by the nostalgia-laced setting. The drive-in was only one of a handful left operating in the state and among drive-in theaters is considered one of the best in the country. The theater isn't as busy as it was in the 1950's and 60's but it still attracted quite a crowd on weekends when hit movies were shown.

At Karen's insistence Jesse drove the two of them a few minutes down the road and parked the old truck at the theater's entrance. It was closed. These days, it only opened on the weekends and entertained only one or two showings of the top movie out at the time. Karen swung the passenger side door open and dropped down to the gravel on the side of the road.

"Come on," she exhorted, waving him out of the cab of the truck.

"That's it," He said following her up the gently sloping paved road that led into the drive-in. "I think, you've lost it. This is a movie theater, not a bar, and it's closed at that."

"Will you just trust me?"

"I thought, this place didn't even serve alcohol."

"It doesn't. Just trust me and stop whining."

The two followed the hill around the massive screen facing away from the road. As the pathway ascended, the area in front of Jesse opened up into a mix of dirt and gravel where visitors parked their cars. Seven acres of empty space stared back at the two as they stepped into the lot. One lone building, advertising, popcorn, soda, burgers, and fried Oreos interrupted the expanse. Above them, an endless array of bright stars shone down on the two figures traversing the parking rows.

"Wow," Jesse exclaimed, taking in his surroundings. "It sure looks different when nobody's here."

"Yeah, it's not too bad is it?"

"I can't believe this place is still around. You know, I can specifically remember seeing *Return of the Jedi* here when I was younger."

"Nerd," she replied, jabbing him in the ribs with her elbow while they walked.

Karen stopped next to a small metal cover at their feet. It was an access point for plumbing valves on pipes running beneath the ground. Karen knelt down, not caring that the edge of her blue sundress was in the dirt surrounding the lid, and pried it open. She reached one of her slender arms into the dark hole in the ground and pulled out a plastic jug of clear liquid.

"What in the world is that?" Jesse asked.

"Moonshine."

"Moonshine? Why on Earth are you hiding moonshine at a drive-in theater?"

"I'm not, Tanner is."

"Who the hell is Tanner?" Jesse took a quick look around them, paranoid that someone would see them extracting hard liquor from a hidden compartment at a family theater.

"Tanner's my co-worker's son. He works here on the weekends. His uncle makes whiskey and Tanner sells it to people here who want something stronger than a Diet Coke."

Karen sat on the ground next to the open hole and stretched her long legs out in front of her, crossing her ankles and kicking off her high heels. She set the jug down and patted the ground next to her, inviting Jesse to join her.

Jesse sat down, but not before taking another look around them. "Well, isn't Tanner going to be mad?" he asked.

"Oh, he'll be pissed. But he doesn't need to know it was us. Besides, he's got a huge crush on me so even if he knew I did it, he wouldn't say anything."

"So what, we're just going to chug moonshine out of a jug?"

"Of course not, we're not hillbillies." From her small purse, Karen produced two lowball glasses and handed one to Jesse.

"Where did you get these? Do you carry whiskey glasses with you at all times?"

"Of course not. I may be from Blue Ridge but I'm not a drunk," she replied. "I took them from the restaurant."

"When did you... So not a drunk but definitely a thief. You know, you're a nurse and I'm a lawyer, we're supposed to be respectable members of the community."

"Respectable isn't any fun," she said as she poured a small amount of liquid into both cups. "But I do feel kind of bad for taking them. I'll probably sneak them back in tomorrow sometime."

Jesse put the glass to his lips and took a sip, not knowing what to expect."

"Wow," he exclaimed. "That's smooth."

"Yeah, Tanner's uncle is an artist."

The two sat back, staring at the stars shining above them and the empty movie screen. There was no chill in the night air but the heat of the day had subsided and Jesse was perfectly comfortable leaning back on the dusty ground. They sipped the moonshine and enjoyed the slight breeze which moved across the empty lot. Jesse was captivated by Karen, although he tried desperately not to be. But as she sat in the dim light, sipping moonshine from a stolen glass, Jesse could think of nothing else. Not even work or fishing.

"You know Karen, of all the people who we knew growing up I'm surprised you're still here. I figured you'd have gotten out of town." Jesse said, swirling the potent liquid in his glass.

"Does anybody ever really leave this town?" she asked. "I mean look at us. I went off to Atlanta, you went to New York but here we both are."

"Well..." Jesse started, preparing to correct her that his stay in Blue Ridge was only temporary, before allowing her to finish.

"I wanted to get out. I wanted to see the world. Atlanta was just a stepping stone. But here I am. I came back. We always come back, no matter how much we want to stay away."

"You want to stay away?" he asked. "Don't you like your work and being close to your family.

"Of course I do. I love being a nurse and I love my family. But I could be a nurse anywhere and I would stay close to my family no matter what. I love it here. It's my home. But I can't help but think about what my life would be like if I had just said no to Roddy and stayed away."

Jesse remained quiet, allowing her honesty to sink in.

"So what about you Cavanaugh?" she asked.

"What do you mean?"

"You know all about me and Roddy. All these years and you never thought of settling down?"

The question, while fair considering their prior conversation, caught Jesse off guard and snapped him back to the realities of the present.

"Actually, I did for a while."

"Oh, I'm sorry, I didn't know."

"No, it's fine. It's just been a while."

"What was her name?" Karen asked.

"Um, her name was Miriam, and like you, we were pretty young. Probably too young when we got married."

"What happened?"

"Oh, you know," Jesse replied, swirling the whiskey in his glass and watching as it spun around and around, reflecting small amounts of light in the darkness. "About the same as you. Like you said, marriage is messy and we just weren't ready."

"I'm so sorry," Karen said, and placed her hand gently on Jesse's shoulder.

Jesse quickly changed the subject and the two sat, emptying the plastic jug by small amounts. For hours the two spoke, laughing and conversing about everything they could. In the distance, heat lightning streaked across the edges of the horizon.

CHAPTER 13

Nothing compares to the feeling of mixed ecstasy and anxiety that occurs when a trout rises and takes an angler's waiting fly. That singular moment, though fleeting when measured by standard means, feels joyously endless to the fisherman. For a moment, time itself seems to stop, and the angler is permitted to experience the event in a deeper, more lasting way than the casual observer is able to comprehend. It is, in and of itself, the fisherman's reward. In moments like these, the fisherman transforms into a warrior with a crusader's heart beating beneath his mesh-lined vest. That beautiful moment when the hook sets, and man and beast, both struggling against one another, become literally connected to one another, is the true prize.

The fish itself is simply an additional benefit. The reason that the experience of actually landing a trout on a fly is so rewarding is that it is so rare. Many, including fishermen, would extol the virtue of expressing gratitude for the small and simple blessings that so often beset individuals on a daily basis. However, there is no doubt that a flood of appreciation is not out of order when rare fortune strikes. Some sportsmen will spend hundreds of hours with not so much as a bite in between catches. With so much time spent compared to the amount of fish actually pulled from the river, it is surprising that anyone would fish at all. And yet they do. Because that moment, that reward, erases to some degree all the frustration felt during the time in between.

The sunlight passing through the leaves overhead speckled the surface of the stream with intermittent shadow and light. On the water's surface, a handmade fly floated gently along with the flow. Darting in and out of the shadows, the fuzzy brown creation moved smoothly up and down and from side to side as the movement of the water directed it downstream. For hours the fly had remained undisturbed, moving slowly along before being pulled back in by Jesse's reel and flung through the air to again make another journey downstream. Over and over again the fly soared and drifted along without the slightest evidence of interest by any passing fish. It had settled now in a deep pool in the river where the water moved almost imperceptibly slow. Jesse watched from afar as it inched lazily across the clear water.

Seemingly from nowhere, a trout rose to take the drifting fly. Instantly it disappeared from sight. Only the tip of the fish's nose breached the surface of the water as it snatched the fly before disappearing into the depths of the river as quickly as it appeared. Jesse didn't have any time to react before line started flying off his reel, being pulled along by the fleeing trout. Hoping not to jerk the fly away, Jesse gently began to turn the reel, stalling the line from following after the fish too rapidly. In an instant Jesse's rod bent in protest as the line between them tightened. Jesse could feel a slight twitch in the line which told him exactly what he wanted to know. The hook had set and was now embedded in the fleshy inner wall of the fish's mouth.

Jesse was surprised by the sudden turn of events, but probably not more so than the trout struggling on the other side. One moment both were seemingly alone in the stream enjoying the beauty of their surroundings and the majesty of the river, the next moment they were locked in an existential battle against one another. For the fish, the conflict was clearly life or death. Instinctively it fought against the line, knowing that as it was pulled further upstream it moved closer to its demise. To the best of its knowledge, losing the struggle meant a certain end. In reality, this was not true. Like many sportsmen, Jesse had no intention of killing the fish against which he labored. It was never his prize in the first place.

For the fisherman, the struggle also seems existential at the time. While he doesn't work to thwart a physical demise he contends with the fish to preserve his spiritual and emotional life. A life which, at the time, seems to be very seriously at risk just as the fish believes its physical existence is threatened by the struggle. And like the fish, the fisherman's fears are untrue. Hooks become dislodged, lines break, and fish get away. And life moves on. But to the angler at the time, that is unimportant. They feel they are battling for their very soul as they fight against the determination of nature itself.

Jesse kept tension on the line, allowing the tip of the thin rod to remain slightly bowed as the filament crept off the reel slowly towards the fish struggling against it. Suddenly he felt the tension begin to disappear as the fish swam toward him and the line. Quickly, but without sharp movements, Jesse raised the tip of the rod slightly and pulled in some of the excess line created by the trout's sudden change in direction. At this critical juncture Jesse was not concerned with landing the trout just yet but only with keeping a conservative amount of tension on it while it expended its valuable energy.

Jesse was still unable to ascertain the size of his catch but he was impressed by the amount of fight it was producing. It weaved back and forth from one side of the stream to the other and Jesse's line cut across the surface of the water in pursuit. He briefly glimpsed the shadow of the fish beneath the surface of the water as it darted through a large swath of light. It seemed enormous to him. Jesse understood that he had only glimpsed it for a fraction of a second but visions flashed across his mind of landing a trophy catch.

He could feel the twitches from the line which told him that the trout was shaking its head in an attempt to free itself from the hook buried in its mouth or throat. A barbed hook would have assisted in making sure that the fly remained firmly in place. But Jesse was fishing with a barbless hook according to his father's customs and the arbitrary requirements of an Appalachian Slam as explained by Abram and Bennie. In further research into the Appalachian Slam Jesse had learned that barbless hooks were not strictly required by all adherents but were preferred by many so he continued to use them. Now he worried that he would lose the trout and wondered whether he had doomed himself to failure for that decision.

In an effort to counteract the fishes attempts to jolt itself free Jesse made small adjustments in his technique. Too much tension and the line could break, too much slack and the fish would be successful in removing the hook. He moved his rod slowly up and down giving slightly more space to the fish before taking it back again. The shaking ceased, and Jesse breathed a sigh of relief as he realized the hook was still attaching the line to the trout without any sign of loosening. Jesse began to reel in his catch little by little, pausing between every few spins of the reel to ensure that the fish would not attempt another sudden escape. It was still fighting, but not as hard, and the pauses in between each set of movements were growing longer and more frequent. A few more spins of the reel brought the trout a few feet closer.

When the fish was roughly ten feet from Jesse he finally had an opportunity to get a close and vivid look at it. It twisted around on its back as it darted from side to side, exposing its bright lateral scales to the sunlight overhead. As it twisted Jesse was also able to see a flash of its white belly against the muted browns and greens of the rocks and sand of the riverbed. The light shining between the branches flashed brightly off the reflective scales of the rainbow trout. Jesse's sunglasses were sliding slowly down the bridge of his nose as sweat beaded across his tan face but he couldn't spare a hand to push them back where they belonged. Finally the trout, still thrashing slightly every few seconds, was brought to the water gently swirling around his knees. Making sure to maintain tension in the line Jesse carefully reached behind him and retrieved the net which was fastened to his waist. In one smooth motion he reached down to the slow-moving stream and cradled the trout in the net, pulling it out of the water with almost no sign of resistance.

By this point, Jesse had caught a number of fish in the rivers and streams surrounding Blue Ridge. Certainly not as many as he would have liked, but enough to have developed a sense of the trout in the area. But this one was much heavier than the ones he had landed so far. No wonder it had given him such a thrilling fight. Jesse waded to the shore with the net in hand. After placing his rod on the riverbank he pulled the trout from the net to revel in his catch. He estimated that the rainbow trout was a little over a foot long. Its colors were vibrant and well defined. Jesse had noticed that some of the rainbows that he had caught seemed dull and subdued. But this one had a dark green and brown head contrasted starkly with the bright pink stripe running on either side of its silvery body. Stretching from head to tail, dark spots were speckled across the fish.

He held the trout out in front of him with both hands, admiring the beautiful fish. Not too long ago Jesse wouldn't have considered any fish to be beautiful. Now, gazing upon his catch he appreciated its dignity. It was not the monstrously large fish he had imagined as it had fought against his efforts to capture it. Yet he wasn't disappointed. After viewing its beauty up close he didn't care about its size. For the first time in his life he actually wanted to take a picture of a fish. Normally he simply removed the hooks from their mouths and let them swim free without any documentation. Now he wished he had his phone so he could record the catch to show... somebody.

The trout made a gasping motion with its mouth. Gently he reached down, plunging the fish and his hands into the cool water. He desperately hoped that the fish had not been out of the water too long. Jesse had lost track of the time while mesmerized by the colorful animal. He held the fish loosely in his hands under the water, facing it upstream, so the flow of water rushed over the trout and through its gills, hopefully bringing fresh oxygen into its system. Ever so gently the fish began to move its body from side to side. Jesse wondered whether it was the fish itself making the motion, or simply the flow of the water making the fish appear to move. All of a sudden, the trout darted out of Jesse's hands as though it had never been in any danger and disappeared into the river.

"That wasn't a bad fish right there." The voice of Jesse's dad said in clear admiration.

Jesse turned and looked upwards at the image of his dad standing over him before turning back to the river. The trout was gone. Just moments before Jesse had been holding in his hands one of the most beautiful fish he had seen and in the next instant it was gone. He found it so odd that something so beautiful could just disappear so quickly.

"You don't even have to lie about that one when you tell this story to the boys." His father continued.

Jesse rose from his haunches and waded to the shore to retrieve his waiting pole. "Where have you been?" he asked. "You usually pop into my head every time I end up out here. I haven't seen you in a couple of days now."

"I was afraid you'd throw your phone at me again."

"That's a good one," said Jesse as he examined the fly still attached to the end of his line, assessing whether he should use it again or switch it out with a new one. "You've always had such a great sense of humor Dad."

"After our last interaction I thought it best if I give you some space."

Jesse decided the fly was still good and moved back out into the water. He had been on the verge of moving to a different location upstream but after the catch he just had he figured it would be best to stay here for the time being.

"What are you here to talk about now?"

"You tell me, I'm your fantasy."

Jesse remained silent. He pulled line off his reel in preparation for the process of casting once again. He knew that at any moment the voice of his father would break the silence of his mind with whatever topic was at the forefront of his thoughts. It was inevitable. When you fish, you think deeply and reflect on your life. One always leads to the other. He wanted to soak up the precious few silent moments and savor their comfort. Jesse stared forward, ignoring the imagined figure of his father looming over his own personality and breathed deeply as the last few moments of uninterrupted communion with nature drifted away.

"How come you didn't tell that girl everything about Miriam?"

"Oh is that what we're going to talk about?"

"That's what you're thinking about so I guess so."

"Can't I just enjoy fishing in peace?"

"You tell me." His father's voice replied.

Jesse watched as his line drifted slowly downstream. He pulled a few more feet of line out with his free hand to allow it to drift a little further but eventually began reeling it back in slowly in preparation of another cast. Jesse had been reflecting about the previous night. He and Karen had continued talking late into the night under the stars at the old Swan theater. They reminisced about their time growing up, and the time spent apart since then. Eventually Jesse drove Karen home and the two said goodnight. Nothing more.

Jesse contemplated the evening while he fished. It was more enjoyable than he had expected. Karen had changed over the years, but she was the same girl he was smitten with in high school. All of the quirky, headstrong character traits which had attracted him to her as an adolescent were still there, but with an added grace and elegance that had developed over the years. She was smart, funny, assertive, and beautiful. If he were interested in dating he would anxiously be looking forward to another evening with her. But he wasn't, so he was only looking forward to keeping in touch, and maybe seeing her again briefly before he returned to New York. And yet he couldn't stop thinking about her. How the stars in the night sky reflected in her eyes. Perhaps that explained why he felt so bad about their conversation.

"It wasn't a lie." He blurted out of nowhere.

"What wasn't?" His father responded, sounding surprised as he watched his son expertly land his fly at the base of a small cascade near the edge of the stream.

"The thing about Miriam."

"Oh that. Well, it certainly wasn't the truth."

Jesse glanced at the image of his father through his sunglasses. He recognized the look on the wrinkled face. It was a look of judgment, and he had seen it many times before.

"I didn't have to tell her everything about my life Dad. That's not a requirement."

"So tell her that then. Instead, she pours out her soul about how her marriage ended and then, when she asks about Miriam, all you say is 'Ditto..'"

"That's not what I said."

"Basically."

"And besides, I wouldn't call what she said, 'pouring out her soul.'"

"I don't know, Jesse. It may not have seemed that way but you don't think that was difficult for her?"

"So is this what you're doing now?" Jesse asked. "You're playing the part of my conscience."

"Someone has to."

Jesse clenched his jaw and focused on his line.

"Well, if my conscience is embodied by you then I'm in real trouble.

"That's for sure. You know, that conversation was tough for her Jesse, regardless of how short it was," his father continued. "And you care about her. She deserved to have you open up as well. You didn't have to tell her every little detail but a little more explanation about what happened would have been good for both of you. You didn't even mention Elle."

"And what about what I deserve?" Jesse asked, clearly frustrated with the mental back and forth. "Don't I deserve to not have to wade through the details of my failed marriage whenever anybody asks?"

"You do deserve that," His father's image sighed as he folded his arms and watched the flowing water. "But this is different. If you can't open up to people you care about then you'll just keep being alone."

"You know I like my life Dad. That may be hard for you to accept because you never did much with yours but I like being who I am and doing what I do. And I like doing it by myself. Besides, Karen is just an old friend. Nothing more."

"That's why you've been thinking about her all day?"

"She's a particularly good-looking friend."

"Well I can see that. Shoot everyone can see that. Why do you think your mother was so excited about your date with her? But that's not why you've been thinking about her all day. You care about her as more than some old high school friend."

"I'm done with this Dad. Can you just let me fish?"

From the corner of his eye Jesse glimpsed a look of disappointment on his father's imagined face. He thought it so odd that his mind would utilize his father as the mouthpiece of its inner thoughts. And even odder that it would express emotions like disappointment. He turned away and with a few flicks of his wrist he placed the fly tethered to the end of his line directly beneath a low hanging branch where he had been aiming.

"Not bad." His father's voice whispered quietly.

CHAPTER 14

The wooden rocking chair creaked back and forth beneath Jesse as he moved it gently with his feet. The sun had just risen, but Jesse had been awake for some time now. Jesse was an early riser, he always had been. As a teenager he tried his best to sleep in because that's what he thought teenagers were supposed to do. Most mornings however, he woke early and lay in bed while the small window flooded his basement room with light. Eventually he gave up and accepted the fact that he was a morning person. He was grateful now for the habit. By the time his colleagues stumbled into the office, nursing overpriced coffee, he was already hard at work.

He knew from whom he inherited the trait. He could still remember lying awake in bed early in the morning listening to his father moving around in the house above him. The floorboards in the old home groaned as his father attempted to quietly move about as he prepared for the day. Jesse's mother and sister were usually fast asleep and would remain so for some time. But Jesse and his father were always awake early. Jim spent the morning on the back porch, watching the world spring to life while his teenage son stayed in his room, waiting for his father to leave for the day before he ventured upstairs.

Now, with his father still attached to life support in the hospital, there was nobody to avoid, and Jesse took his father's place on the back porch. He sat alone, contemplating the sunrise by himself. Walt was curled up in the rocking chair next to him. The animal was completely covered with wavy black fur and when he curled up like he currently was, it was difficult to determine exactly where the dog's head was. The only evidence that Walt was a live animal, and not a decorative pillow, was the soft sound of breathing coming from the furry mass. Jesse didn't know the dog. His parents had adopted him as an abandoned puppy three years before. He didn't know how the dog normally acted, but to Jesse he seemed depressed. Jesse imagined Walt sensed that something happened to his master and missed Jim's company.

In the fishing journal, Jim wrote often about his mornings spent on the back porch with Walt. Throughout his entries Jim wrote fondly about sitting alone in his rocking chair on the porch with his morning coffee, listening to the sounds of the daybreak as he mapped out in his mind where he would fish throughout the course of the day.

He didn't sit and study the book like a devout religious follower. When he did open it momentarily to glance at the next entry, he would promptly flip to the next day if it appeared that his father was going to attempt to write about life as though he were some profound sage. Jesse was only interested in the valuable insight his father had to offer about fishing in the North Georgia hills. He was not concerned with the man's conceited attempts at philosophy.

Opening the small book, Jesse thumbed through the journal until he found an entry from June of last year. He hoped that his father had recorded techniques and flies that had proven successful then. He calculated that the same might prove beneficial this year.

June 11th.

Yesterday wasn't too bad at all. I spent most of the day up at Noontootla. I caught three rainbows and had a brown on my line. Couldn't land him though. He wasn't too big but he fought good. He wiggled free at the last minute. Still, not a bad day. They were striking all day long. The rainbows were especially active. I caught two of them on the brown stonefly nymph and the other on a zug bug. I got strikes on the nymph and the zug like crazy. The brown grabbed hold of a hare's ear nymph I was trying out at the end of the day. I'll start out today with that hare's ear but I'll also stick with the stonefly and the zug. There's no need to change it up until they stop biting.

I haven't gotten the Slam but it's coming. Every day I get better about judging what I need to do to bring them in. The water temperature, the air temperature, the weather, the time of year, I'm getting a better feel for it all every day. I'm picking the right flies, going to the right spots. Now all I need is for the right day to come around. I've been catching rainbows left and right and I'm not doing so bad with the browns either. But the brook trout, those are the tough ones. I've only caught one of them in the last month and a half. It'll happen though. One of these days the river's going to flow my way.

Jesse leaned his head back and stared at the ceiling fan rotating lazily above him. He could already feel the heat of the day creeping in around him as he watched the blades of the fan spin around and around. He made a mental note of what little useful information contained within the short entry from the journal. Brown stonefly nymph, zug bug, hare's ear nymph. He knew them all. Jesse was not sure what Noontootla was. He remembered seeing it on a map somewhere so he assumed it was a creek in the area. He made a mental note to look into it.

There would be no fishing today. He promised his mother he would visit his father in the hospital with her and he knew she planned on making it a long visit. He had been neglecting to visit his father as regularly as he promised, but with his almost hallucinogenic rendezvouses with the man on the river, he felt as though he had put in his time. Granted he couldn't tell his mother that, he would sound crazy. And besides, crazy or not, she would likely make him go anyways.

Jesse hated hospitals. Particularly this one where he had to watch the man with whom he shared such a complicated relationship languish in hopelessness. But as a general matter, Jesse avoided hospitals whenever possible, which was easy since he was a corporate attorney. It was a profession that kept him as far away from the medical field as possible.

Jesse considered himself a reasonable man. In fact, those that knew him would likely describe him as overly rational. He almost never allowed emotions to play a prominent role in his decision making. But there were aspects of his life where, even perhaps unknowingly, Jesse allowed emotion to trump rational thought. Over the course of almost two weeks Jesse had become consumed by fly fishing, a sport which can only be driven by emotion. Finally, he allowed himself to embrace a distaste for hospitals. He understood this was completely driven by his emotional experiences with them. And he didn't care.

He could still vividly remember the sterile smell of the hospital room where he sat, exhausted, listening to the doctor explain the situation to him and Miriam.

Total Anomalous Pulmonary Venous Return.

It was a congenital heart defect. And as explained to Jesse and his young wife of three years, it was a critical condition that required immediate attention. Jesse remembered being overwhelmed by the information, he was exhausted from standing by Miriam's side through the last nine hours. Day had passed into night and then day again without sleep. As the doctor explained the situation, everything seemed muted and blurred. The doctor's voice sounded as though it was coming from somewhere far away even though he was standing directly in front of them. At some point Jesse heard Miriam begin to cry but he did nothing. All he could do was stare forward while trying to make sense of the information.

That day was supposed to be the happiest day of their lives. Miriam had been amazing. She never breathed a word of complaint even though she was in obvious pain and discomfort throughout the entire process. All Jesse could do was encourage her and grip her hand. After what seemed to be an eternity, Miriam gave one last push and their daughter was born. They had decided on a name weeks before.

Elle.

Total Anomalous Pulmonary Venous Return, or TAPVR for short, is a heart defect affecting the pulmonary veins which connect with the heart. Blood vessels which are meant to bring oxygen-enriched blood from the lungs to the heart via the pulmonary vein do not connect properly. Instead they attach with the heart by way of an anomalous connection. In Elle's tiny heart, oxygen-rich blood was not being returned from the lungs to her left atrium as intended. Elle was not getting enough oxygen to her system and without a potentially dangerous surgery it was explained that she would die from the condition.

Jesse remembered the moment they placed Elle onto Miriam's chest. She was blue and grey. The same color as the thin blue smoke he remembered wafting out of his father's wood-burning smoker in the backyard when he was a child. Jesse had always heard that newborns were odd colors just after being born and he assumed it would fade away just as the smoke had. But it didn't. At least not without the assistance of modern medicine. Her pulse was low, and she clearly had difficulty breathing. After hospital staff detected a heart murmur she was sent off for further tests and Jesse, with bags under his eyes, followed.

An echocardiogram confirmed the presence of the defect and Elle was immediately transferred to the NICU. Jesse and Miriam were left feeling helpless and for days the two lived in the hospital. Jesse was angry. Not at anyone in particular, just angry at the world. As the hours dragged on he became increasingly flustered while speaking with the never-ending stream of doctors and nurses. How could they not have seen this in the ultrasounds?

Later Jesse would find out that it was common to not learn about these types of defects until birth, but at the time it made him furious. Night after night Jesse remained in the NICU while Miriam rested. He watched helplessly over their daughter as she struggled against the machines and monitors attached to her frail body.

Elle was born a week early so no family was in New York at the time. However, as soon as they learned of the diagnosis, Miriam's family came into town. Jim and Helen Cavanaugh were not far behind. As soon as their family arrived, Jesse and Miriam were separated. Miriam had three sisters, all of whom wanted to spend every waking second by her side, helping her in any way possible. The two wouldn't be given time alone until after the ordeal had ended.

Jesse remembered Elle opening her eyes just barely and peeking at him past a tube taped onto the cheek which ran into her small nose. They were all alone as Miriam slept. Aside from the beeping of medical equipment, the area where Elle laid was quiet. Her eyes had a steel gray hue as they peered through the soft lights of glowing monitors. It felt so long ago. Jesse tried to think about Miriam's eyes. He couldn't remember what color they were anymore. How could he not remember the eye color of the woman he married? The woman he had loved. Who forgets that?

The vision of Elle staring up at him, on the other hand, was burned into his memory. She didn't look scared, or angry, or any of the other emotions that Jesse was feeling at the time. She peered at him lovingly. Jesse wept openly as he looked down at her. Hot tears rolled down his face as he reached out and allowed her tiny hand to weakly grip the tip of his index finger.

The next day Elle underwent an operation to repair the defect in her heart. She passed away during surgery.

Elle Cavanaugh lived eight days. The weeks that followed were a blur. Miriam was devastated and often started sobbing uncontrollably at random. Jesse was distraught in his own right but reacted differently. He felt withdrawn as though he were going through the motions of life but was not in control of his own body. He wanted to reach out to Miriam, to comfort her, to show her he loved her. But he couldn't. He felt like he was a spectator watching from afar as he allowed his wife to grieve without his support. He and Miriam attended the appointments with their therapist, but he felt more like a concerned bystander than an active participant.

After a short leave from work, he returned. He was a young attorney then, within the beginning stages of his successful career. His job had been demanding from his first day at the firm but he had always made time for Miriam. The two had been deeply in love and Jesse had cherished the feeling of leaving the office every day to return home to her.

After Elle though, things changed. Jesse threw himself into his career. He took on the most complicated and time-consuming projects that the firm undertook. He looked for every opportunity to bury himself deeper into the cold embrace of his career. He left before Miriam arose in the morning, and returned after she was fast asleep. If he returned home at all. Eventually the only time he saw his wife was at their weekly therapy sessions.

When Miriam brought up the possibility of divorce Jesse didn't even fight it. He didn't fight for her. The worst part was that he wanted to. Jesse still loved his wife when he signed the divorce papers. His entire soul screamed at him to throw the pen down and fight to get back what they once had. But he couldn't. Or at least he didn't feel like he could. Everything about the divorce was amicable. Property was divided agreeably, no alimony was sought, and there was no need for child support or custody to complicate the process. He met Miriam on a Tuesday at a cafe near her work to sign the papers. He remembers it was beginning to get cold outside and she was wearing the blue scarf he had gotten for her on her birthday a couple of years before. He couldn't remember the color of her eyes but he could remember the blue scarf draped around her neck as she kissed him on the cheek and walked out of the cafe.

That was the last time he saw Miriam. There wasn't a day that passed when he didn't think about that day or the day Elle died. Every day at some unexpected point they returned to him.

Over time he stopped feeling as though he was watching his life unfold from afar. He began to feel like himself again but something in him had changed. Every day he was haunted by those two days when he lost the two people with whom he was supposed to spend the rest of his life. He knew it wasn't truly necessary that the death of his daughter should lead to his divorce. But it had. There was nothing he could do about it now yet it weighed heavily on his mind.

Jesse rocked back and forth in the rocking chair, listening to the sounds of birds beginning their morning chorus of songs. He hated thinking about the events surrounding Elle's death but he couldn't keep them from invading his mind on a daily basis. Finding the unexpected gift in the basement with her name on it certainly didn't help.

One of the aspects of the entire ordeal that Jesse remembered so vividly was how supportive and involved Miriam's parents were. Her mother called her constantly, but not in an overbearing way. Her father expressed constant love and support both to Miriam and to Jesse. The man truly treated Jesse like a son and for that, Jesse was grateful. Jesse's own mother was as saintly as she always was. It was in her nature. Her own eyes were wet with tears as she comforted her grieving son and daughter-in-law. Aubry was still in college at the time but made her support for her older brother known often. There was only one person who was absent: Jim Cavanaugh.

Amid all of the outpouring of love expressed by family and friends, Jesse's father remained quiet and aloof. Shortly after Elle was born he arrived in New York with Helen. But her personality overwhelmed the room as it so often does and he was content to remain silent and distant. He expressed his sorrow and had embraced Jesse in an awkward hug but not much more was offered beyond that. After the funeral, when his parents had returned home, Jesse never received any phone calls or messages from him. Sometimes when his mother would call, she would force the two to speak briefly before Jim passed the telephone back to her. But nothing else.

Jesse continued to rock, torturing himself with the memories of his ex-wife and daughter. He felt anger begin to rise in his chest as he contemplated his father's lack of compassion and support at the time of his Elle's death but quickly attempted to suppress it. He had battled for years to put the emotions of the ordeal behind him, but it was not uncommon for them to arise for brief periods of time.

Jesse glanced at the journal which he still held in his hand. Elle had died over eight years before, but his father had begun recording his thoughts in the book before then. Jesse wondered what his father had written during the emotional time period. Did it merit one of his long entries outlining his thoughts and feelings? He thumbed through the pages, moving quickly back to the date of Elle's birth.

It was empty. There was no entry. Or on the days that followed. The handwriting jumped from the week before Elle's birth to a few weeks after her funeral. Jesse furrowed his brow as he felt the same anger begin to burn in his chest again. There was no entry in the journal about Elle's birth, her death, or about Jesse and Miriam. Jesse thought to himself that he shouldn't be surprised. Just as he had in reality, Jesse's father completely ignored the life-altering trial. He completely ignored his son and the pain that overwhelmed him.

CHAPTER 15

On the small, outdated television hanging in the upper corner of the hospital room, Drew Carey was explaining the rules of the Showcase Showdown to two excited contestants on *The Price is Right*.

I miss Bob Barker.

Jesse loved the show. Or at least he used to. He couldn't remember the last time he had watched it. Certainly not since Bob Barker had retired.

Hearing the music reminded him of days spent home sick from school. He would sprawl out on the ugly, floral-print couch in front of his family's old TV while he recovered from whatever other ailment he had contracted. Most of the time, the illnesses were real, but on some occasions Jesse just needed a day watching *The Price is Right*. He had become a master at faking illnesses to avoid school by the time he was a sophomore. Almost as good as his sister. Briefly, he wondered if the show, with its current host, was worth ever taking a personal day like when he was a teenager. Not that he ever would now.

The lonely television sat mostly ignored in the corner with its volume turned down to the point where it was barely audible. However, Jesse could still hear the unmistakably upbeat music of the game show filling the background of the quiet room. It was interspersed with the pumping of the ventilator attached to his father and various beeps and clicks from other medical equipment and devices.

Jesse turned away from the TV and glanced at his father. The frail, old figure lay stretched out across the hospital bed. Nothing had changed since the last time he had visited. Just as he had expected. Wondering why he was even there, Jesse turned his attention back to the Showcase Showdown.

Drew Carey seemed to be doing a good job. But it just wasn't the same. Jesse wondered if the new host carried on Barker's tradition of imploring the audience to have their pets spayed or neutered at the end of the show. He pictured the elderly game show host giving his trademark request as the credits rolled. Jesse smiled. It was the only pleasant thought which had entered his mind since entering the hospital room a few hours before.

Since Jesse had arrived home, he had grown to dread the time his mother forced him to spend at the hospital. He couldn't do anything to help, there was never any improvement, and he lacked the connection with his father that the rest of the family had. To them, these moments were special times to be enjoyed and remembered. To Jesse, it was just time passing like any other moment in the day. His visits ended up being nothing but long, quiet, awkward stretches of silence. He did it to appease his mother. So that she felt that her husband was not alone.

But today was different. Jesse had actually looked forward to this hospital visit. Not because he wanted to see his father. Now there was more at the hospital for him than just the unsettling image of his old man being forced to cling to life. A soft knock sounded at the door and Karen's face appeared in the doorway of the room. Jesse shot to his feet as *The Price is Right* instantly disappeared from his mind.

Karen smiled and stepped into the room, leaving the door cracked open behind her. Through the crack, the faint sounds of the small hospital drifted in. Her dark hair fell loosely on the shoulders of her purple scrubs.

"I got your message and thought I'd drop by."

Jesse had texted Karen, letting her know he would be in the hospital and invited her to come and see him.

"I'm glad you did," Jesse responded as the two of them stepped closer to each other, meeting at the foot of Jim Cavanaugh's hospital bed. Karen glanced at the old man lying still in front of the two.

"Sorry," Jesse remarked, instantly regretting inviting Karen into the depressing room. "I should have met you downstairs, you didn't need to come up here and see this.

"No Jesse, it's fine," she said, reaching out and touching his arm. "I'm a nurse, none of this is new to me. I just... I can't believe your dad... I... I'm so sorry."

"It's fine," Jesse responded, trying to lighten the mood. "It's nothing that can't be dealt with. Thanks for coming by. I was going crazy in here by myself. Do you want to maybe get out of here for a few minutes?"

Jesse began moving toward the open door.

"Oh, I wish I could. I'm slammed right now. I'm surprised I was able to break away at all."

"Oh, that's fine," Jesse responded awkwardly as he stopped moving toward the exit.

"I just wanted to drop by to see what a girl needs to do to get a second date around here," Karen said confidently, staring into Jesse's eyes as she leaned against the back of a chair.

"Um... well... I." Jesse sputtered, not expecting her to be so direct.

"Sorry to put you on the spot but I had fun the other night," Karen said smiling. "What are you doing tomorrow?"

"No real plans," Jesse said, "I was just going to go fishing for a little bit in the afternoon but I can..."

"Pick me up just after lunch then."

Jesse was surprised.

"You want to fish?"

"Cavanaugh, I'm a Fannin County girl. I could fish circles around you. In fact, I probably will."

Jesse chuckled, "Alright, I'll drop by after lunch."

"Can't wait."

Karen smiled at Jesse and turned towards the door. She stopped briefly and looked at Jim Cavanaugh lying in the bed in front of them. For a brief moment the clicks and whirs of the hospital equipment, which had been overshadowed by their conversation, again filled the air with subtle noise. Before exiting the room and pacing quickly down the corridor Karen reached out and touched Jesse's arm again.

"Hang in there Cavanaugh."

The next moment Karen was gone and Jesse was left standing at the foot of his father's bed, listening to those same machines interspersed with the quiet sounds of the game show coming from the TV.

"*... and remember to have your pets spayed or neutered.*"

Jesse glanced at the television as credits began to scroll across Drew Carrey and the winning contestant. *Hmmm,* he thought, *I guess he does still say it. Good for him.*

***

Eventually Jesse was relieved of his post when Aubry showed up a few hours later. He felt like a child getting out of school as he practically ran out of the hospital to freedom. Unlike her brother, Aubry was happy to sit with their father. Both of the two were avid readers and Aubry spent her time at Jim Cavanaugh's bedside, reading from his favorite book, *The Brothers Karamazov*. Jesse had walked in on Aubry reading passionately to their father from the old novel a few times. On those occasions Jesse felt a stab of jealousy before pushing the emotions away. Eventually he would succumb to the silence of the room as his sister left him to quietly endure his father's looming presence.

Knowing that his mother was at home, and not wanting a long conversation with her at the moment, Jesse got behind the wheel of the truck and pointed it northwards. Every time Jesse returned from solo trips to the hospital his mother wanted to hear every detail of the uneventful visits. He knew she was hoping that Jesse would develop some sense of connection with his father and that their relationship would be miraculously repaired through these visits. But Jesse was tired of disappointing her with the same answers to the same questions. He attempted to remain positive in his responses to her interrogations but he knew she could see through him. She always could. That's what mothers do.

He didn't know where he was going, which was rare. He was the type of man who preferred to have every detail of an activity planned well in advance. His days at work were meticulously organized and he rarely deviated from his plans unless absolutely necessary. This isn't to say that he was inflexible, only that he made it a priority to manage risk and avoid uncertainty. Even when traveling to a new location he rarely relied on turn-by-turn voice navigation, in case data coverage was limited, preferring instead to memorize directions ahead of time. But not today.

For some reason Jesse felt compelled to drive out of town and search for a fishing spot without directions or previous planning. Compelled wasn't the right word, at least Jesse didn't think so. He didn't believe that anyone was ever compelled by unseen forces to do anything. He simply felt predisposed to find his own spot today.

It was odd, he understood that. He didn't know why that day, of all days, he should decide to drive into the mountains without any particular place to go. Earlier that morning, while reviewing a hand-scrawled list of creeks, streams, and other locations he had gleaned from his father's journal, a new thought had come to him. *Why am I fishing these places where Dad fished?* He asked himself. *The man spent years chasing after that worthless Appalachian Slam and never got it. Maybe he doesn't know what he's doing... Maybe I should find a new spot. Somewhere he never tried.*

Granted, finding a new spot to fish near Blue Ridge was impossible. People had been fishing the waters across the rolling mountains since mankind first wandered into the valley. There was no spot to be found along the river, or its many streams, that had never been visited by a hopeful angler at some point in the past. But that was no concern of Jesse's. He didn't need a spot unseen by man. Just maybe a spot unseen by one man in particular. It was petty of him to make that a priority but it was a priority nonetheless. Perhaps he hoped that by finding a location where his father had not recorded in his journal, he would be able to fish in peace. Maybe the visions of his father which had been accompanying him couldn't follow to an unknown location. He knew that was unreasonable. The unwelcome specter was a resident of Jesse's mind, not of any physical location. But he had decided to venture into unreasonable waters today, so he was not opposed to the strategy, as unlikely as it appeared.

Warm air whipped across Jesse's forearm, which rested on the open driver's side window of his father's truck. The breeze felt cool as it rushed through the hairs on his arm and swirled into the stuffy cab. But make no mistake, it was sweltering outside. Periodically, when Jesse brought the truck to a rest at some deserted intersection, he could momentarily feel the stifling heat as it crept back into the old vehicle. No music played on the radio. The only sounds in the truck were the rhythm of the tires on the burning asphalt interspersed occasionally by the singing of birds and the chattering of squirrels in the foliage overhead.

There was no rhyme or reason to the route Jesse took across the tree-lined mountain roads. He turned left and right at sporadic intervals only making the decisions to do so when the road he was on abruptly intersected with another. The roads wound around mountainsides, crossed over streams, and passed under thick canopies of intersecting branches blocking out much of the bright sunlight overhead. At one point Jesse reached a large road sign welcoming him to Tennessee. Knowing that his temporary, non-resident fishing license was only valid in Georgia, Jesse turned the truck around at the border and continued his wandering drive southwards.

After almost an hour of directionless driving, he pulled the pickup onto the side of the road and came to a rumbling stop. Dust enveloped the truck as it came to a rest on a worn patch of dirt and gravel next to the two-lane road. Light streaming through gaps in the trees overhead pierced through the dissipating dust cloud, illuminating it like laser beams cutting across the air. A few yards ahead the deserted road passed over a stream of water. This spot had obviously been used as a parking spot in the past. In the brush to the right of the bridge, a narrow opening in the overgrowth showed a small path which lead down to the water's edge. In Fannin County a strange path cutting through the weeds and bushes next to a bridge only meant one thing. This was either a fishing spot or a place where teenagers came to smoke pot undisturbed. Possibly both.

Jesse didn't know who owned the properties on either side of the bridge. His eyes scanned the tree line nearest him. There were no "Keep Out" or "No Trespassing" signs attached to any of the trees. He had come to learn that, for the most part, Fannin County landowners didn't mind the occasional fisherman as long as they stuck to the river and respected their property... and their privacy. Fishing was part of the culture here and so, it was tolerated fairly liberally within reason. Feeling confident by the well-worn nature of the trail ahead of him, Jesse threw his waders over his shoulder, grabbed his pole and plunged into the forest.

It didn't take long to move down the uneven trail to the pebble-strewn riverbank below. Jesse stood in the shade of the bridge overhead as he donned his waders and boots. The water didn't even reach his knees as he carefully moved out to the middle of the slow-moving stream. Downstream the water moved under the low bridge. The property on either side appeared to be cow pastures based on the few brief glimpses available through the trees. Upstream the water emerged around a bend, obscuring Jesse's vision of the creek any further than a few dozen yards. Against his better judgment Jesse began wading against the flow of the water, towards the depths of the woods and away from the inviting open air of the downstream fields.

Moving carefully, so as not to lose his footing on the underwater creek bed, Jesse trudged slowly against the water. He knew that he was alone on the river but he couldn't help but feel as though he wasn't. He had come to learn exactly what that meant and he tried to ignore the inevitable. But his mind conjured from nowhere the image of his father wading by his side against the force of the stream.

"Ugh, I hoped you wouldn't be able to find me here."

"Well, you see, that doesn't make any sense because..."

"I know why it doesn't make sense. You don't have to explain it to me." Jesse stared forward as he continued on. His father walked along next to him for a few tense moments.

"So, you just want to walk then?" the ghostly vision asked.

"Yes, thank you, I'd like that very much."

The smooth pebbles, which littered the creek bed under the clear water shifted under Jesse's boots as he strode cautiously up the stream. By this point, he was well aware of the need to stay alert while navigating the uneven beds of the mountain rivers. Some days, particularly after rain, it is impossible to see what awaits under the vivid surface. The waters in the South are different from the wide, sweeping rivers crawling across the great expanses of the West. There is almost always a hint of red Georgia clay in the otherwise pure water, making it difficult to know with certainty what obstacles lay beneath.

In relatively short time, Jesse, accompanied by the silent vision of his father, made it to the bend of the river which curved around a tall, stone cliff jutting out of the water on his left. Placing his hand on the rough surface of the immense rock face, Jesse stepped gently over a small log which was wedged in between a number of rocks protruding from the current. Once again, the pebbles under his boot shifted as soon as his foot made contact and the rocks moved, throwing him off balance. Instinctively Jesse reached out and grasped the rock wall with his left hand, making sure not to lose the fishing pole he was gripping tightly with his right. He stopped moving briefly, listening to his heart beat wildly in his eardrums as he contemplated how to proceed without falling in.

Ahead of him he heard his father laughing softly to himself.

"I guess that's the benefit of not really having legs," he said, motioning downwards to where the vision's legs disappeared into the moving water.

Jesse ignored the old man as he made his way across the loose bed of pebbles and sand and continued moving upstream as soon as his feet found secure footing.

"Oh come on, you have to admit it, that was funny! ... well, you should have seen your face."

The silence was awkward and palpable, as Jim's chuckles faded away into the babbling of the running water. Finally, after a few more yards, Jesse broke the silence between the two.

"What are you exactly?"

Jesse couldn't see the look on the elder Cavanaugh's face, as he kept his eyes focused intently on the moving water. He didn't want to see the reaction, he only wanted to hear the answer.

"Well, I think you know exactly what I am. In fact, you've pointed it out to me a number of times that I'm just an expression of your imagination, or subconscious, or something."

"Alright, well what do you want? What are you doing here?"

'Hmmm... Now that, I think, is a better question. And to be honest, I'm not sure."

Jesse couldn't help but roll his eyes slightly, the same way he would in high school when his Father had attempted to lecture him.

"Great, that's helpful."

"Actually, I think it's quite helpful," the old man said, moving into Jesse's peripheral vision as he walked. "If I don't know, it means you don't know. That's probably not the answer you're looking for, but it's a least somewhat revealing."

"Well, thanks for the breakthrough Doc."

"You're obviously looking for something, otherwise I wouldn't be here. Maybe I'm here to try and help you find it."

"The only thing I'm looking for is some peace and quiet."

"Well..." there was a slight pause in his father's speaking, "you could have picked a worse spot than this."

Jesse, who had been looking down at the rocks and pebbles below him, noticed that his father was staring straight ahead, upstream as he spoke. He raised his eyes to follow Jim's gaze. The view before him was stunning. The stream opened up and straightened out after the bend from which Jesse had just emerged. It stretched in front of him until it disappeared into the forest somewhere in the distance. As in all of the streams he had fished, the water was covered by a ceiling of branches forming a natural tunnel cutting through the woods. Like the creek below the bridge, Jesse could see that this section was also surrounded by bright fields just barely visible through open patches in the leaves. Golden, afternoon sunlight broke through the trees and stretched across the entire length of the long expanse, causing the moving water to glint and sparkle as though it were covered with rare jewels from one end to the other.

"Wow," Jesse audibly exclaimed in an almost reverent whisper.

He stood quietly in the water for a moment, taking in the unexpected beauty of the scenery staring back at him. After a minute or so of trying to absorb the view before him he heard his father's voice at his side.

"Jesse, I... I'm...," the old man seemed to stumble over his words as he tried to get them to leave his mouth in an orderly format, "I'm sorry you and I never came to places like this together."

Jesse didn't avert his gaze from the creek in front of him, mesmerized by the way the light danced across the surface of the water. Finally, after a few more seconds he responded. "You can't be sorry," he remarked, "you're not real."

"You're right," the old vision replied thoughtfully, "maybe I'm not then. Maybe you are."

CHAPTER 16

"Hey, what does a fish say when it hits a concrete wall?"

Jesse had heard the joke before. Years ago, sometime before he moved to New York. He couldn't remember where he had heard it but he could remember the answer. It was simple, dumb, and, in his opinion, not very funny. But he didn't have the heart to tell Karen, who seemed excited, as though she had just remembered it herself for the first time in a long time.

"I don't know," giving his shoulders a subtle shrug, "what does it say?"

"Dam!"

Neither one of them laughed. They just stared at each other through the dark lenses of their sunglasses. Karen had paused in the midst of tying a new fly on to the end of her line when she started telling the terrible joke. Jesse was a few feet in front of her, slowly pulling in some of the line he was letting drift in the water. Both of them were standing up to their knees in the unusually cold water of a slowly moving creek.

They continued to stare at one another, completely motionless. After a few seconds, Jesse finally cracked, and a smile crept across his stubbled face. He gave a small snort as he shook his head and turned back to his line. It wasn't a pity laugh, and it certainly wasn't a laugh at the quip. Karen's deadpan delivery had forced its way into the joke making it much more humorous than it actually was.

"I knew I would get you with that one Cavanaugh!" she exclaimed triumphantly, "admit it, I'm hilarious."

"I won't admit that in the slightest," he responded as he arched his line back and forth overhead, finally landing it in the perfect spot upstream. "That was your one freebie. From now on every laugh has to be earned."

"You used to like that joke," Karen said as dropped the end of her line into the running water to test how the fly moved across its surface.

A shadow of recognition moved across Jesse's thoughts as a faint memory began to form hazily in his mind.

"Wait," Jesse said, smiling again as his mind retraced Karen's comment. "You've told me that joke before."

"Oh, how nice of you to remember." She responded, zipping her line upstream, landing it in the exact spot where Jesse's had been only moments before. "I'm telling you, you thought it was funny back then."

"I'm sure I didn't. I was probably just being nice like I am now. When was that again?"

"Oh come on," Karen said, feigning offense, "you really don't remember?"

Jesse gave another shrug in response. "Sorry. It's not like it was just yesterday."

"No, I'm just giving you a hard time. I wouldn't expect you to remember that. Around here we're used to living in the past. You know, Friday night football, cheerleading, Rebel pride and all that."

"Oh man, if my coworkers in New York knew that my high school mascot was the Rebels I think I might be out of a job."

"Yeah that probably wouldn't sit too well at the country club, would it?" Karen said with a small laugh.

"Well, I'm not a member of a country club but no, it would not."

Jesse and Karen had been slowly working their way upstream for almost an hour. To Jesse however, it felt like they had only been together for a brief moment. Earlier, as he had approached her house in his father's truck he almost convinced himself to keep on driving as his heart started beating faster and harder. But he knew he couldn't do that. In a town like Blue Ridge, it would only have been a matter of a few hours before word that he had stood Karen up reached his mother. Jesse shuddered thinking about the consequences and so, reluctantly, he parked the truck in front of her small, white house.

There was no reason why he should be nervous. He was Jesse Cavanaugh. He was a handsome, successful attorney who had spent the better part of the last decade becoming well acquainted with the sometimes vicious New York dating scene. Nothing and nobody in Blue Ridge, Georgia should intimidate him. As he reminded himself of this his heart rate returned to normal. Before he could open the door, Karen appeared on her front porch and the pounding in his chest returned.

Jesse had the entire afternoon planned out. Or at least where they were going. Based on his father's notes he had compiled a small list of creeks which he had not had an opportunity to visit in the short time he had taken up fishing. Sitting in the truck outside Karen's house Jesse unfolded an aged map he had found in between the seats upon which he had circled the locations of the fishing spots.

"This is crap."

"What do you mean?" Jesse responded, pointing to the map laid out between them. "These seem like good spots to try out."

"No, these are the worst. No wonder your Dad hasn't caught his Appalachian Jam."

"Slam."

"What?"

"It's called an Appalachian Slam."

"Whatever," Karen said as she began to fold the map. "I've got a better spot. Head straight and take a left on Second Street. And who the hell uses a map these days? Are you Amish or something?"

"My phone has had some issues lately, I'm getting a new one."

Karen led him out of town into the forested backroads which Jesse thought he had grown to know so well in the past couple of weeks. But as she directed him to turn left and right and left again all over the hills he realized he didn't know them as well as he thought. In no time at all he was completely disoriented and utterly dependent on her guidance. At one point he cracked a joke about her leading him out into the middle of the woods to kill him. Not skipping a beat, Karen admitted that was her plan all along and commanded him to turn off the road onto a rock-strewn path. The path was barely wide enough for the truck to fit through. Karen urged him to ignore a *No Trespassing* sign, with more than one bullet hole, and they disappeared into the woods together.

The stream swirling around the two as they moved against the current was warmer than the other waters which Jesse had been spending time in lately. It was calm and lazy as though time was purposefully slowing to match the lazy drift of the creek. Even their surroundings seemed to match its slow creep downriver. There was a breeze but it blew gently, birds chirped but in a more melancholy, leisurely pattern, not the usual, incessant chatter Jesse had come to know so well.

Like Jesse, Karen was dressed in a pair of waders protecting her from the water which flowed around her legs. If Jesse had been forced to identify the least flattering article of clothing a person could wear there was no doubt in his mind that he would have chosen fishing waders. The garment, if it can even be called that, is completely utilitarian in its design. Perfectly effective in serving its intended purpose, but not an item one would typically wear to impress another person. He understood that women's waders were cut differently from the bulky design of the men's options but still, only so much can be done with a pair of chest-high rubber pants.

Or so he thought. Jesse was already standing in the water when Karen had come around from behind the truck wearing her worn in, tan and green pair. He had left her at the tailgate to pull them over her clothes while he prepared his reel and fly. He was stunned by how elegant she looked. Something about Karen allowed her to carry the outfit with as much beauty as though she were wearing a ballroom gown and stepping down a marble staircase instead of stepping down into a muddy riverbank. The waders hugged every curve of her body as though it had been tailor-made for her athletic frame. Over the course of the next hour, he couldn't keep his eyes off her as she stretched back and forth, arching her line over the waves of dark hair bouncing across her shoulders with the motion.

On they moved, together up the narrow stream, being careful not to entangle their lines with one another's as they flicked them across the water's surface. There was no awkward silence between the two of them. Moments of silence were abundant as they enjoyed the company and the setting, but none of it was awkward. The silence was as natural and intimate as the deepest of conversations. The afternoon was interspersed with various snippets of conversations, more bad jokes, and exclamations of frustration when one of them (usually Jesse) got their line caught in a bush or low hanging tree. But for the most part the time passed in relative silence.

Ahead Jesse could hear the sound of rushing water and he noticed that the stream passing by his legs was doing so at a quicker tempo. A dozen or so yards ahead of them the creek disappeared around a slight bend obscured by a curtain of green leaves still growing from a felled sweetgum tree protruding part way into the stream. The water cascading through the branches and around the tree was moving at a quicker pace still, telling Jesse that just beyond that bend waited some type of rapids, likely meaning an end to their upstream hike. The water was also getting deeper as they moved on. Jesse would have thought that a spot like this would be perfect to find trout willing to strike a waiting fly. But so far he had come up empty handed, having only felt one or two small strikes on his line. Karen had been able to reel in a pitifully small brown trout early into their excursion but otherwise had the same luck as Jesse. On any other day Jesse would have been disappointed but today he gave it no thought.

As they approached the bend Karen again broke the silence of the moment. "Hey, I know this is going to come off really weird and corny but I'm glad you came back. I mean, that sounds bad because I know you came back because of your dad and I'm not glad that he... you know... I'm just... I'm glad you're here."

"You're right," Jesse responded, "that was weird and corny." The two laughed briefly.

"No, but really, Jesse. It's been great seeing you. Nothing else here seems to change. This whole town can feel like it's in a rut and most of the time when people leave you don't see them again."

Jesse smiled, "It's been good seeing you too. I'd probably go crazy if I only had my family while I was here."

"So... do you know when you've got to go back?"

Jesse was wondering when Karen was going to ask something like this. He reeled his line in a little bit as he prepared to flip it across the quicker moving water yet again. "I don't know. Probably pretty soon. I've got a lot of work that doesn't get put on hold just because I run away to Georgia."

"What about your mom?"

"I don't know. My dad's condition certainly complicates things. He could be like he is for a few more hours or a few months. I just can't know. It would suck to get to New York just to turn around for a funeral but I might have to do that."

"Well, for what it's worth, I wish you could stick around a little longer."

At that moment the pair rounded the fallen tree and turned together to view a beautiful waterfall cascading over an outcropping of rock barely taller than Jesse into a clear pool surrounded by ferns, rocks, and trees. The waterfall sent a spray of mist over the pool, giving the scene a mystical feel as rays of light shone through the mist onto the water's surface.

"Wow!"

"I know," Karen responded as the two of them gazed on the waterfall, "I love it here."

"I'm going to change up my fly," Jesse said, eyeing the deep pool under the churning water as a possible break in his bad luck. With his free hand he attempted to unzip the pouch on his chest wherein his recently tied flies were stored in their case. The zipper, however, resisted, catching on the fabric surrounding the pocket. Jesse lowered his chin trying to see what was causing it to stick.

"Here, let me," Karen said as she moved close to Jesse, almost completely against his broad chest. Jesse put his free hand on her waist, steadying the two of them against the shifting sand beneath their feet. After a few moments Karen successfully opened the pouch but didn't move away from him, only looked up into his face. "There, you don't need a law degree to know how to do that."

"You know," Jesse said, staring into her eyes, "The fishing here is terrible."

"Yeah, this place is the worst for fishing."

"Then why'd you bring me here?" he asked.

There was a slight pause before she answered, in which their eyes never broke contact with one another. "It's private."

At that, Jesse bent his neck slightly and pulled Karen closer to him with the hand still gently placed on her waist. As their lips met he could feel that she had wanted to do this for as long as he had, maybe longer. She leaned into him with a passion that even exceeded his and the sensations of the afternoon disappeared around them.

***

That evening Jesse sat alone on his parents' back porch. Walt curled up dutifully on the chair next to Jesse's as the fading rays of the setting sun streaked through the screen surrounding the porch. Ever since parting ways with Karen just a few hours earlier he couldn't stop thinking about her. Since Jesse's divorce he had dated sporadically, spending a significant amount of time with a few women across the years. But none made his heart race like Karen did, or caused him to dwell on them for as long afterward. But now, since he had sat down on the old rocking chair, Karen wasn't the only person to occupy his thoughts. Just like that, as though an invitation had been formally presented, Jesse felt his father's presence and the old man stepped out of the shadows created from the sun setting behind them.

"Well, now that was some fishing trip," said Jim as he stepped closer, folding his hands behind his back like Jesse remembered him doing when he was younger. Jesse almost thought he saw Walt's ears perk up ever so slightly at the imaginary voice.

"And there you are," responded Jesse, making his annoyance obvious. "I'm not at the river, isn't this a little far from your jurisdiction?"

"Hey, I've got nothing critical to say. I just wanted to tell you good job. Nice technique."

"Alright, we're done here. Thanks for ruining the evening." And with that, Jesse began to rise from his chair.

"No, really Jesse," his father said, putting his hands up as though in surrender. "Tell me about her."

"Hey, why didn't you show up out there today?" he asked. "I was worried you were going to appear and I was going to have to try to not look crazy. You're always out there when I fish."

"I don't know, you didn't invite me. I guess your mind was clear, or at least occupied by something good. It's funny what happens when you aren't actively hating me."

Jesse didn't appreciate the jab but he sat back down in the chair. He wouldn't admit it but his father was right. Aside from worrying that the ghostly vision would appear next to Karen in the water, he hadn't thought about his father, or at least he hadn't thought about their troubled relationship. Even now, sitting here, part of him wanted to dwell on the animosity he still felt teeming below the surface. But visions of Karen flashed before his eyes and his mind moved on.

"So tell me about her."

"What's to tell?" Jesse asked. "You know everything I do. You're me for heaven's sake. And besides, you... the real you, knew her for real. Or at least the two of you met on occasion."

"So what?" the old man retorted. "What's it going to hurt to talk about her? I think you want to anyways. Come one. What's she like?"

Jesse paused, staring at the hallucination as he rocked back and forth, debating whether he wanted to continue conversing or not. Finally, without even coming to a conscious decision, he opened his mouth.

"Well, for one thing, she's funny, I mean really funny, in a charming way..."

For the first time since his father first appeared to him at the river, Jesse spoke freely without the interruption of internal tension.

***

A few miles away Helen Cavanaugh kept dutiful watch over her husband's lifeless form. She was curled up on the uncomfortable couch, wrapped in a hospital blanket with an open book threatening to fall from her hands as her eyelids fought exhaustion. In the background she barely noticed as the beep of a monitor picked up its slow cadence.

Jim's finger twitched. Ever so slightly at first, but then all of the fingers on the hand laying at his side moved slowly in unison as though he were carefully gripping an unseen object and then releasing. The movement caught Helen's eyes and she jolted upright. In amazement she turned from the hand to the face of her husband where she witnessed his wrinkled eyelids flutter open. He slowly turned his head and looked at his wife as best he could. The book slipped from her hands and fell to the cold floor as she jumped from the chair.

CHAPTER 17

Never in the history of Blue Ridge had such a minor action set off such a swirl of activity as the minuscule hand and face movements made by Jim Cavanaugh. Unless you count the time when Winnie Roebuck wore the same outfit as Helen to the church spring ladies brunch. Although the battles that stemmed from that were all hidden, passive-aggressive interactions.

The scene in the hospital immediately following Jim's movements, on the other hand, was a flurry of chaos for quite some time. Immediately Helen called her two children who came to the hospital as quickly as they could. By the time Jesse arrived Aubry and Marco were already there. Aubry was talking hurriedly with their mother while Marco was speaking calmly with one of the many doctors they had seen over the past couple of weeks.

More than one person in the group, including Jesse, had attempted to tactfully suggest to Helen that what she saw was simply a result of her lack of sleep. Dark lines under her watery eyes betrayed the fact that she was incredibly tired. However, she became more and more irritated every time someone made the suggestion until she brought the room to a screeching halt by declaring loudly and emphatically "I saw what I saw!" while pounding her small fist on a bedside table.

Gradually the various conversations picked up again. Jesse was most interested in hearing what a professional had to say on the matter and so, joined Marco in listening to the doctor. The man explained, in a lower voice now, how by all indications their father did not have the capability to move his hand, head, or eyelids. The physician, a small, balding man with thin, stylish glasses continued to explain that even if Jim were to regain that kind of muscle movement, it would not be at this point but would come sometime in the future, after extensive therapy.

At that moment Aubry gave an audible gasp from her father's bedside. "Marco! Marco!" she practically screamed, "Jesse! I saw him move!"

Jesse and Marco moved quickly across the room and the two of them, along with his Aubry, Helen, and the doctor, stared intently at the man lying on the bed in front of them. Seconds passed at an unbearably low speed. After some time, Jesse realized that he was inadvertently holding his breath and began to breathe in and out slowly. Jesse found the scene almost funny. Five grown adults, including a doctor, hovering around one man's bed, each as confused as the next while they stared unflinchingly at an old man in a coma. The more he thought about it, the less funny it seemed. The seconds continued to pass and Jesse wondered how long they were going to stand there, quietly watching his father. He glanced to the side and caught Marco's eye. The two shared a look indicating that Marco was wondering the same thing.

Just as Jesse opened his mouth to speak, the old man's fingers twitched ever so slightly. The movement was almost imperceptible but it seemed to send a seismic wave through the group of onlookers. Helen clutched her chest and steadied herself on her daughter's shoulder with her free hand. Aubry's eyes welled up with tears as she covered her mouth and nose with her trembling hands. Marco's face broke out into a wild smile and he put his arm around his wife. Jesse didn't move, keeping his arms folded in front of him as his stare remained fixed on his father.

"Well, I'll be..." mumbled the doctor, whom everyone seemed to have forgotten about, until he was quickly interrupted by Helen.

"I told you!" she boomed, pointing her finger at the others in the room. "You all thought I was just being some crazy old woman but I knew what I saw. I knew it!"

In unison the group began assaulting the doctor with a barrage of inquiries. All of them, with the exception of Jesse, rattled off question after question, never letting the poor man finish one answer before a new question was lobbed at him. Finally, and with an admirable level of patience and control, the man was able to quiet the three individuals moving closer and closer around him like wild panthers preparing to spring on their prey. One by one he was able to calm them down until finally, Helen herself paused to listen to what he had to say.

"Listen, there's no doubt about it," the doctor said to the group, "this is a good sign. I am just as happy as all of you to see this. I was obviously not expecting this given the state he's been in, but it looks to me like you've got a fighter here."

At this, the small group gave another grateful sigh. Helen and Aubry began speaking to one another about how they felt when they first saw his hand move. Before he lost control of his audience again, the doctor interjected.

"That being said, as I'm sure you understand, he's not out of the woods yet. He's not even near the edge of the woods. But there is some light shining through the trees. We need to run some more tests, I want to get another colleague of mine in here to take a look at him with me. But you should feel very happy about this progress. For now, he's stable, I'm going to have his nurse visit him a few extra times tonight just to check for anything else, but I recommend you go home, get some sleep, and we'll see what we can find out in the morning."

With that, the doctor bid them farewell and quickly left the room, looking relieved to get away from the over-excited family. Just as the door was almost closed behind him Jesse slipped out unnoticed, carefully closing it behind him. The doctor was a few paces ahead of Jesse moving towards the nurses' station at a quick pace. Jesse jogged in the same direction to catch the man's attention before he made it too far.

"Yes Mr. Cavanaugh, do you have another question?" the doctor asked.

"Not really," Jesse said leaning in close to the man as though he were afraid that someone might listen in to their conversation. "I just wanted to say thanks for that in there?"

"What do you mean?" the doctor replied with a confused look on his face.

"I mean, you know, my family, they're excited and I appreciate you letting them be excited but you know you don't need to do that with me."

"I guess I'm still not following."

"That whole *light through the trees* thing. I'm glad you said that. It was good for them to hear it, but you can be honest with me. You don't need to sugar-coat anything. I understand the situation. This kind of thing, the moving, the hands, that's probably something you see in a lot of people who are in the same condition as my dad right?"

"Mr. Cavanaugh, I'm honest with all of my patients and their families. I was being honest when I said that there is still a long way to go but no, I don't see this ever with anyone in as bad a condition as your father. He suffered an enormous stroke. That muscle movement is way more than I would have expected from him right now. So I'm not sugar-coating it when I say that it is a very good sign, regardless of the work that still needs to be done."

Jesse wasn't sure how to process the information the doctor was giving him. When he first learned of the severity of his father's medical condition he accepted quickly the fact that his father would die. He had been sad, yes, but he always wondered if that sadness was just a product of him being told for years through television, books, movies, and his own interactions with other people that he was supposed to be sad when a relative died. How much of it was real and how much of it was simply following what he felt he was required to feel given the situation? Now, learning that his father's death was not inevitable churned all of those emotions up again and introduced a few new ones to complicate things further. The most potent and unexpected one, which made itself ever more present in his mind as the doctor spoke, was relief, and dare he say, even happiness.

"Get some sleep, Mr. Cavanaugh. Things are looking up."

When Jesse returned to his father's room his mother and sister were both in tears and smiling. After much protesting, Jesse, Marco, and Aubry were able to convince Helen to return home with them for the rest the doctor had encouraged her to get. Only after the promise that one of them would drive her back first thing in the morning did she relent and allow them to leave her husband's side.

The ride home was a quiet one. Jesse drove his father's truck while his mother stared out the passenger window at the passing streetlights. The look on her face was one of peace and satisfaction. A few miles from home she shifted in her seat on the long bench of the old truck and laid her head on her son's shoulder. The two didn't say a word as she reached over and held on to his arm. Jesse knew what she was doing. It didn't need to be said, she was saying she was glad he was there and not in New York.

The next few days were a blur for Jesse and the rest of his family. Spirits were high and all of them seemed excited about any news they could possibly find out from the hospital. Helen still insisted on someone staying by her husband's bedside as much as possible but it was a much less dreary affair. Flowers in the room were replaced with freshly cut bouquets and it was not uncommon for a few people to visit every day in order to wish them the best of luck. Helen and Aubry must have spread the news quickly because it did not take long until handwritten notes of encouragement began appearing tucked into the Cavanaugh's screen door while they were out. Most surprising of all, Jim's signs of improvement continued. His fingers or eyelids or toes continued to twitch every few hours while brain activity, as monitored through specialized equipment that Jesse didn't fully understand, rose dramatically. A pair of doctors from Emory University Hospital in Atlanta even visited briefly to make notes of his activity and review Jim's progress first hand.

Jesse spent much of those next few days with Aubry and her family. Even though they had known each other for many years, Jesse had never spent a significant amount of time with Marco. He had never really wanted to. Not that he didn't like Marco, he did. He had just never felt an overwhelming desire to spend time with the man. Especially since doing so meant coming home to Georgia. Jesse was pleased to find that Marco was not so reserved, and he was welcomed into his brother-in-law's home as though he were the type of uncle that visited often. As short summer rains put a damper on any fishing plans Jesse might have had he passed the time playing with his nephew, making traditional Cuban meals with Marco, and looking through embarrassing old photographs with his sister.

In between time spent with his mother, his sister's family, and visiting his father at the hospital, Jesse was in frequent communication with Karen. Knowing that the Cavanaugh family, including Jesse, was going through a difficult and emotional situation Karen attempted to keep a respectful distance. The morning after their fishing date she sent Jesse a long and obviously well planned out text message apologizing for coming on to him at the waterfall. She asked his forgiveness for not being sensitive to the fact that Jesse's father was in the hospital and encouraged him to spend time with his family instead of her. Jesse smiled as he read it, wondering how long it had taken her to craft the lengthy message and convince herself to press send. He appreciated her concern but even given the good news they had received, he welcomed the opportunity to remove himself and his mind from his family. He dismissed her message and simply responded by asking what time they should meet that evening.

The two found small moments to see one another. Lunches, dinners, mountain hikes, and the occasional hospital supply closet. Jesse felt like they were in high school again, having to sneak around in order to avoid the prying eyes of his family. Karen was still petrified that what they were doing was wrong given the circumstances that brought Jesse back home. Even though Jesse didn't mind, Karen was convinced that Helen would not approve of the two of them becoming involved while her husband was clinging to life.

In the back of his mind Jesse knew the secretive nature of their relationship was for the best. However, he had come to the conclusion for different reasons. Soon, whether his father recovered or not, he would return to New York and he did not envision a relationship with Karen surviving the distance. He had no interest in even attempting such a thing, regardless of how much he cared for her. He certainly had a deeper connection with her than anyone else since his divorce, but his life in New York simply did not have room for a nurse from Fannin County. Keeping their relationship between the two of them would make it easier on Karen when he left.

Four days after the family had gathered around Jim's hospital bed, Jesse found himself entering Daddy Ray's Bait & Tackle. The rains, which had lingered in the area for the last few days, had subsided and Jesse slipped away from his mother and sister to the shop, using a flimsy excuse that he needed more fly making material. If either of them were to glance at his father's cluttered workbench they would learn that wasn't true, but Jesse imagined that neither of them would wander into the basement while he was away.

Water, which had been soaked up by hot pavement and thick, red, Georgia clay quickly evaporated causing the humidity in the region to skyrocket in the aftermath of the summer showers. Simply walking from the truck to the front door of the small shop caused Jesse to break a significant sweat. Luckily the inside of the shop was cool. Still muggy, but cool thanks to an ancient, overworked air conditioning unit and two out-of-sync ceiling fans. A small bell attached to the front door announced his arrival and he was immediately met by Abram's friendly voice emerging from the rows of fishing gear, outdoor accessories, and magazines.

"Back here, Jesse."

Jesse strode up the side aisle, past the checkout counter where Daddy Ray was once again asleep in his chair. As Jesse walked past him he briefly paused and then turned back around, standing directly in front of the owner. Every other time he had been here Daddy Ray had been snoring loudly. Now the old man was silent and still, with his head leaned straight back and his mouth wide open. Jesse moved closer and listened carefully. A few tense seconds passed before Daddy Ray gave a loud violent snort and adjusted his head and neck as he slept. Satisfied that the elderly proprietor was alive and well, Jesse continued to the back left corner of the shop.

Jesse was met by Abram who was leaning against a shelving unit waiting for Jesse. The old man greeted him and handed him an opened, glass bottle of Coke before diving right in. "Well well well counselor it looks like you caught something out there a little more interesting than a trout. At least better looking and a lot more fun."

Abram elbowed Jesse playfully and led him around the corner of the shelves. Jesse couldn't help but smile at the situation unfolding before him. Karen sat on a bar stool at the counter in front of the large window on the far wall. Bennie was seated next to her. The two were turned towards one another, Karen's elbow rested on the counter with her hand outstretched towards Bennie who was gently holding it with one, massive calloused hand, moving his thumb across her outstretched palm.

It appeared Bennie was attempting to read her palm since Jesse heard his deep, rough voice whisper phrases like "life-line" and "love-line." It was obvious by the way that he was looking directly into her eyes and how he gently caressed her arm with the back of his other hand that he was doing the best he could to hit on Karen who was attempting to suppress a fit of laughter. Jesse had to admire the man. He didn't let a small roadblock, like the fact that he was thirty-five to forty years her senior, dissuade him.

"You'll have to forgive Bennie," Abram said, leaning over to Jesse, "he considers himself somewhat of a ladies' man. It's really your own fault bringing a woman like that into a place like this."

Catching the two of them watching, Karen turned to them while still allowing Bennie to stroke her open palm. "Jesse. Look, your friend here is telling me how long I'm going to live."

Bennie instinctively pulled his hands away from Karen's, almost knocking over his mug in the process. The two of them stood, Karen gracefully as she glided across the old wooden floors towards Jesse, and Bennie more awkward and sheepish.

"Jessie, I didn't hear you come in. We've been getting to know your friend here."

"Thanks for keeping her company guys, sorry I'm late."

Jesse smiled as Bennie moved back to his usual position on the sofa and attempted to avoid eye contact with Jesse. He and Karen had taken to finding creative ways to avoid his family and Jesse could think of no better place than the bait shop. He knew his mother would never be seen in a place like this. After some more playful banter with the two men, Jesse and Karen made their exit. They had no schedule for the day but only planned that they would spend it together. As they walked away through the aisles of the store towards the exit Karen did something she hadn't done before. She reached down and held Jesse's hand as they walked, inter-twining her slender fingers with his.

In many ways this felt more intimate that their rendezvous at the waterfall or their brief moments together hiding from his family. This was public. This was on display for all the world to see, or at least for all the bait shop to see. Jesse's first instinct was to graciously let go of her hand but it passed as suddenly as a cool breeze on a hot summer's day. As soon as it did, a new instinct took its place, and Jesse closed his hand around hers, gripping it gently, and lovingly as he opened the doors and stepped out into the sunshine with her by his side.

CHAPTER 18

Montana. Why on Earth would Jesse's father be so obsessed with Montana?

It was referenced everywhere throughout the elderly fisherman's journal. From determined statements that he would visit someday to interesting facts he apparently learned over time (Jesse was surprised to learn that the land-locked state was home to a large population of pelicans). But the old man never provided any explanation in his journal as to why he was so consumed by the idea the Western state. It was obvious that Montana was an outdoorsman's paradise. The hunting and fishing in the region were legendary. But it was just as legendary in Colorado, Utah, and Idaho. Why Montana?

The question rattled around Jesse's mind. It wouldn't go away. And much like his father, when Jesse got something in his head it was difficult to concentrate until he was able to deal with it. So he figured there was no reason not to ask. Even if what he got was a made up answer imagined from the recesses of his own thoughts, it was better than nothing.

"Why Montana?"

"What?" the vision of Jim asked from his spot seated on a log stretched out along the riverbank. The man seemed genuinely surprised by the question.

"What's the deal with your fascination with Montana?"

Jesse was in the process of releasing a small trout back into the moving waters of Cooper's Creek. The fish had hardly put up a fight but when Jesse scooped it out of the water his heart began pounding in excitement. The fish's bright pink fins and belly, contrasting with its green and brown sides, were unmistakable. It was a brook trout; the rarest of the three species Jesse was after.

It was always fun to catch a brook. Their elusiveness made each catch exhilarating, but this fish was particularly exciting because Jesse had caught a large brown trout just an hour before. This meant that he was already two-thirds of the way towards landing an Appalachian Slam. The only fish left to catch was a rainbow trout. Rainbows in these waters were a dime a dozen. Jesse was surprised he hadn't caught one already. In all the other instances where he had almost got the Slam he had caught multiple rainbows throughout the day with only a brook or a brown remaining. Now all he had to do was get lucky enough to bag the most common fish around. He had never come this close. His blood was pumping excitedly as he continued to ride the adrenaline high from the brook trout.

But it still hadn't kept his mind from his father's unusual desire to visit Montana.

"Jesse, we can talk about that later. You need to focus. You're this close to catching a Slam." Jim held his finger and thumb out indicating the small amount left for Jesse to obtain what he himself had been unable to.

"Come on, it's fishing, it's not like I need a lot of concentration," Jesse replied. "If anything, I just need to relax and fish. This could help."

"What about all that, *I need peace and quiet, leave me alone,* you've been spewing at me? You need to focus on the task at hand. You're one easy fish away from doing it. Don't screw it up now because you have some complex where you feel like every word I write in that stupid journal has to be deciphered and analyzed. That journal is just noise. You've got a goal in sight. Focus on that."

"Well, now you're stressing me out." Jesse shot back bitterly as he felt his nerves began to tighten with the thought that he was so close. Jesse replaced his net, washed his hands in the babbling creek and moved out into the flow of the water. But Jesse wasn't willing to drop the subject. After a moment of silence, briefly interrupted by the swishing of his line, he asked again. "Come on, why Montana?"

Jesse didn't watch his father, instead preferring to keep his eyes concentrated on the spot towards which he was arcing his line. However, he did hear him sigh in exhaustion as he answered.

"I don't know. Montana is Montana. It's a great place to fish. Or so I've been told. I've seen pictures of people fishing on the Madison River. That place looks great. You should see the trout they catch out there. They're huge. They make these fish look like minnows."

Jesse could understand that to some extent but he still didn't see the appeal. It seemed so random. "Yeah, but why Montana? Have you ever even left Georgia before?"

"I visited you in New York a couple of times with your Mother. And I went up to Harvard when you graduated law school."

"Oh yeah," Jesse mumbled as he continued flipping his line. "I forgot about those. I guess they didn't exactly leave a lasting impression on me."

"And I've been to some insurance conferences out west. But mostly Vegas and California. But that's not why, it's just..." Jim's speaking faded away as he tried to conjure up the right words to express his thoughts on the subject.

"Well, you make a compelling argument. Maybe you should have been the attorney in the family."

"You don't get it Jesse," the man sitting on the log said slowly and deliberately as he watched his son whip another cast across the water. "It's not something you can explain. It's something you feel. Montana represents for me opportunity. Unlimited opportunity. It's big sky country. The rivers are wide without these trees crowding over them, the land is vast and far-reaching. You can see all the way to the horizon. Here you can only see as far as the next tree line unless you get up on top of a mountain."

"It's beautiful here though" Jesse responded, admitting it for the first time.

"Yes it is, but it's not about beauty. It's about what that open space represents. A man can do what he wants and be who he wants to be under a sky like that. A new environment of open-ended potential. For me, it's more than a place. It's an idea, or rather an attitude. And it's not a bad place to fish, which doesn't hurt. But that kind of opportunity is what draws me there. You can't find that opportunity here or in New York for that matter."

"Okay, listen I know you always hated that I moved to New York but I'm just fine with it. I have enough opportunity there."

"Are you sure about that?" Jim asked. "It's not about New York, or Georgia, or anywhere else. It's about being a new person. Becoming a new man. Perhaps the person you wanted to be but never became, or weren't strong enough to be. It's about the excitement of somewhere and something new and the undeveloped promise that's waiting for you there. Wanting more opportunity and change and potential is different for everyone. For me, it's Montana."

Listening to the fantasized answer delivered in his father's voice, Jesse felt sadness for the man lying in the hospital miles away. For the first time in Jesse's life he considered the fact that the man Jim Cavanaugh had become was perhaps not the man he intended to be. In Jesse's mind, the man now struggling for his life was cold, aloof, and distant. But then again, some might say the same about him. He certainly didn't want to be that way or have his friends and family think that about him. Perhaps his father didn't care at all or perhaps he did and the image of who he had grown to be was not what he had wanted out of life. Jim must have had dreams beyond selling insurance policies in Blue Ridge, Georgia. There must have been something else that he wanted out of life. If the man could really speak to him in an honest and open way (which he never did) he had to believe that there would be some expression of disappointment and regret.

Jesse began to understand Montana.

"So why didn't you go?" he asked.

"What?" Jim seemed surprised by the answer as though the thought had never occurred to him.

"Why didn't you ever go? You've got the money. It's not that hard to get there. You don't really have anything else going on. Why didn't you go."

"Oh, you know, there's always so much to do. And besides, I still need to catch the Appalachian Slam. I told myself that maybe after I get that then me and your mom would go out to Montana."

"That's not it," Jesse responded as he continued to work his line. "You're scared."

"Don't be ridiculous."

"No. Why else wouldn't you go? You talk about it being something new and representing so much opportunity for change for you but you've never shown any interest in that. You're scared that if you go out there you'll have to face your demons."

"Well, it sounds like maybe you should take a trip out there yourself," Jim responded, showing mild annoyance at his son's judgments.

"Believe it or not Dad, not everyone would love the wide open spaces."

"Yeah, I get it," Jim answered, "there's nowhere to hide out there. Here I've got my trees, up in New York you've got your buildings. But out there you're exposed. And being exposed can be difficult."

The two fell silent. A few tense moments passed and Jesse forced himself to remain quiet. Out of nowhere the tip of Jesse's rod bent low towards the creek and his reel began to spin as line was pulled wildly from it. There had been no nibble or sign that the fly was about to be taken. No rising leap to snatch the lure from the top of the water. The trout simply struck without warning.

"You got him now!" Jim screamed as he leaped from the log and practically ran into the water towards his son.

Jesse was surprised by the sudden turn of events. In an instant he forgot about Montana and focused on the rod he was gripping tightly. The fish was fighting aggressively against the tension of the line and Jesse maneuvered himself across the creek to bring himself closer to the fish. It was massive. It had to be the way it was fighting.

"Let him run! Pull him in! Move over there! No, back here!"

The ghostly vision shouted directions at Jesse. Each one contradicting the last. Jesse had met every other fishing suggestion or instruction doled out by his father's vision over the past few weeks with disdain, anger, and frustration by Jesse. But not now. There was no time for that.

Slowly Jesse began to pull the fish in against its protests. Inch by inch it crept closer to where Jesse stood in the water. Back and forth it moved under the water attempting to shake the hook ensnared in its mouth. Finally, it moved close enough to see as it darted under the surface of the sunlit water.

"It's a rainbow son!" his father's voice boomed in his ears. The old man reached out and in excitement placed a weathered hand on Jesse's shoulder as he continued to work the reel. Jesse couldn't feel the hand but could see his father anxiously holding on to him. "You're doing it. You've got the slam."

Jesse retrieved the net in preparation to take his prize. As he did so, the trout changed directions rapidly. The tension eased and there was an audible *pop*. Jesse felt the hook dislodge from the fish's mouth as the line went slack. In an instant the rod sprung straight again as the fly whizzed out of the water on the end of Jesse's line, almost hitting him in the chest. Briefly the rainbow trout breach the surface of the creek as it flipped its tail and disappeared under water. Jesse stared in disbelief, frozen by the painful image.

"Oh come on!" his father's voice groaned in frustration.

For the first time in years Jesse made a lighthearted joke with his father. "It still counts right?"

The two of them laughed. There was nothing left to do. Getting mad wasn't going to help. Yelling at his father wasn't going to help. Jesse was surprised. He didn't feel as disappointed as he expected after falling short so close to his goal. He felt oddly content.

"I'm sorry Jesse. I really thought you had it there."

"It's fine really. It just wasn't meant to be. There's always tomorrow, right?" There was still light left in the afternoon and Jesse had no plans to stop fishing for the day but the experience had a feeling of finality to it. He could tell that he was not going to have any other chances that day. Sometimes a fisherman just knows.

"That's right," Jim said as the two watched the water move swiftly by them. "There's always tomorrow.

For the first time in a long time, and certainly for the first time since coming home, Jesse actually looked forward to seeing his father the next day. He was sure that if he dwelt on the issues the two of them had the same old emotions would come to the surface. They always did. But he chose not to. He appreciated that for a moment in time, however brief it was, he was able to think about his father without the usual wave of anxiety and anger consuming him. Standing there with him, looking forward to the next day Jesse understood Montana a little more.

CHAPTER 19

James Cavanaugh was dead.

Jesse sat next to his sister's family and his mother on the front pew of the First Baptist Church as the organ signaled the beginning of his father's funeral services. Jesse glanced around him at the mourners who had come out to show their support for the Cavanaugh family. It was a large crowd. Larger than he had expected. The mood in the church was what you would expect at a funeral. Somber and despondent. There wasn't a dry eye in the building. Except for maybe himself and Jayden. The five-year-old was too young to fully grasp what had happened. Jesse on the other hand, didn't have the same excuse. He hadn't shed a tear since the moment his distraught sister had informed them of their father's death. His eyes hadn't even begun to well up. Should they have? Was something wrong with him for not crying along with these strangers?

Aubry and Helen reassured friends and fellow churchgoers who expressed their consolations that Jim had passed swiftly and painlessly as he slept. It was a nice story and provided these kind individuals with some sense of relief. But it wasn't true. The old man had suffered a painful and violent death, assuming that he could feel anything at all from the midst of his coma. It was unclear if he could. But from the way he thrashed about it appeared that he felt something. A hospital orderly had been in the process of changing linens in his room when his eyes flew open and immediately rolled back in his head while his whole body seized.

The second stroke was even stronger than the first. Doctors and nurses immediately flooded the room, and every effort was made to save the man's life. But after a few short minutes and one last violent surge of muscle spasms, he was dead. Helen had been at her home, Aubry was visiting Marco on a construction site, and Jesse had been fishing. There were no final words, no parting action or special moment shared with his family. It felt like the moment should have more gravity but it didn't. One moment he was alive and the next, he wasn't.

The entire Cavanaugh family was taken aback by the sudden and jarring news. It was as though a door which was beginning to open had suddenly been slammed shut. Enough hope had been introduced into their lives with his signs of improvement that when it was removed it felt like he had died for the second time.

No one was more distraught than Helen. At the onset of the ordeal she had insisted on remaining by her husband's side. Then she relaxed that rule, insisting instead that someone from the family be with him. Then, only that they have someone with him as much as possible. Now, with her husband dead she felt that her failure to stay by his bedside at all times was a betrayal of the man she loved.

"I should have been there," she sobbed through tears as the family gathered at the hospital. "I abandoned him."

Jesse, Aubry, and Marco attempted to impress on her the error of that sentiment. They insisted that she would not have been able to save or help him if she had been present and that witnessing the event would have done nothing more than to magnify the loss. But nothing tempered her grief or her guilt. Jesse hoped that time lived up to its reputation and would, in fact, heal all wounds.

On the day of the funeral Jesse's mother's eyes were red and puffy. Throughout the service, tears would well to the surface of her eyelids and subside as though she were consciously willing them not to fall. Jesse didn't know if it was a result of her remarkable ability to remain composed in front of society or if she had cried so much in private that she didn't have any more energy to do. It was a stark contrast to the hysterical woman who had broken down in front of her family at the hospital. This woman was grieving but graceful, whereas the woman at the hospital had teetered close to a nervous breakdown as she collapsed from shock and heartbreak into her daughter's arms.

Even though Jesse had a front-row seat he felt as though he were watching the funeral unfold from afar. The sensation felt very familiar. He assumed that the service was progressing as normal. He could smell the flowers and hear various mourners sniffle as they fought back emotions. At the pulpit of the church, the local pastor stood above the coffin, speaking to the crowd. Jesse drowned out his words until his voice sounded simply like white noise in the background of his mind.

All Jesse could think of was how he was always surprised at how quickly funerals were planned, scheduled, and executed. His father had only been dead for three days before he would be lowered into the hard Georgia clay. One day a person was dead and three days to a week later they were in the ground. There never seemed to be enough time to grieve before they were gone forever.

The last three days had been a whirlwind of activity. Jesse, Aubry, and Marco did everything they could to take as much off Helen's plate as possible. They divided up duties between the three of them and quickly plans were made with the funeral home and the church. Floral arrangements were chosen, programs were printed, and an outfit was selected for the recently departed. This last item of business reminded Jesse that he had not packed appropriate attire for the occasion. For some reason he hadn't been planning on a funeral even though he was convinced when he set out from New York City that his father would not recover from his affliction. Briefly he wondered why he had failed to pack for mourning. Had some part of him hoped that it would not be needed? He had worn his father's old seersucker when he was forced by his mother to attend church, but the light, springtime suit seemed inappropriate for this situation. And so, the day before the funeral, Jesse drove to the nearest department store. He didn't have time to have a suit properly fitted so he settled for the closest fitting black suit jacket and trousers.

The suit almost fit his tall frame which, he decided, was worse than it being a completely wrong size. Instead, something just felt off at all times without being able to pinpoint where. Jesse had selected the most expensive suit he could find but was still annoyed by what he deemed substandard quality. He tried not to be an elitist in general, but Jesse's successful career had afforded him certain luxuries in which he was more than happy to indulge. One was a closet full of high-quality clothing hanging in his Manhattan apartment. His mind went through the perfectly fitted suits waiting for him as he fidgeted with his clothes in the hard pew.

All of a sudden the crowd around him stood as music from the church's organ began to play. Jesse instinctively stood along with them, surmising that the services had concluded. He couldn't have reported a single word that was said throughout the entirety of his father's funeral if he had tried. Had the pastor been the only person who spoke? Was there someone else who delivered a eulogy? How long had it lasted? What hymns did they sing? Jesse could remember following along in a hymnbook while people around him sang but he couldn't remember the melody or the lyrics.

Jesse wondered what had been said about his father. He could take a guess that it was probably all the same clichés that are churned out at these things as though it were a requirement. *Jim was a fantastic insurance agent and fisherman, but was an even better husband and father. Jim was a kind soul who always went out of his way to show others that he cared. God needed another angel which is why he called Jim home.*

These people didn't know his father. At least that's what Jesse told himself. They may have grown up with him, worked with him, fished with him, or worshipped with him. But from Jesse's point of view they didn't know him. They didn't know how it felt to be ignored by him when your child dies, or when your marriage falls apart. Jesse had come to the conclusion that that's how you truly get to know someone. When you are encompassed by grief, sadness, and stress and you're just hoping that the phone will ring with them on the other side of the line. When that ring never comes, that's when you get to know who they are.

Jesse took up the rear as his family walked behind his father's casket out of the building. Jesse didn't know these people and didn't care to. In a few short days he would be gone. He was appreciative that they were here to support his mother but their faces meant nothing to him. As their solemn procession moved through the church Jesse did recognize Winnie Roebuck, his mother's arch nemesis and former friend. The two women had waged social battles for years over potluck recipes, brunch outfits, and positions on various church committees. As the family moved slowly past her row, Helen Cavanaugh reached a gloved hand out to the woman who squeezed it briefly as tears ran down her face. The gesture was silent and short-lived but did not go unnoticed by those who witnessed and were moved by it.

The drive to the cemetery was short and quiet. Close friends and families followed the hearse in a line of cars that weaved through the streets of Blue Ridge. Following the southern custom, other cars driving on the same road pulled off to the side to show respect for the dead as the funeral procession passed. Jesse had forgotten about this practice and was surprised to see that it had survived to this day. *Some things here never change*, he thought as they continued on. At the gravesite a few more words were said, a prayer was given, and then it was done. The slate gray casket was lowered into the open grave and the small crowd began to dissipate.

Abram and Bennie were in attendance at the gravesite. Jesse had noticed the two fishermen standing in the back of the group. After the service they approached Jesse to pay their respects. Abram was calm and collected as he shook Jesse's hand firmly, expressing his grief over his loss. Bennie, on the other hand, was beside himself. Tears streamed down his cheeks and trickled through his neatly trimmed mustache. Jesse would have thought the vision of the barrel-chested military-style man reduced to a puddle of tears was funny if the setting hadn't been so serious. Jesse graciously thanked them for attending and was met with a rib-crushing bear hug from Bennie. After a few moments of the large man sobbing on the shoulder of his new suit, Jesse patted his back, gave him a "there, there" and sent the two men on their way.

"Friends of yours?" Aubry asked with a puzzled look on her face.

"I guess," he responded, watching them walk across the cemetery grounds, Abram's arm around Bennie.

There is always food at southern funerals. Lots of food. Luncheons and communal meals are a part of funeral services all over the modern world but nowhere is it more pronounced than the Deep South. When Jesse's family returned to his mother's home they found a large number of people waiting for them as well as platters filled with food. Jesse assumed that Aubry had arranged the spread in conjunction with the church women's group. The dining room table was covered with plates of ham, potato salad, deviled eggs, funeral potatoes, peaches with cottage cheese, three bean salad, three types of homemade macaroni and cheese, and rolls. As Jesse ventured into the kitchen he found that the counters were equally full of cobblers, pies, brownies, and a large Gatorade cooler filled with iced tea. Jesse didn't attend church anymore but he had to hand it to the Baptists, they could cook.

Helen immediately shifted into host mode. She made sure that everyone's Dixie cups remained filled and that all plates remained full. Every person she helped insisted that she leave the logistics of the gathering to those who organized it but she refused. Helen was a socialite and a host by nature. She was not about to allow a party in her own house, even if it was meant for her, go hosted by any person but herself. Jesse watched as she buzzed around the small home, picking up spare plates and utensils, wiping children's faces, and refilling platters of food. Her tears had dried up, the puffy circles and redness had retreated from her eyes. She was operating with tunnel vision, only focusing on the tasks at hand in tending to her guests, much to their discomfort.

Jesse assumed her behavior was not a healthy reaction to her husband's funeral. But what did he know? He wasn't exactly known for dealing with grief in the healthiest of ways himself.

Jesse spent the reception trying to avoid people as much as possible. He attempted to retreat into the basement but was caught by his mother and herded into the living room with the other guests. Eventually he found himself stuck in a corner with one of his father's old business partners. Jesse picked slowly at a slice of pecan pie while he listened to the man tell story after boring story about him and his father's adventures in small-town insurance sales. Eventually he was rescued by a hand tapping his shoulder.

"Jesse," Marco said, getting his brother-in-law's attention. "Sorry to interrupt but I think there's someone here to see you."

Jesse followed Marco's gesture through the open front window to the porch where he could see the silhouette of a woman through the thin white drapes moving in the breeze. Thankful for the excuse, Jesse apologized to his father's business associate, abandoned the pie on the nearest table, and snaked his way to the front door. Karen was seated with her legs crossed on a wide banister that encompassed the large porch. There were a few visitors scattered across the porch in small conversations with one another but Karen sat alone. She was dressed in a tasteful black dress fitting for the occasion and although it was no more formal than any other attire at the event she had a way of making it seem as though she were overdressed in her pearls and heels.

Immediately Jesse felt a surge of relief in seeing her. A flood of emotions rippled through his chest as he approached her across the creaky porch. Karen had called and texted him immediately upon hearing the news of his father's passing, but Jesse had only replied that he was busy making arrangements and that he would get back to her as soon as he could. This was, of course, true to some extent, however, he hadn't reached out since. Picking up the phone and calling her seemed all of a sudden like an enormous burden to bear. One he was not willing to shoulder.

Karen gracefully rose to her feet and embraced him. "Jesse, I am so sorry," she said and placed a discreet kiss on his cheek.

The tempest of emotions subsided with the feel of her body against his and the smell of her perfume. The only feeling left was peace and he put his arms around her in return.

"I was at the church," she continued as she stepped back from him, "I didn't want to interrupt the family and I didn't want to come inside and distract you here while you were talking with people."

"Are you kidding? You saved me from having to be in there." Jesse motioned at the house and realized for the first time that through the shapes of visitors in the windows he could clearly see his mother and sister peeking through the drapes. "Come with me," he said and the two walked down the front walkway towards the sloped road lined with cars.

"Jesse I can't stop thinking about you. I can't imagine what you're going through. I know you've been dealing with a lot but I wanted to see you today to make sure you were okay and to let you know that I'm here for you." Karen reached out and took his hand. Jesse knew that this obvious romantic gesture was well within the view of his family's prying eyes but instead of letting go he closed his fingers on hers and held tightly on to her delicate hand.

In an instant the detached feeling returned. He recognized the sentiment. It was how he felt after Elle died. Back then he felt as though he were watching his life from a distance and not controlling his actions. He had felt the same way earlier that morning as he watched the funeral proceed from afar. Now he watched, almost in disbelief, as he let go of Karen's hand and stepped back from her a few steps. *Oh no, it's happening again.* Immediately the image of Jim Cavanaugh appeared out of the corner of his eye staring directly at him while Jesse looked into Karen's big, beautiful eyes.

"What are you doing Jesse?" the old man said, his imagined voice only audible to his son. "Don't do it. Not this time."

But there was nothing he could do. Jesse wasn't in control or at least he felt as though he wasn't. He wanted to scream out and tell himself to hold Karen close and not let go. He wanted to reach out to her and tell her how much she meant to him. But he had been here before. There was no point.

Resigned to his fate he simply sat back and watched the spectacle unfold from somewhere within the recesses of his mind.

"Karen," Jesse said. "Thanks for coming. I'm glad you're here. I've had a great time these last few weeks."

"Stop it Jesse!" his father raised his voice in his ears. "She doesn't deserve this. You don't deserve this!"

Jesse ignored the vision's protests and continued. "I don't think I would have made it through this without you. I can't express how much you've done for me."

"Okay," Karen said, obviously wondering where he was going with this.

"Things have been crazy here. I'll probably be leaving in the next few days to head back to New York and I doubt things will die down before then. I just wanted to let you know I'm so grateful for all that you've done for me and for keeping me sane during this time."

"Oh, I didn't know you'd be leaving so soon." She was taken aback, not expecting the announcement at that moment. "Well, can I see you before you leave?"

"Um, yeah," he said softly, nodding his head. "I'll try to give you a call before I leave town." There was a slight pause where Jesse could tell she was trying to think of what to say next. Deciding not to drag the conversation out longer than it needed to be, he cut in before she could speak. "Thanks for dropping by Karen. It means a lot."

With that, Jesse turned and walked past the vision of his father towards the disappointed faces of his mother and sister in the windows of the house. There was no parting kiss, or hug, just sudden disconnection. Jesse wondered what emotions her face showed at that moment as he walked away. Confusion? Anger? Sadness? Did she stand and watch him leave or did she turn and leave herself? He wasn't sure and couldn't know. He didn't want to know. He never turned around, but instead walked quickly up the path and disappeared into the house.

CHAPTER 20

Ghosts are real in Georgia. Or at least they play a real part in the history and culture of the state. Even though most put little stock in them now, ghost stories are as much a part of the traditions of the South as its architecture, cuisine, and checkered past. Tales of strange apparitions stretch from the northern mountains to the southern swamplands and crop up in every small town in between.

On Crybaby Bridge, in Columbus, they say you can hear the ghost of an infant who was killed there crying on the night breeze. On Booger Hill in Cumming, at the alleged site of a gruesome lynching of wrongly accused slaves, legend has it that if you shift your car into neutral after dark it will be pushed to the top of the hill by the spirits. An old sorority house in Athens is supposedly haunted by a suicidal bride from the nineteenth century, leading any girl who lives in the engagement suite where she died, to become engaged to her boyfriend by the end of her time there. In Savannah, the state's first capital, ghosts are so integral to the city they have become big business. One of the most popular activities for tourists are the many competing "ghost tours" which transport visitors to haunted locations across the town.

In Blue Ridge, Jesse was confronting a different type of ghost. The vision of his now deceased father haunted him everywhere he went. At one time, the specter was contained to the rivers and creeks where Jesse fished, peppered by short visitations elsewhere during times of quiet introspection. Now, Jesse saw the ghostly figure no matter where he was, or what he was doing. He knew the old man, who seemed so solemn and disappointed, was not a physical or a spiritual manifestation. This was a mental issue, and one which Jesse was determined to solve through the time-honored practice of ignoring the problem.

Jesse found if he buried himself in whatever task he undertook, he could almost shake his father's looming presence. Almost. Something was always there. At times, the man was in his presence, speaking with him in that same condescending manner which Jesse knew so well from his life. Other times, all he saw was the man's outline watching him from his peripheral vision as he interacted with other people. Jesse would intently pay attention to the person with whom he was speaking but he could always see his father standing at the edge of the room and feel his aggressive silence.

The dark figure reminded him of Edgar Allan Poe's "The Tell-Tale Heart." He remembered reading the story in middle school. The narrator in that writing had committed a murder and concealed the victim's remains under the floorboards of his home. However, he is besieged by the imaginary beating of the victim's heart, leading him to confess to his crime.

The story seemed too on the nose for Jesse to ignore. Jesse also was being plagued by imagined sensations which reminded him of the dead. However, Jesse had nothing to feel guilty of. He hadn't killed his father. He hadn't crafted the wedge which had driven them apart. Guilt should not play a role in Jesse's actions as he approached the end of his stay in Blue Ridge. There was no reason for him to feel haunted by the man, and yet, everywhere he looked, his father was waiting for him. He felt as real to him as the beating heart sounded to the murderous antagonist of Poe's story.

Quietly, Jesse began to make preparations to leave his hometown once more. His clothes were neatly washed, folded, and placed in his unscuffed luggage. A pressed pair of slacks and a button-down shirt intended for the day of travel were draped on top of the bag which was stored at the foot of his bed. Jesse knew he would be staying for at least a few more days but he was happy to live out of the suitcase in preparation to leave as soon as it felt appropriate.

Since arriving in Blue Ridge, Jesse had allowed his beard to grow. He had kept it reigned in but had maintained a scruffy, few days' growth. It was modest and fairly neat but still more than he was used to back home. Additionally, he had allowed his hair to grow out long enough to touch his ears for the first time since college. A quick shave and a trip to Marco's recommended barber corrected the situation and he now looked again like the lawyer who had wandered into town a few weeks ago.

In addition to making preparations for his physical travel back to New York City, Jesse undertook to ensure that he was not the only one prepared for his departure. Ted had specifically sent Jesse back to his hometown to make sure that his mother was okay in the wake of his father's stroke. Jesse regretted that he had allowed his own issues between himself and his father affect his mother over the years. It should not have taken prodding from his boss to force him to come visit her but it had. Of all the things that may have caused Jesse guilt, this was one of the only actions which he recognized as a legitimate source of regret. Jesse sat with his mother at the kitchen table and poured over paperwork. He made sure that bills were taken care of, payments were scheduled, and life insurance policy claims were commenced.

After finding an estate attorney that Jesse felt he could trust to begin the process of probating his father's will, he reached the conclusion that everything that could be done to help his mother had been taken care of. With the click of a button on his new phone, he purchased a plane ticket home. He would be leaving in four days.

By the time he arrived back in the city he will have been gone for almost a month. Jesse had never spent nearly that amount of time away from work since he first started at the firm. Part of him was excited to get back in the office. He recognized that feeling. It was his default setting. Another part of him dreaded going home. Every time those feelings surfaced he recognized the familiar outline of his father standing over him. Watching him.

He pushed those apprehensions, along with the ominous vision, away from his thoughts and considered what to do with his remaining time. All preparations had been taken care of. There was nothing remaining that he needed to take care of. Sitting on the back porch, rocking back and forth as Walt snored next to him, Jesse scrolled through his new phone until he landed on Karen's contact number. Her beautiful face smiled up at him from the profile picture glowing next to the phone number. Karen had texted him a number of times since the funeral and left a few voicemails. Not one had received a response. After a few days they ceased altogether. His finger hovered over her phone number. Sighing in defeat, Jesse turned off the screen and dropped the phone back into his pocket.

Hearing the front door open he understood that it was time he break the news to his mother that we would be leaving. He brought her to the back porch where they sat in the shade from the afternoon sun. She did not take it well. The two argued. It was subtle, it was polite, but it was still arguing.

"Mom, you're not some frail old woman. You can take care of yourself. We've gone over everything together. You're taken care of."

"I'm not worried about me Jesse. I'm worried about you."

Jesse grunted under his breath, taking offense to the statement. "You don't need to worry about me Mom. I don't know if you've caught on but I've lived in New York for a while now."

"You know what I'm talking about. I'm worried about you being alone. You shouldn't be off by yourself. Dad just died Jesse. I've got Aubry and Marco and Jayden. I'll be fine. Who do you have?"

Jesse was uncomfortable with the question. He wasn't worried about being alone, in fact, he looked forward to it. But he still didn't want a spotlight shined on it by his mother. "What did you think Mom? That I was going to all of a sudden love it here and want to stay forever?"

"Of course not. You know that's not what I'm saying. Forgive a mother for worrying about her son."

"You've got nothing to worry about Mom," he responded sipping on a cold glass of lemonade she had brought him. "Believe it or not, I actually like being alone. No offense."

"Offense taken," she said, drinking from her own glass. "What about Karen Hunter? I thought you were hitting things off with her."

"Karen's a friend from high school Mom. It was good seeing her while I was here but we never really kept in touch before. I can't imagine we will now."

"She seemed like more than a friend the other day. What happened out there?" His mother was obviously referring to the awkward goodbye she had witnessed from within the house, but Jesse paid it no attention.

"Don't worry about it, Mom." A few silent moments passed between the two until Helen abruptly redirected the conversation.

"I'm sorry about you and your father Jesse." It was an unexpected declaration for which Jesse felt unprepared. "I wish you two could have been closer while he was around."

Jesse swirled the lemonade in his glass, watching the liquid and the ice cubes spin while he thought. He wanted to tell her they had been plenty close but his mother was astute. There was no fooling her about the disconnect he had always felt with his father. "That's not something you need to worry about either, Mom."

"You know he loved you, don't you?" she asked. "He did. He just couldn't express that to you the way he did with Aubry for some reason. It ate him up that the two of you didn't have that kind of a relationship."

"Yeah, he seemed pretty broken up about it." Jesse retorted sharply.

Helen's tone changed at her son's disrespectful sarcasm. She assumed that authoritative aura which afforded her so much power over her children. "I'm serious Jesse. When Elle died, when Miriam left, it just destroyed him."

He appreciated his mother's sincere efforts to posthumously reconcile the two men but Jesse was not fooled by her distortion of the facts. "If he was so distraught where was he?" Jesse asked. He knew he was wading into dangerous territory here but he didn't feel like biting his tongue any longer. "Why couldn't he reach out to me if he cared so much?"

Helen should have been angry with Jesse for sullying the memory of her husband so recently after his death but she maintained her composure.

"I suppose," she began slowly, "that the two of you were just too similar. It was easy for him to connect with Aubry but it's tougher when the person you want to reach out to is so much like yourself."

Nothing could have assaulted Jesse's pride more than the accusation that he and his father were alike in any way. He was noticeably angered as he placed his glass on the small table between their chairs.

"I know what you're trying to do Mom. You're trying to repair something that was broken a long time ago. I appreciate that. But I don't need it. We don't have to pretend that something was there that wasn't. He and I were nothing alike." At this Jesse stood, indicating that he was done with the conversation.

"You must be joking?" Helen said calmly from her seat as her son began to walk away. "You're practically the same person."

Jesse ignored his mother's words. He was angry with the insulting thought that he and the man he had spent so much time hating shared anything in common. He was tempted to walk away from her without uttering a word, but he couldn't bring himself to do it. The anger within him was still boiling but subsided briefly as he attempted to leave the porch. He paused before stepping into the kitchen and put his hand on his mother's shoulder. She gently grasped it with her perfectly manicured, yet weathered hand. "I love you, Mom."

"I know you do."

The feelings of anger and frustration lingered but much like the unwanted vision of his father, Jesse was able to push them away for brief moments. He needed to get out of the house. He couldn't bring himself to call Karen so there was really only one option left available to him. Jesse threw his fishing equipment into the bed of the pickup truck and headed for the river.

The Appalachian Slam seemed so petty to him now. Like the cares of a child. Jesse had abandoned his pursuit of the goal as soon as his father died. Whatever it represented to him died along with the man who had spent so much time chasing it. It had seemed so important to Jesse before. Now the only thing he cared about was getting back home. He hadn't been fishing since he received news of his father's passing. Too much had taken place and required his attention. Now, needing a place to run to, the river seemed like his only option.

He didn't go far. No more long, winding drives through the mountains. He simply wanted to get to the water as quickly as possible. Without the drive to catch the three trout species he had been seeking, there was no need to consult his father's journal or try some new spot. Instead, he simply set out for the park he had visited when he first began.

The same two fishermen which had been there on Jesse's first day were sitting in the same spot near the most logical entrance to the slow moving river. Next to the large, bearded man the same ugly dog sat, scratching at fleas and staring blankly at its master. Jesse wondered if these people ever left. Upon entering the shallow waters Jesse waded a dozen yards or so downstream where he began flipping his line across the water.

It had only been a few days since wetting his line last but Jesse could feel tension in his shoulders begin to disappear within moments of his first cast. A tightness in his chest immediately began to ease as he breathed in the soft aromas of the mountain air blowing across the smooth waters. The Appalachian Slam may have held no more interest for him but he had to admit, it felt good to be back on the river.

Jesse expected that his father would appear shortly in an attempt to bring the stress he had just shed back into his life. Instead, Jesse heard the distinctive two-toned wolf-whistle that often accompanied cat-calling after an attractive girl and turned to look back upriver. His sister Aubry, dressed in her own fishing gear, was wading towards him past the two men seated on the riverbank. One of the fishermen had undoubtedly shot the whistle in her direction. For a brief moment Jesse felt protective of his sister being objectified by the strange men.

"Hey Ernie, how's the fishing today?" She asked as she continued slowly moving toward Jesse. These men were obviously not strangers to Aubry and it was clear she did not feel threatened by them in any way.

"It ain't too bad," he said through quite a few missing teeth as he held up a string from which four limp trout were hanging. "Hey, when you gonna leave that husband of yours and run off with me?"

"Any day Ernie. Any day. As soon as you get a house that ain't on wheels."

The man snapped his fingers as though he had just missed the opportunity of a lifetime and Aubry shortened the distance between herself and her brother. It wasn't long before she reached him, drew out her line, and cast it effortlessly upstream. "How'd you find me?" Jesse asked once she got settled in.

"It wasn't that hard," she said shrugging her shoulders. "I could see you from the bridge. Mom said you had gone fishing so I figured I would just head towards the bait shop then I saw you out here stumbling around. I figured you could use some company."

"Why does everyone think that?" Jesse retorted. "Don't you and Mom know that it's okay to be alone sometimes?"

"I'm sorry? Do you want me to leave?" she asked defensively.

"No, you can stay."

"So," Aubry said, drawing the word out as she pulled in some of her excess line. "Mom says you're heading back to New York?"

"That's right. Are you going to try and convince me to stay?"

"No. I just wish we could have spent more time together without having to deal with everything with Dad. I would have liked to come out here more and really teach you how to fish."

Jesse smiled. She was obviously better than he was. A lifetime of living in Blue Ridge will do that to a person. In reality, he didn't mind the company. The environment continued to chip away at the anxiety he had felt building at home and he enjoyed spending time with his sister. The two of them talked as they continued downstream, each of them catching a few small rainbow trout which they released back into the river.

Aubry was in the process of telling Jesse about her son's upcoming first day of school when his phone buzzed in the inner pocket of his waders. Jesse awkwardly retrieved it while holding his fishing rod and glanced at the illuminated screen. Once again, Karen's face smiled up at him, this time as an incoming call. The world around him seemed to go quiet as he drowned out his sister's voice. For a moment Jesse contemplated taking the call. His spirits had lifted as he fished, perhaps he was being foolish in ignoring her attempts to reach out. He wanted to answer and hear her voice. But something pulled him away. With a forlorn feeling Jesse pressed the red button and silenced the phone.

"Who was that?" Aubry asked.

"Nobody," Jesse responded. "Just work."

CHAPTER 21

An eerie glow pushed back the darkness. The recesses of the basement were still obscured by the black of the night but the blue-tinted light of Jesse's laptop shone from the workbench. The computer screen cast an unearthly ambiance across the large room. Boxes, tools, furniture, and other junk basked in the faint light and long shadows which distorted, even more, the misshapen forms. Dark basements are inherently ominous and foreboding but the dim light made it more so, adding to the already menacing aura.

At the workbench, the screen of the laptop illuminated Jesse's face brightly. It was late. Well past midnight. And Jesse was tired. Dark circles, which had appeared under his eyes over the course of the last few hours, were accentuated by the glow of the laptop in the darkness. Jesse would rather sit at the table upstairs or in one of the other unused rooms of the old house. But the last few hours had grown increasingly stressful and in an attempt to avoid the prying eyes of his mother he had retreated, once again, to the damp smelling basement. There he sat, moving back and forth from his computer to his phone as he responded to a barrage of emails and phone calls.

In reality, Jesse would rather not be staring at the documents and tables illuminating his screen at all. He would prefer to be in bed, sound asleep, burning away a few more hours until he could finally return to New York. But crisis had forced him to delve into the intricacies and stresses of his career prematurely.

Not long after returning home with Aubry, Jesse received a phone call from Gabe back at the office. The deal which Jesse had left in his care, the one he had devoted countless hours and long nights at the office to, was collapsing. The only reason he had agreed to leave the deal in Gabe's hands was because it was essentially finished when he left. There was really no more work that needed to be done. When Gabe had indicated that there were issues with the deal, Jesse had taken his colleague at his word that everything was fine. But it appeared that wasn't the case.

As Gabe had revealed earlier, Carvalho S.A., Jesse's client, and the smaller of two merging metal supply companies, had failed to disclose a few contracts with governmental entities. The contracts were immaterial. They had been entered into and then abandoned without any recorded reason. However, even though they were expired by now, they raised the question of whether Carvalho was exposed to any liability through them. The other party was convinced that the agreements had been deliberately withheld during due diligence. Further inquiry showed that those suspicions were not without their merits. The other party wanted an entirely new due diligence period initiated with extra care to ensure that there was nothing else hidden from them. The proposed solution would almost certainly kill the deal.

For the remainder of the evening, Jesse was glued to his phone, speaking with individuals involved from all over the world. Rio de Janeiro, New York City, Birmingham, England and Birmingham, Alabama as well as half a dozen other offices. Gabe had done the best he could but it was Jesse that had built these relationships in the first place. He had developed the trust necessary to make a transaction with so many moving parts a reality. Without him, the parts stopped moving when faced with a problem. Only Jesse could get them working properly again.

Ted was still not aware that Jesse had been looped into the communication. His boss was, perhaps, the only attorney in New York who would have continued to push for Jesse to be left undisturbed in the face of such a meltdown. Jesse appreciated the gesture but was more interested in making sure the deal he had crafted and cared for came to fruition. Additionally, while Jesse was frustrated, he wanted to make sure that his friend did not unnecessarily bear the burden of the downturn. Their boss had let Gabe know in no uncertain terms that while Jesse would not be held accountable for the deal's failure, Gabe's career was on the line.

Jesse was exhausted. Staring at the bright computer contrasting sharply against the dark room around him only added to the feeling of fatigue which was steadily sweeping over him. Finally, after answering and sending more emails than he could count and spending too many hours on the phone trying to convince corporate officers there was a way forward, Jesse felt like he had done all he could do. At this point, the people involved had to make personal decisions about whether they trusted him enough to proceed.

Jesse's eyes began to blur as he poured over the multiple open tabs on his laptop's screen. Gabe had insisted he could handle the final document review but Jesse figured if he was in it this far now, why not see it all the way to the end? So he trudged on, reading every line of the heavily modified documents. Little by little, he tweaked them so they resembled more the contractual masterpiece he had crafted before coming to Georgia.

He was surprised at how disdainful he felt towards the situation. He normally didn't dislike his work. It was the one constant in his life and he felt he had a closer relationship with the practice of corporate law than he had with any person. No one loved working through the night but he had done it plenty of times in the past and felt only an underlying sensation of satisfaction. But tonight was different. Something about it felt meaningless. Next to the adrenaline rush of landing a monster trout after an exciting struggle, the thrill of closing a large corporate deal suddenly felt counterfeit and hollow.

Jesse rubbed his eyes harshly and gave out an overly dramatic sigh. There was no one else in the basement to hear him and his mother was asleep two floors above him. He had taken the opportunity all night to be louder than normal with angry exclamations peppered with language he would never use if his mother could hear. Jesse was generally a very patient man, almost never showing a temper in front of his co-workers. But in private he couldn't resist expressing his frustrations to the darkness. Tonight had been no exception and a few hand tools found themselves on the far side of the room where they had been violently projected against the concrete wall.

Jesse pushed the computer away a few inches, causing all of the shadows in the room to shift. His eyes were drawn to the gap between the workbench and the corner wall and he couldn't force himself to look away. It had been out of the field of light cast by the laptop's screen but now that the illumination had changed, the deep blackness of the void gaped back at Jesse.

He felt pulled towards it as though he might fall in himself if he didn't take decisive action. After a moment of staring at the shadows he reached his hand in and pulled out the wrapped gift he had abandoned earlier. Jesse had been so angry when he had seen the package before. Until now his resentment had outweighed his curiosity and he had hardly given the present a second thought. But as he turned it over in his hands he figured that he was already frustrated now, so decided to indulge his curiosity.

His hands tore through the brittle, yellowing wrapping paper and peeled it from the long, rectangular, cardboard box. He tossed the used paper aside and it rolled into the dark, unseen recesses of the basement. Slowly, Jesse removed the top of the box and peered inside. Staring back at him rested the smallest fishing rod and reel Jesse had ever seen. It was broken down into two lengths of pole but even so, the entire rod was probably only a third the length of a normal fishing pole. The reel was bright pink and silver. Additionally, there were four small, hand-tied flies, each made with artificial pink feathers, stuck into a piece of foam next to the fishing rod. Nestled in between the reel and the old tissue paper filling the box, Jesse saw a small card written his father's handwriting. With one swift motion Jesse unsealed the card and read the note.

Elle,

Your Grandma and I are so excited to meet you. We can't wait to show you how much we love you. I love fishing, and I think I will love it even more when I get to do it with you. This rod and reel should be enough to get you started when you're old enough. I made these flies especially for you. I can't wait to take you out on the water and watch you grow up to become an amazing woman.

Love,

Grandpa

The handwritten note was sweet, heartwarming, and heartbreaking. It was also infuriating. Jesse didn't know why. Perhaps it was the hours of stressful negotiations, the exhaustion, or something else. But the more he stared at his father's handwriting, the more upset he became. If anything, the note should have been endearing and for most, it would humanize a distant father. But for Jesse it had the opposite effect. His anger was unrealistic, it was misplaced, it made no sense. But for once in his life, Jesse was tired of pushing it away. He let it wash over him and his shaking hand began to crumple the note as he felt white-hot fury rise in his chest.

Slowly, as he allowed his temper to smolder like a dying fire springing back to life, he became aware of the familiar feeling that he was not alone. Jesse turned away from the glowing computer screen to face what he knew was waiting behind him. Jim Cavanaugh's image stood in the darkness, looking at his son with a sorrowful expression in his eyes. The dull, manufactured glow of the laptop barely illuminated the man, whose features were sharply contrasted with the shadows around him. The old man looked more like a ghost to Jesse than ever before.

Already Jesse could feel warm tears creeping into the corners of his eyes as he gritted his teeth at the man standing before him. "How dare you?"

"What?"

The response wasn't an innocent query. There was no honest question in his father's voice. Jesse understood exactly what it meant from his tone. It was an invitation to finally say what he had been feeling for so many years.

"What?" Jim's voice echoed again across the basement. Firmer this time. "Why on earth would a gift from a grandfather to his granddaughter make you so angry?"

"How dare you keep this down here all this time?" Jesse's lips were tight as he forced the words out of this mouth. "You had to know that one day I would find it, or that someone would find it. Why would you keep this?"

"I couldn't force myself to get rid of it. I couldn't force myself to forget about her."

Jesse clenched his jaw again and diverted his eyes. "No, I'm not doing this. I'm not having an argument with an empty room."

"Oh come on Jesse, you never had the spine to say it to my face when I was alive. Here I am." The old man extended his arms to the side as though inviting his son to take a swing at him. "You get something not many people do. You get a second bite at the apple. Take it."

Jesse was on his feet although he barely moved closer to the ghostlike man standing in front of him.

"I hate you." The words were calm and deliberately delivered. Jesse had never said it to his father, or even about him. He had wanted to but he never could. This was the first time. And it felt indescribably good.

"No you don't, you hate yourself."

Jesse glared into the dark, sunken eyes staring back at him.

"Your mother was right you know? You and I are the same. You may hate me, but if you do it's only because you hate yourself."

"I am nothing like you," Jesse retorted sharply.

"Oh is that right?" his father asked, "Please then, enlighten me on why you despise me so much."

Jesse held up the handwritten note still crumpled in his sweaty fist. "Look at this. You are so willing to show compassion to everyone in your life except for the one person who needs it. Me!"

"Is that so?"

"Yes!" Jesse didn't mean to yell as loud as he did but it came out involuntarily. "Mom acts like you're some perfect father. Aubry adores you. Those people who came out to that church for your funeral, they were crying like they lost some damned saint! And this note. You had never even met your granddaughter but you're writing notes telling her how much you loved her."

"Is that what this is about? You don't think I told you I loved you enough or gave you enough hugs?"

Jesse could sense the sarcasm in his father's voice and did not appreciate it. "No. It's because when I needed my dad he wasn't there. You weren't there. When Elle died, when Miriam left, I had everyone supporting me except for the one person I needed. You were nowhere to be found."

"And there you have it," Jim said sternly. "It seems you're more like me than you could ever imagine."

"You don't know what you're talking about." But Jesse could sense the truth in his father's assertion and a lone tear escaped his eyelid and rolled down his cheek.

"When Elle died were you there for your wife?" The words stung Jesse and he almost felt a physical pain as they were delivered.

"Stop it."

"No, let's do this Jesse. Let's really take a look at who we are. When Elle died what did you do to comfort Miriam? Did you reach out to her? Try to help her? No, you retreated into your own suffering." Jim aggressively pointed his finger at his son, accentuating each point. "You were there but she grieved without you. How many times did you listen to her cry herself to sleep alone? But what did you do? You just watched it happen from afar. Sound familiar?"

"That's different and you know -"

"Oh, is it? How about when she finally left you? You don't think your mother was in pain? Or the rest of your family? But where were you? You buried yourself in that job. The next time you came up for air you were a different person, and not for the better. You wouldn't even be here now if your boss hadn't forced you to come visit your grieving mother. We couldn't have helped you back then if we wanted to. And believe me, we wanted to."

"You've made your point -"

"No, I don't think I have. You see, nothing has changed. Nothing. What about Karen? After all you've been through you finally find someone who makes you happy and what do you do? You push her away. Jesse, there is a woman who cares about you right here. Just across town! Who wants to be with you! And all you can do is sit in a basement alone."

Jesse had never been so furious. He wanted to turn and walk away but he couldn't bring himself to do it. Besides, he didn't think it would do any good. So he just stood there, staring at his father through tearful eyes.

"Nothing's changing Jesse. So you hate me. So what? I'm dead, do you think I care? Do you think you've won some victory over me by hating me? The only reward you get from hate is more hate. Every day you become more and more like me. With every relationship you let crumble and die you become more like the man you despise so much."

"I can't forgive you for abandoning me when I needed you."

"You'll be surprised by what you can do kid," Jim said, with a hint of pleading in his voice. "But I'm not asking you to forgive me. For now, I'm just asking for you to let go. Elle is dead, Miriam is gone. I'm dead. You don't have to forget them, or forgive me. I'm just asking that you let go of your hate, let go of your pain and move on. Let yourself be happy. Stop being so much like your old man."

"This is a lie," Jesse said motioning to the man standing in front of him as another tear rolled down his cheek. "My father would never bear his soul to me. He would never talk to me about Elle, or Miriam, or Karen. This thing you're trying to make me remember him as, this isn't him."

"So what?" Jim asked. "So what if this isn't your father? What good is it for you to spend the rest of your life dwelling on how bad a father I was if it's just going to cause you to turn away from the people who love you? Is that really better than giving me some redeeming quality, even if it isn't real?"

Silence again invaded the space in between the two men as Jesse pondered his father's words. After a few strained moments Jim continued but with a softer tone to his voice.

"I kept that gift Jesse because I couldn't bring myself to do what I really needed to do. You and I had drifted apart for years before Elle was born. We never clicked the way fathers and sons are supposed to. I was so excited when you and Miriam were going to have a baby because I thought it was my last chance to have something with my son. She was supposed to bring us together. To make things easier. I envisioned us all three fishing together. Being together like you and I were never able to. When she died, that dream died with her. I should have reached out to you and been the dad you deserved. I'm sorry that I wasn't. Instead, I retreated down here. And now you're doing the same thing."

The light shining behind Jesse dimmed as the laptop began to power down from inactivity. Jesse stared into his father's eyes. They weren't mournful anymore. It was as though a heavy burden had been lifted from the old man. There was still a sadness behind them but they appeared content. Jesse, who hadn't moved from the time he stood up, took a step towards the man, and then another. The computer's screen finally went black, plunging the basement into darkness once again.

CHAPTER 22

The smell of bacon is permeating. It is thick, rich, and envelopes any space within the vicinity where the food is cooked. It is such a pervasive smell it tends to linger in a house for hours. The smell of bacon can arouse the heaviest of sleepers and enticed them to the breakfast table. And so Jesse found himself being lured awake by the dense smell of bacon sizzling in a pan upstairs. The kitchen was not close to Jesse's basement room but still, somehow the smell wafted under doorways and through vents to reach him. Slowly it pulled him upright as though it were raising him from the dead.

Jesse had been lying sprawled, fast asleep, across the sagging twin bed. He was surprised at how deeply he slept. After the imagined confrontation last night with his father, Jesse figured the vision's cutting words would keep him awake. Instead, he couldn't even remember retiring to his bed. Sleep had served him well, although he ached at his joints.

Helen had not called down the stairs for her son to join her which meant she had not finished preparing breakfast. But the smell of bacon drifting into the basement was enough for Jesse. With a slight groan and a few extra pops from his back, Jesse pulled himself to his feet and shuffled into the bathroom. He brought himself to the sink and splashed two handfuls of cool water on his face, hoping that the shock would help him fully wake up. It didn't, but it did feel good.

As he turned back to the bedroom, Jesse caught a glimpse of his reflection in the mirror. He stopped momentarily and stared intently at the man looking back at him. The person standing before him looked old. Bags under his eyes and flecks of grey in his hair. He was reminded again that he was, in fact, much older than he felt. Or at least, in that moment, his age, and its harsh reality, became uncomfortably clear to him. His father's accusations from the night before screamed across his consciousness as he saw the old man's face briefly reflect in his own features.

You and I are the same. You may hate me, but if you do, it's only because you hate yourself.

The words stung again. Not nearly as bad as the night before when they echoed across the dark void of the basement and in his own mind. But they still stung nonetheless.

Breakfast passed without incident. Although it was noticeably more subdued than most mornings. Helen, who was normally so animated and verbose, was quieter than usual. Jesse had expected this. His own relationship with his father was complicated but Helen's was not. She had loved the man unapologetically for decades. While her large personality had dominated the household, there had never been any sign of tension between his parents. His father's death was an enormous loss for her and it showed on her expression as she moved throughout her morning routine. It wasn't grief or despair necessarily. It was just loss. It stayed with her as an ever-present, and unwelcome companion. It influenced her actions, mannerisms, and words until the feeling of loss permeated the entire house like the smell of bacon in the morning.

Jesse had planned on spending the day preparing for his return to New York. He hoped to leave his mother with as few chores and worries as possible. However, he found it difficult to find projects to undertake. Following the customs of the South, neighbors and fellow churchgoers had mowed the lawn, pulled weeds, cleaned the garage, and filled the refrigerator and freezer with enough food to last a month. Jesse had hoped to find a task which would prevent him from checking his phone every few minutes. But that seemed nearly impossible as he continually glanced at the small screen out of instinct. He was no longer nervous about whether the deal would fall through or not. He had moved past that. All he wanted now was to know, what happened. Regardless of the outcome.

Every passing hour was a painful exercise in self-control as Jesse undertook minor chores around the house. He cleaned up the workbench which was strewn with fly-tying materials. Wires, strings, and threads were wound up and stored in cubbyholes which were now cleaned, organized, and labeled. Feathers, foam, hooks, and beads were tucked away as finished flies were placed in the clamshell case Jesse had carried with him across the mountains and rivers. Even the waders which he had purchased for himself were hung on a nail next to his father's old, and now unused pair.

Jesse contemplated going fishing. It just seemed natural now that he had trained himself to make it part of his daily routine for almost a month. But as soon as the thought entered his head it was driven away by a glance at his phone, looking for news of the merger. His father's foolish pursuit of the Appalachian Slam was the farthest thing from his mind. He had allowed it to almost become an obsession of his, just like his father had. But now it seemed so juvenile.

He had to get out of the house. With nothing to occupy him while he dwelled on his work, the building felt more like a prison than a home. There was nowhere he needed to go. No one he needed to see. His family members were all occupied as they tried to return to some semblance of normalcy, and there was no one else who wanted to see him now. So he pointed his father's truck towards town without a destination or a purpose.

He drove aimlessly through the city. His path took him past old businesses from his youth and new ones which had moved into the spaces of those which hadn't survived. He passed houses of friends from high school and even thought he recognized a few faces in the pedestrians ambling around downtown. He expected to be hit with a wave of nostalgia but it didn't come. Jesse wasn't particularly excited about returning to New York but nothing about what he saw made him want to stay in Blue Ridge. Apparently he just wasn't wired like that.

You and I are the same.

His father's voice snuck into his mind at unexpected intervals while he drove. He made an effort to ignore the voice and keep driving. After almost an hour it became clear that his trip down memory lane was serving no purpose. He pulled the truck into the parking lot of an Ingles grocery store because there was nowhere else to go. His mother's church members had provided her with an abundance of casseroles and frozen meals but the least he could do was restock her essentials before he left. He didn't know if she needed milk, eggs, and bread but it wouldn't hurt her to have extra. And it gave him an excuse to stay away from the house for a few more minutes.

As Jesse prepared to enter the grocery store he noticed something he hadn't during his tour of the city. His father's journal sat on the seat next to him. Jesse must have left it there after his last fishing excursion. He pulled the book out from under an assortment of fishing magazines and began to flip haphazardly through the pages.

Montana. Appalachian Slam. Rainbow trout. Creek. River. Brown trout. Mountains. Brook trout. These words were repeated over and over again. They jumped out of the pages as Jesse turned them. He couldn't believe he had wasted so much time reading the journal and trying to follow any clues it might have. There was nothing there. Jesse glanced again at his father's last entry, most likely written just minutes before his stroke. It was still unreadable. Jesse didn't know why he even tried again to decipher it.

Without warning his phone began to buzz loudly. Jesse dropped the journal onto the seat next to him and hastily retrieved the vibrating phone. Instantly, upon seeing the name of the caller Jesse answered in excitement. "Gabe! Tell me you've got good news."

"Do they have champagne down there or just moonshine? Because this deal is done buddy."

Jesse felt his heart rate rise and then fall back to normal. "You sure?" he asked.

"What do you mean, am I sure? I know you think I'm incompetent but I know when a deal is closed."

"I know, I'm sorry. I just want to make sure it's taken care of."

"It's all done. Everything's been taken care of."

"That's great news," Jesse said casually.

"C'mon man!" Gabe exclaimed. "Get excited! This is a big deal. Everyone here who worked on it wants to celebrate. I convinced them to wait until you got back though so don't make any plans for that first evening."

" I won't. And I know it's a big deal. Thanks, Gabe for filling in while I've been gone."

"Well don't ask me to do that on the next one. By the way, the people at Carvalho said they've got some other things they want you to handle for them when you get back. I told them to shoot you an email and you'd get back to them in a few days."

"Thanks, man."

"No problem. I just wanted to call and let you know it was done. Congratulations. I'll see you when you get back."

"I'll see you at work."

Jesse hung up the phone and stared down at it until the screen turned black. He felt like he should shout with joy or punch the steering wheel. But he didn't want to. He should be overcome with a sense of relief and satisfaction. He had been stressing about this for so long and now it was done. But the feeling didn't come. He thought about all he had done to make this happen. He had done good work. He was proud of the work he had done. But the victory seemed hollow and fleeting. Now he would move on to the next deal. And the next. And the next.

You and I are the same.

Jesse ignored the bite of the words and sat in silence for a moment, continuing to try and enjoy the moment. But he didn't. After a few minutes, he began to scroll through the contacts list in his phone. For the first time in a while, he wanted to talk to someone. He wanted to reach out. The impression to do so hit him strongly and suddenly. His first reaction was to fight it but for some reason he chose not to. He scrolled to Karen's name and paused briefly before moving on. Eventually, the screen came to rest and his thumb hovered over another name.

Miriam.

Her name glowed up at him. He couldn't look away, like a moth being attracted to a light bulb. *Did she even have the same phone number?* He didn't know why he had never deleted her contact information after the divorce. It had never even occurred to him until now.

It was as though an unseen force was compelling his actions. He had to prove to himself he wasn't like his father. Or at least he had to show that he wasn't going to be like him anymore. He pressed the call button and the phone began ringing as he pressed it to his ear. *What are you doing? Stop! Hang up!* His heart beat faster and faster with every ring. Beads of sweat began to form on his brow. He hoped she wouldn't pick up. He prayed she wouldn't.

"Jesse?"

At the sound of her voice it all came rushing back to him. Every emotion. Every twinge of pain. Every regret. It all hit him as though he was remembering it for the first time and the edges of his eyes began to water in response.

"Jesse? Is that you?" He realized he hadn't yet answered her and tried to regain his composure.

"Yeah. Yeah, it's me. Hi Miriam."

"Oh my... I... I... how's it going? How are you?"

"I'm good," he lied. "I'm doing okay. I'm actually in Georgia right now."

"Oh. How's your family? You'll need to tell them hello from me."

"Yeah, Mom's doing okay. She's good. Dad actually... well, Dad passed away which is why I'm down here."

"Oh my God, Jesse, I'm so sorry."

There was genuine concern in her voice. That was something he had always admired about his ex-wife. She had a compassion he lacked. When she expressed concern for somebody it wasn't out of a sense of duty. It was real. Jesse responded, physically shaking his head even though she couldn't see him. "No, it's okay. Don't worry about it. We're fine. I'm fine."

Jesse still didn't fully understand what compelled him to call the woman he had driven out of his life so long ago. He would have never guessed that morning that he would be talking to her while sitting in a grocery store parking lot. But he was determined to prove that the voice echoing in his head was wrong.

"Listen, Miriam, I know this is awkward and I'm sorry for calling but I feel like I needed to talk to you."

"Of course Jesse, what do you need?"

"I just... I just wanted to let you know that I'm sorry."

"What?" She seemed truly caught off guard. One would have thought that being contacted by her ex-husband for the first time in years would have been surprising enough. But she sounded more surprised from this statement than from the call itself.

"I'm sorry Miriam." More tears began to form around his eyes. "I'm sorry for everything. I... I should have been there for you. I wasn't, and I should have been. I know I can't do anything about it now. But I just wanted to tell you I'm sorry." He wanted to say more, to elaborate, to explain. But he couldn't. It was difficult enough to say what he just had. He didn't have it in him to continue.

There was a pause from the other end of the line. It was longer than he expected and with every passing second he worried that she might hang up. He listened for the click which would signal the end of their conversation. He wondered what was going through her mind as she attempted to make sense of his unexpected apology.

"Thank you."

There was a shakiness to her voice as she whispered the words into the phone. The two didn't speak for a few moments as they both processed what had just happened. A simple apology followed by a simple expression of gratitude. It probably wasn't what either had expected but there was a feeling of catharsis to her words. Jesse's heart was still pounding in his chest but there was no more dread.

From Miriam's end of the line another voice, the voice of a little girl called out from the background. "Mom! Look at this!"

"Liv, wait just a second. Mommy's on the phone."

Jesse smiled. The unexpected voice made him happy. He would have thought that the emotions it brought would be complicated. But they weren't. Hearing that Miriam had a child was a relief to his soul. For a moment he considered that maybe he hadn't ruined her life. He wondered if she had been able to have the family, and the support she had never been able to have with him. He hoped she had. But he couldn't ask her for more details. He didn't have the right to pry into her personal life. He could only hope that the voice meant she was happy.

"I'll let you go, Miriam," he said with a smile on his face.

"Jesse, are you okay? I know it's tough when you lose someone. Do you need to talk more?" She was concerned. Why wouldn't she be? His father had just died and here he was reaching out to her out of nowhere. He understood why she would be worried about him.

"No, Miriam, I'm fine. I really am. I just needed to call and tell you that."

"Well, you don't know how much that means to me." In the background, he could hear Miriam's daughter still vying for her attention.

"Goodbye, Miriam."

"Take care of yourself, Jesse."

It was over. The call lasted only a few minutes but adrenaline continued to course through Jesse's veins. He listened for his father's voice. He waited for the assertion that the two men were alike. Waiting to feel that stab of self-realization pull him back to reality. But it never came. The cab of the truck, and Jesse's mind, were quiet.

He had felt alone for so long that he had become used to it. But this was different. This wasn't loneliness or loss. It was comfort. Quiet solitary comfort. Jesse didn't want to examine his feelings towards his father. He knew they were the same and were still there, lurking under the surface. But for now, they were quiet and still.

CHAPTER 23

Catch and release. The standard among true fishermen. If permitted, it isn't uncommon to keep a particularly beautiful trout now and then. And there are plenty of anglers who put their catches to good use in a frying pan. But most adopt the practice of releasing the fish they catch back into the stream. Some do so by choice, but many creeks and rivers are designated as mandatory catch and release areas.

Noontootla Creek is one of them.

Jesse crouched in the water of the creek and gently removed a hook from the mouth of a rainbow trout. He gripped the fish tightly until the hook was completely out and then stretched the prize in front of him to admire his catch. It was a trophy fish. Easily one of the most beautiful specimens he had seen during his time there. Bright hues of pink, green, and silver shimmered as the fish lurched slightly in his hands. Jesse estimated the fish to be at least fourteen inches long, maybe longer. A treasure to be sure.

But Jesse knew he couldn't keep the fish. And besides, he was returning to New York the next morning. What use was a dead fish to him now? Jesse lowered the trout into the water at his feet and moved it back and forth until it beat its tail and surged off into the safety of the stream. It was his second catch of the day, both rainbow trout. But this one had been special. It was large, beautiful, and strong. The kind of fish that motivates a fisherman to keep returning to the river.

Nobody else was fishing this stretch of the creek. Jesse had almost turned the truck around when he pulled up to the water at one of its public access points. He figured the lack of others fishing the creek was a bad sign. Now he just wondered if no one was there because most were more interested in catching something they could put on their plate. He hadn't been disappointed so far. The creek itself was small, but it had already proven a good source of rainbows at least.

The thick canopy of hemlocks and mountain laurel hung low over the clear water, and dense undergrowth crowded the space from either side, making it difficult to cast a decent line. Jesse had already lost a few flies to the heavy foliage in the last hour and a half. The creek was best suited for skilled fisherman well beyond Jesse's experience, but he was enjoying his time nonetheless.

The stream was fairly shallow but with enough deep pools to sustain a sizeable trout population. Noontootla Creek originates near the southern county line. It twists and turns northwesterly until it finally dumps into the Toccoa River above the reservoir. It only runs a dozen or so miles. But within that relatively short distance, monster trout of each species are caught and released into the year-round cold water.

Jesse had sworn off fly fishing. But like most who swear off the hobby, here he was again, standing in the middle of a mountain stream with a rod in his hand. Although it was different now. He was no longer driven by obsession. A week before he would have been doing all he could to catch the Appalachian Slam, just like his dad had. It would have consumed his thoughts while vying for attention alongside his father's condescending voice. Now his father was dead, and the Appalachian Slam didn't seem to matter anymore. He was there for just one reason. To say goodbye.

"That was a gorgeous fish." his father said.

Jesse sighed and pushed himself to his feet with a slight pop in his knees. "I figured you'd come."

The vision of the old man stood before him in the water just as it had so many times in the preceding weeks. Even though the man wasn't really there was a palpable tension in the air. Jesse had visions of the explosive argument which had taken place between himself and the apparition.

You and I are the same. You may hate me, but if you do it's only because you hate yourself.

The words cut into Jesse again as he gazed on the specter of his dad. He had dwelled on them little since speaking with Miriam yesterday. But the words were still there, hiding under the surface, waiting to strike.

"I got the impression you were done with this whole fishing thing," Jim said, gesturing at their surroundings. "I'm surprised to see you out here."

"Well, that makes two of us," Jesse responded as he ensured the wooly bugger, with its barbless hook, was still secure on the end of his line.

"So what are we doing here, Jesse?"

Jesse nodded up the creek as he began moving against the water. "You want to fish?" he asked, stepping past his father, who stood quietly for a moment before joining his son.

The two marched upstream in silence for a hundred yards or so, climbing over rocks and ducking beneath low hanging branches. In a short time, they arrived at a section of the stream just above a small cascade where a deep pool of water stretched along one side of the creek. With a few flips of his rod, Jesse let the wooly bugger fly and landed it expertly on the other side of the pool, between two large rocks.

Jim let out a long whistle. "Not bad at all, son. You know I think you might be better than me now."

"I know," Jesse responded confidently as he jerked the fly across the water.

Jesse allowed the fly to float aimlessly across the surface of the creek for a few minutes before he pulled it in and cast it back over the water.

"You want to tell me what we're really doing here?" the older man asked.

Jesse sighed and pulled the brim of his baseball hat low over his face. "I figured we shouldn't end things the way we did the other night."

"End things?"

"Yeah, Dad. After today I'm done." Jesse whipped his line over his head and landed it even further up the pool than before. "This whole creepy ghost thing you and I have going on is over."

"Hmm... is that something you get to decide?" his father asked. "It's not like you willed me to be here. I'm pretty sure I pop up unintentionally."

"I know," Jesse responded tersely. " I don't know what it'll take, therapy, or just strong willpower. I don't know. But you and I won't be talking anymore. So if you've got anything to say, now's the time to say it."

"Jesse, I think I said all I needed to the other night."

"Yeah," Jesse answered. "Me too."

There was a long pause between the two men. Jesse kept one eye on his line, which was gently floating downstream, and another on the image of his father standing next to him. Jesse hadn't realized how loud the forest was until there were no words being exchanged between them. A chorus of birds singing in the trees above his head pierced the silence with boisterous melodies. The distractions made it difficult to think about the odd exchange taking place within Jesse's mind. But Jesse didn't want to think about it and was happy to let the sounds of the forest take over.

"You know Jesse, I'm proud of you for calling Miriam yesterday."

"No, you're not." He spat out quickly. "You're not real. My father might have been proud. He might not have. There's no way to know. He's dead."

"You're right," said the old man, keeping his eyes pointed upstream at his son's fishing line. "Then I guess you're proud of yourself for doing it. Oh well... that's probably all that matters."

The silence invaded again as Jesse pondered the statement. Together they watched as the fly lazily drifted beneath an overhanging tangle of branches and twigs. Almost imperceptibly the floating string hesitated in its drift where it plunged below the surface of the water. The slight change in direction was all Jesse needed. He pulled back sharply on his rod and began reeling in excess line. He could feel the vibration through the line as the hook set and his rod bent against the movements of the fish on the other end.

"You got him!" Jim yelled in support. "Let him run but keep the line tight!"

"I know!" Jesse yelled back in frustration. He moved closer to the pool and secured his footing against a large stone under the surface of the moving water. The fish was moving in long, arching zig-zags across the creek. Jesse maneuvered his rod back and forth to keep the line between them tight. All the while he slowly reeled the line in inch by inch.

The dark outline of the fish darted just a few yards in front of his feet. Its tail splashed out of the water as it rapidly changed direction. It was another large one, maybe the same size as the last. His heart began to race as he pulled it closer and closer. Its movements became less erratic as it slowly lost energy. Finally, in one smooth motion, he scooped the fish out of the water with the net which had been hanging at his side.

The trout was perhaps twelve and a half inches in length. Jesse was expecting a brightly colored rainbow trout to be thrashing against the net. However, as he inspected his catch he was surprised to pull out a brown trout, with its unmistakable mix of brown skin and dark, ringed spots. The fish was weakened but still had enough strength to jerk against Jesse's grasp as he lifted it up to the sunlight breaking through the canopy overhead.

"Look at that," his father's voice exclaimed in a hushed tone. "You know what that means don't ya?"

Jesse looked over the exquisite trout one more time before lowering it into the current and setting it free. He pulled himself to his feet and began preparing his line for another cast. "It doesn't mean anything Dad."

"Whatever you say son," the old man said with a smirk. "Two down, one to go."

"Can we just fish?" Jesse asked firmly. "That's what we're here for isn't it? I don't need you trying to imprint your obsessions on me more than you already have."

"Lead the way," said Jim, deferring to his son as he motioned upstream.

And so Jesse did. He led his father against the flow of the stream. The two trekked onward for hours, battling slippery rocks, overgrowing thorns, and long, discouraging periods without any strikes. At one point Jesse considered turning back, knowing that he would have to hike back to the truck anyways at some point. However, he was reminded by his father that "the brookies live upstream." So they continued on as the afternoon shadows began to lengthen.

Along the way Jesse kept his line in the water as much as possible, flipping it across the stream and catching it in the trees here and there throughout the process. Hoppers, stoneflies, caddis, and worms. Jesse was burning through the arsenal of flies he had amassed over his time home. Two additional rainbows found their way into Jesse's net as he continued upstream. At the edge of a large pool, Jesse observed what was clearly another brown take his fly in its mouth for what felt like an entire minute until it coughed it up.

As the younger Cavanaugh fished, the two men talked. Jesse rigorously avoided the sensitive subject of their relationship as much as he could. For the most part their conversation consisted of fishing, with a little baseball thrown in for good measure. It was awkward, forced, and broken up by long stretches of dense, almost palpable silence. Jesse wondered if these manufactured conversations were at all similar to how average fathers and sons communicated with one another on fishing trips. He determined that they had to at least be comparable although not completely so considering his father was dead.

The sun wasn't setting yet, that didn't happen until very late this time of year. But it had descended far enough to inform the two men that the clock was ticking on the day's excursion. Jesse had a flight to board in the morning. He couldn't spend all day on the river as he had during the past few weeks. He planted himself on a large boulder, took a long drink from his water bottle and opened his fly case. He had just lost a fly on a stubborn, submerged log and needed a replacement. He scanned his depleted collection and his eyes came to rest on his father's four, hand-tied, pink flies. That morning, in preparing for the day, Jesse had removed them from the gift to Elle and placed them in the case, resisting the strong urge to throw them in the garbage. He pulled one from the foam, examined it in the sunlight, and began to tie it to the end of his line.

"Now you're bringing out the big guns," his father said, rubbing his palms together in anticipation. "You may be able to cast better than me but nobody ties a better fly than your old man."

If Jesse were a teenager he would have rolled his eyes. The creek was very narrow at this point, with the trees intruding heavily from each side. Jesse wasn't sure how far they had traveled but he could tell they were much closer to the headwaters of the creek. He waded out into the middle, which was deeper than he had anticipated. The cool water rushed over and around his knees, causing him to shiver momentarily in response. His cast just barely missed a sweetgum branch and the pink fly landed on top of the water.

"Do trout even strike at pink?" Jesse asked.

"There's only way to find out."

The two were quiet as they watched the bright lure float downstream before Jesse pulled it back in and cast it again.

"You know," Jesse said cautiously. "This doesn't change anything. I'm not forgiving you. This is just fishing."

"I know," Jim responded, keeping his hands in his pockets. "It certainly doesn't change anything for me. I'm dead. There's nothing you can do about that. There's nothing that's going to change anything for me. But maybe this'll change something for you."

"Like what?"

"I don't know. Maybe it'll change how you think, or how you choose to remember things. I'm not saying you need to lie to yourself and pretend that we were closer than we were. But maybe you won't let my mistakes define how you live. Maybe you can start to let go and focus on things that matter. Like people... and fishing."

"Oh, fishing is something that matters now?"

His father didn't respond to the question. "You know Jesse, I know you're not going to forgive me. I don't expect you to. But fishing feels a lot like forgiveness to me. Being here with you, that's good enough for me."

Jesse bit his bottom lip, expecting anger to boil up to the surface. But it didn't come. He could feel it lurking within his soul but that's where it stayed for the time being. He almost wanted to allow his frustration and his hate to flow freely. He wanted to reiterate all of the things his father had done wrong. But he didn't want it enough. Surprisingly, he was content fishing.

The fly disappeared below the surface of the water where it had been idly drifting. Jesse snapped into action and set the hook. His rod bent, his reel creaked, and the struggle began. The fish was active and strong. It darted and pitched, moving back and forth across the creek. Jesse allowed it room to run but pulled it in sharply when he felt it move in his direction. Unexpectedly, the fish darted to the left and breached the surface of the water, jumping through the air.

Jesse's heart stopped.

Framed in the patchy daylight for one, short moment he recognized the vivid orange belly and pink spots of a brook trout.

"Did you see that!" Jim yelled in excitement. "You've got yourself a brookie! Don't lose him now!"

Jesse steered his rod from side to side with the brook trout's movements. He caught another glimpse of the fish as it turned on its side, flashing its bright underside to the surface for a brief instant. The fish was small, as most brook trout are in the area, but it was a fighter. Every dart and pull threatened to escape the barbless hook of the pink fly. Jesse had to remind himself to breathe as he continued to fight the fish.

"You've got this, Jesse!"

After what seemed like an eternity, Jesse had the fish splashing at his knees and he lunged after it in his net. In one quick moment it was over and Jesse pulled the fish out of the water in the dripping net. With shaking hands he removed the pink fly from the fish's mouth and clumsily threw his rod, along with the net, onto the nearest bank. The smaller than average fish was, for all intents and purposes, unremarkable. But as Jesse held it up between himself and the vision of his father, tears began to well up in his eyes.

"You did it, Jesse," his father said respectfully. "You did it. I never could but you did."

Tears flowed freely down Jesse's face, dripping from his chin into the clear water. He sobbed loudly as he gazed upon the fish he was cradling in his hands. He didn't know why he was so emotional. He couldn't explain it if he were asked to. It was just a stupid fish. But to him, it felt like more. It was more than the Appalachian Slam. There was a finality to it that he couldn't describe.

One by one he felt every demon which had plagued him storm out of the recesses of his mind, envelope him momentarily, and then wash away with the flow of the water. Anger, fear, hate, regret, pain, sadness, loss. Little by little they lingered, then melted away.

Through his blurred vision he took notice that the fish was struggling less and less. Its mouth gaped open and shut regularly but then slowed as Jesse continued to weep. Jesse felt his father place his hand tenderly on his shoulder. He actually felt his hand. He was shocked to feel the warmth of a physical touch.

"Jesse, it's catch and release. You've got to let it go."

Jim was crouching in front of his son, staring into his tear-streaked face. The man reached out and gripped his son's shoulder as their eyes met. Jesse closed his eyes tightly, squeezing tears across his cheeks. He lowered the fish to the surface of the water but paused before dipping it in.

"Jesse, life is catch and release. Hold on to what matters and let go of what doesn't."

Jesse plunged the trout under the water and allowed it to slip from his grasp. It didn't move. It's body bobbed in the current for a moment as it began to drift away. Finally, the tip of its tail twitched, it righted itself, and in one powerful movement, it disappeared into the stream.

Jesse grinned, wiping the tears from his eyes. He straightened up and watched as the shadow of the fish darted away until he couldn't make out its shape anymore. Jesse glanced over to his father, expecting to hear his thoughts on the Appalachian Slam. But he wasn't there. His father was gone.

CHAPTER 24

It was a long hike back. Jesse made the trek down Noontootla Creek alone in silence. His few remaining flies were stored carefully in their case and his line wound tightly around its reel. The weather and water conditions were optimal to continue fishing but Jesse was done. The creek had served its purpose. There was no need to stay any longer.

Eventually, he came to the flat, pebble-strewn bank where he had entered the water a few hours before. For a moment Jesse looked back upstream, wondering if he would see the image of his father watching him through the trees. But the forest was empty. He followed the water as it swirled around his ankles and wondered if he would ever step foot in the rivers and creeks here again. Perhaps. He was bound to return to Blue Ridge at some point to visit his family. But something about stepping out of the water at this moment felt so irrevocably definitive. The feeling didn't sadden him, but he did become acutely aware of the otherwise simple act of stepping out of the creek. With one last look upstream Jesse walked up the bank to his father's truck and drove away.

Jesse awoke early the next morning as he always did. His flight wasn't scheduled until almost noon, however, he was prepared to leave the house before the sun broke over the treetops. Helen was still asleep upstairs as Jesse crept through the kitchen, made a pot of coffee, and settled in to a rocking chair on the back porch. Against his protests, Aubry had insisted on driving him back to Atlanta. Just like before, she wouldn't allow her brother to arrange other transportation. However, she wouldn't arrive at their mother's house for at least an hour. Jesse had plenty of time.

The scene which Jesse viewed from the comfort of the screened porch reminded him of New York. There was a stillness that accompanied the sunrise. Here, however, the rays of pink and gold streaked over the tops of pine trees instead of skyscrapers. The tranquility was broken by a constant background noise which was only noticeable when Jesse closed his eyes and focused on it. Cicadas, tree frogs, and katydids took the place of car horns, construction work, and pedestrians talking into their cell phones. But they were both there, ever-present. Jesse closed his eyes and listened to the noise. Most of it was jumbled confusion but periodically they blended together briefly enough to form a cohesive melody. Just like the sounds of the city.

"Mind if I join you?" Helen's voice startled him and in an instant the background chorus which had been enveloping him disappeared.

Without waiting for an answer Helen leaned back in another rocker next to her son. Unlike Jesse, she was still dressed in her pajamas, having likely just woken up. She was holding a cup of coffee from the pot he made and sipped gently on the hot beverage. As she did so, she followed her son's eyes through the screen. The two watched as the sun rose over the backyard until Helen again broke the silence.

"You know, this is where I usually found your father in the morning when I would wake up?"

"Is that so, Mom?" Jesse was tired of her comparisons and felt no desire to entertain the idea in yet another conversation.

"Yeah, he would always be sitting in that chair you're sitting in if he hadn't already left by the time I woke up." Jesse could hear her voice quiver as she choked back her emotions. "Just now when I came downstairs there was a pot of coffee waiting, the back door was propped open, and you were sitting here just like him. For a minute it was like he was still here."

Jesse felt bad for his mother. After today she would be left alone in this house, dealing with the loss of her husband alone. But Jesse couldn't stay. He was determined to do his best to support her and visit more frequently now that his father was gone. But he couldn't stay. It wasn't that his work was calling him back to New York. His passion for his career had faded in the last few weeks and for the first time in his life, he dreaded returning to the office. But that wasn't enough to keep him here. He just couldn't stay any longer.

Sensing his concern, Helen reached over and clasped her son's hand. "Don't worry about me, Jesse. I'll be fine."

"I know you will Mom."

"What about you?" she inquired, gripping his hand tighter. "I worry about you up in New York. Do you really think you belong there?"

"Oh, you think I belong here?"

"No, not at all. I can see plain as day that Blue Ridge isn't for you. But trust me, a mother knows when her child is going down a path he's not meant for." He could tell she was serious as she punched each word of her admonition with a sharp emphasis.

"I think I'll be fine Mom. I've lived in New York for a long time now. If I don't belong there I don't belong anywhere."

"You belong where you want to belong Jesse. Where you make yourself belong. I know that's not here, but I'm not so convinced it's up there either."

Jesse refused to admit how correct her words felt. He couldn't help but feel that the life waiting for him back home wasn't what he was meant for. Or at least it wasn't anymore. Seemingly nothing had changed. But returning to New York felt different. He could feel something pulling him somewhere else. He had felt it before, when the river called him. It was incomprehensible and impossible to describe. The feeling gnawed at the edge of Jesse's thoughts for a few moments until he pushed it away.

Helen stood to leave, announcing she had to prepare for the day before Aubry came to pick Jesse up. As she was walking back into the house Jesse stopped her. A thought sprang to his mind and he produced his father's fishing journal from the pocket of his sports coat. "Hey Mom?" he asked as he flipped to the final entry of the book. "You know Dad's handwriting better than I do. I've been trying to figure out what he wrote here. I can't read a bit of it. Can you interpret what in the world he was trying to say here?"

"Jesse, why are you looking through this old thing?" she asked as she took the book from Jesse's hands and squinted at the page.

Jesse had pored over the journal for weeks now. Some of his father's writings were difficult to read but none like his last, enigmatic entry. It stuck in Jesse's mind, given how close he must have written it to his stroke. He wondered if his father could sense his upcoming demise and how that might have affected his thoughts. Did he write about Jesse? Elle? Miriam? Or did he just continue to write about fish?

Helen continued to stare at the illegible script until, in frustration, she held it out for her son to take. "I don't know Jesse. You can read this as well as I can. I have no clue what he wrote here."

"C'mon Mom, you've got to be able to make something out in it?"

"Why do you care Jesse?"

"He wrote some good tips in here about the fishing around here," he lied. "I thought there might be something in this one also."

"I figured you'd be done with fishing now that you're leaving." Helen looked down her nose at her son and Jesse could tell she knew why he was interested in the contents of the journal. Finally, she sighed and handed the book back to him. "Jesse, I don't know what he's writing about there and to be honest, I don't feel like examining every letter to see if I can make it out. All I know is that it doesn't matter. You don't need to worry yourself with what he did or didn't concern himself with. You've got everything you need."

With that, Helen retreated into the house and left Jesse with his thoughts. Jesse held the journal for some time. He wanted to open it again, to see if he could get one, last insight into his father's thought process. But his mother's words reverberated in his mind. Jesse's desire to understand his father's final thoughts faded like morning fog on a river. He stared intently at the book as he thought about how pointless it was to care about the legacy it might contain. He had other things to care about, other things to occupy his obsessive mind. But Jesse was unable to think of what they were. His thoughts turned to his career and the work waiting for him back home but they seemed as pointless as obsessing over the journal entry. Only one thing felt important now.

Jesse hesitantly placed the journal on the table next to him and rose. He quickly walked through the house and bounded up the stairs where he found his mother in front of her bathroom mirror, curling her hair. "Mom, can I take the truck?"

"What?" she asked, with a confused look on her face.

"Can I take the truck?"

Helen continued to look shocked as she tried to comprehend what he was asking. "Yeah, of course you can. But Aubry will be here any minute."

"I know Mom, tell her I'll catch her next time."

"Wait, what?!" she exclaimed as she carefully but quickly unraveled a lock of hair from her curling iron. "You've got a plane to catch."

"I love you Mom," Jesse said as he wrapped an arm around her and kissed her on the top of her head. "I'll call later."

Jesse threw his suitcase in the scratched up bed of his father's pickup, along with his fly rod, fishing vest, waders, and boots, which he had hastily retrieved from the basement. The dust swirled as the tires kicked gravel across the driveway. Jesse pointed the truck towards town and gunned the engine.

As he drove, he passed Aubry, headed towards their mother's house in her red behemoth. He recognized the confusion on her face as he lifted his hand from the steering wheel in a courteous wave.

It was a short drive to the hospital where Jesse parked the truck and briskly walked towards the entranceway. He hardly noticed the group of women in scrubs leaving through the same doors until one called out to him.

"Jesse?" Karen asked, breaking off from the group and motioning for them to continue on without her.

"Karen, hi... sorry I didn't see you there. I was hoping I'd catch you at work."

"I was just leaving," she said, crossing her arms. "Nightshift."

There was an awkward pause. Jesse was worried that seeing Karen would be uncomfortable. He certainly could understand why she might not welcome his arrival and her body language indicated she didn't.

"Hey, can we talk?"

"Now you want to talk? I thought you'd be back in New York by now."

"My plane leaves in a few hours."

"You'd better get going then," she said coldly, "it's a long drive to Atlanta."

"I'm not going."

Karen's demeanor softened. She unfolded her arms and leaned back in surprise. "You're staying here?"

"Not exactly," Jesse answered. "Karen, I'm sorry. I shouldn't have treated you the way I did. You were there for me and I pushed you away. You have every right to be angry..."

"I'm not angry with you Jesse," she interrupted. "I've been worried about you. I know losing a parent is difficult. Everyone reacts differently. I'm not surprised it affected you so much."

Jesse's chest flooded with relief and the sick feeling in his stomach subsided. He was convinced Karen would hate him after he had ignored her. He shouldn't have been surprised that she didn't. She wasn't like him. She didn't carry the same resentment he had been burdened with for so long.

"Still, I shouldn't have treated you that way. You deserve better... I want to be better."

Karen reached out and tenderly closed her soft hands over his, pulling his body closer to hers.

"Don't worry about it, Cavanaugh. You've always been kind of an idiot."

"I can't go back to New York. Not right now. And I can't stay here. I've got to get away." Jesse paused, knowing that what he was saying was a lot to take in. Even for himself. "And I want you to come with me."

"What? When?" she asked, taken aback by his invitation.

"Right now."

Karen pulled away from him. "Jesse, I've got a job. I've got a life. I can't just drop everything and disappear. How long are you planning on being gone?"

"I don't know, maybe a week, maybe forever."

"Okay, you're obviously going through a lot right now and it's affecting your decision making. Let's get you home."

"No, Karen. I'm thinking more lucidly than I have in a long time. This feels right. It's what I need to do. And I want you with me. Come on, I know you don't want to spend the rest of your life here. Even you admitted that. And you said it yourself, you're not committed to this job. You've wanted to do more for a long time now. So let's do more."

"Jesse, not everyone can afford to make life changes based on rash decisions. Some of us need to have a plan."

"Are you happy with what your plan has led to so far?" Jesse asked, looking hopefully at Karen as she continued to process his proposal. "Karen my dad had a plan. He lived by his plan every day but I'm not so sure whether he was actually living or just following a plan. I've done the same thing, just trading New York for Blue Ridge."

Karen exhaled deeply and ran the fingers of both her hands through her hair. "It's not so easy Jesse. I tried to leave before. But here I am. I just came back. What if I come back again?"

"But what if you don't?" Jesse responded quickly. "What if there's something else out there for us?"

There was a long pause between them before Jesse spoke again. "Karen we can come back whenever you want if that's what feels right but I need some time away from everything for at least a bit. But I need you with me. It's not worth it to do it alone. I need...I... I don't want to go through life alone anymore." Jesse extended his hand to Karen who was still looking at him with uncertainty in her eyes. "Please..."

The next few moments seemed to drag on forever. Karen glanced at his outstretched hand and stared into his pleading eyes over and over again. She bit her bottom lip as she twirled a strand of her hair while she thought. Jesse didn't know what he would do if she rejected him. He had no plan to speak of, he felt like he had bet his whole life on this one moment which was now completely out of his control.

Karen reached out and took his hand.

The two smiled at one another and Jesse pulled her across the parking lot, almost running. Karen listed tasks she had to complete as they ran. Packing, calling her mother, calling her boss. Jesse noted each one but didn't dwell on any of them. He was too focused on the feeling emanating through his chest. He didn't know how to describe it, he didn't even attempt to do so in his thoughts. He simply embraced it. He felt free.

Jesse threw open the passenger door for Karen. As she stepped into the truck she grabbed the collar of his shirt and pulled him towards her. He kissed her passionately until she finally pushed him away and closed the door. Jesse took his place behind the steering wheel, pulling his own door closed behind him.

"So where to now?" Karen asked, reaching over to place her hand in his.

Jesse hesitated. He hadn't given any thought to his plans beyond this moment. The question of where he would go had not even occurred to him which seemed so strange now that he thought about it. He needed somewhere new. Somewhere with promise, where he could try to find some semblance of who he was unburdened by animosity and regret. He thought for a moment, considering their options before responding.

"Have you ever been to Montana?"

THE END

Don't miss out!

Visit the website below and you can sign up to receive emails whenever Doyle Johnson publishes a new book. There's no charge and no obligation.

https://books2read.com/r/B-A-TQOH-GGGX

Made in the USA
Columbia, SC
03 November 2019